THE NINE CIRCLES

James Voorhees

Bonfire Books

ISBN: 978-1-964126-17-3 Hardback
ISBN: 978-1-964126-18-0 Paperback
ISBN: 978-1-964126-16-6 Ebook

Printed by Bonfire Books LLC, in the United States of America

First printing edition 2025.

www.jamesvoorhees.com

To Orianne and Alex: Your talents and efforts

continue to make this dream a reality.

PROLOGUE
Caves of Waku

The Caves of Waku had not had this much disturbance in centuries. The Ambassadors had lured the Jeweled Dragon away from her attack on the city of Mortua and out to the barren openness where nothing lived above ground.

There were sixty-five entrances into the caves that tunneled below the crater and made up the Valley of Kaar. However, Tinker was only interested in getting into one entrance, the one that would allow him to reach his cart. He had abandoned the cart with his collection of gadgets, books, and weapons in that cave entrance to protect them when the beast initially attacked. He entered through the partially collapsed roof and ran deeper towards his possessions resting in front of the magically locked gate.

There was no time to think. The Jeweled Dragon had come to this dimension to destroy humankind. She was unloading her raging fury on the Ambassadors in an attempt to stop them from finding the weapons listed in a prophecy and to punish Vampire by killing Monk.

Tinker had to hurry. Dust was falling from overhead as he ran through the darkness. He reached his cart and began rummaging through his gadgets and weapons. His hands instinctively grabbed a pair of goggles. But then, his brain paused his movements and took a quick inventory of the disheveled objects laid out on the cart. He wanted to take everything. *No time, Tinker. Focus,* he thought. He grabbed a few other pieces, including a rolled up animal hide, a journal and a few timeworn books and stuffed them into his bag. His eyes moved quickly over what looked like a disorganized mess of finished and partially finished projects.

"Where are you?" he asked as his eyes moved rapidly over his treasured creations. "Ah! Gotcha," Tinker said with a wide victorious stare. The Dazer, a weapon of his own creation, peaked out from under the pulled-back burlap cover. *This* was why he ran into the cave.

He had used this weapon during the Ambassadors' first battle with the Immortal beast, back when the Jeweled Dragon attacked and destroyed the city of Dellai. It had stunned the dragon and knocked her off balance while Tinker and the others got away. His plan was to hopefully repeat that momentary success and escape this assault.

As Tinker pulled the fabric further back, an orb that was next to the Dazer caught his attention. "Ileana," he said as he remembered that the exiled Queen of Witches had gifted him this orb when he had secured and delivered to her the Book of Spells, the secret text that held the incantations for all prohibited magic. However, she had not explained the orb's power nor its purpose but instead told him that he was "...bright enough to figure it out". Tinker grabbed the orb and stared at it as the pocket-sized sphere began to pulse with yellow light in the same rhythm as his heartbeat. Tinker quickly stashed it into his jacket pocket. "This might be useful," he said without thinking as to why.

A hard crash shook the cave. Tinker saw more dust falling and grabbed some other strange looking objects. He added them to the collection in his knapsack. *Quick exit,* he thought to himself and then reached for a set of retractable wings that were sticking out of a bag.

The dragon's roar caused more dust and rocks to fall around him. "Time to go, Tink!" He was strapping the retractable wings to himself as he looked back at his cart and the weapons and tools he had created. He was full of regret for leaving them behind. "I can make them again," he assured himself and hit the power button to start the quick fluttering of the mechanical wings. "And improve on them," he told himself with assurance.

Another hard crash from the Jeweled Dragon stomping about loosened what was left of the ceiling of the cave entrance and Tinker was quick to put on the goggles as he took to flight and shot through the dust and falling rock. He held his breath so as not to choke, but was nearing his limit as he reached the closest opening and seemed to explode out of it. He stayed stealth near the ground surface with dust trailing behind him like a wake in the air.

"Tinker!" Cadet, the Leprechaun, exclaimed with relief.

"Come on, Tink. Come on!" Axel encouraged just over a whisper. Axel was quick to look back at another cave entrance, the one where Princess had pulled Aldrick, to escape the Jeweled Dragon's fury and fire.

Cadet and Axel were gathered with the rest of the Ambassadors on the upper edge of the Valley of Kaar, the border formed at the rim of the crater. Monk had run from them to lure the Jeweled Dragon away. They stood anxiously behind the beast's flight path as she chased Monk back towards the center of the crater. Vampire was in quick pursuit.

Ileana, the Queen of Witches who had only recently shown herself to be alive, maneuvered her arms and hands and spoke an incantation. Tinker was unaware that his pocket began to glow. Princess and Aldrick were blinded by the brightness as they peered out of the cave entrance and squinted their eyes with an attempt to understand what was happening.

"Tinker's on fire," Aldrick said with worry, shielding his eyes with his hand.

"I don't think so," Princess countered. She saw Ileana's intricate spell casting and knew that the radiance emanating from Tinker had something to do with her magic. "Come on, Aldrick." She assisted him back towards the others. "I'll help you."

"I can make it," Aldrick assured her and rotated his ankle in an attempt to demonstrate that he was capable of moving on his own. He had twisted it when attempting to escape the dragon and was rescued by Princess pulling him into one of the cave entrances and with Axel using his Earth magic to block the beast's attack. They made their way back to the others with caution to avoid drawing attention from the dragon.

Tinker hit a second button on the chest plate of the wings and flew faster towards Vampire, who trailed the Jeweled Dragon as the smell of bergamot came into the air. Tinker knew that the Immortal beast was about to unleash her fiery breath upon Monk. Tinker was in range and pointed the Dazer. As he was about to pull the trigger, the Jeweled Dragon turned her head and shot her angry flames back towards him and Vampire. He quickly pulled up, out of the way of her fiery breath, but was quick to recover his flight path. Vampire ran through the flames.

Tinker aimed his Dazer and pulled the trigger to release the gun's sonic force. But as the forceful sound waves were released, the beast disappeared into a portal of Ileana's making, closing right after the dragon entered. Tinker watched as the rippling borders of the portal quickly came together and sealed the dragon into an unknown location.

Monk too realized what had just happened and stopped at the edge of one of the openings in the crater's surface. However, he was unaware that Tinker had fired the Dazer; the powerful beam continued through the air and dropped to the ground directly where Monk was standing. As a result, the edge of the opening became unstable and created a seismic effect that began to shake the sand and rocks.

Monk's legs lost their stability on the solid surface, and he slipped over the edge. The feeling in his stomach told him that he was falling into the opening in the ground. His adrenaline rushed but to no avail. He was sliding with the sands. His only thought was for Vampire. He reached out in an attempt to steady himself by grasping for anything solid that could stop his sliding but all he found were loose sands. He was falling.

The jerk on his body was strong. Something had stopped his descent: his hand had caught onto something. He gripped tight and was holding blindly to whatever it was. He looked up at his hand but could not see clearly as the sands and dust blinded him.

"I have you!" Vampire held tight as he saw the relieved look on Monk's face.

With his left hand anchored in the sands behind him, Vampire held Monk's wrist with his right hand as he swayed. The sand continued to fall as if in an hourglass.

Tinker had flown through where the portal had closed and hurried when he saw Vampire struggling to get Monk out of the opening.

Back on the crater's rim, Ileana's expression was full of sorrow. She looked back at Seer and saw his eyes glowing red. Sorcerer and AZ were maintaining their protective instincts in anticipation of what might be coming next, but a small relief took over the group as Axel aided Aldrick and Princess.

"He's quite stubborn," Princess told Axel what he already knew about their brother.

Vampire was straining to maintain his position. At the edge of the opening in the ground, the sands around his anchored hand were sliding into the hole and he found that he did not have a base to stabilize himself. He began to slide towards the blackness. He continued to hold tight to Monk and looked back and forth between the opening and his arm dug into the moving sands. He moved his fingers and leaned towards his arm in the sand, grasping for any stone or hard surface to anchor himself.

The others squinted at the blinding light that emanated from the orb in Tinker's pocket. What they were unaware of was that the tattooed wings on Monk's back also glowed bright and began to burn him. The pain became unbearable, and Monk lost his grip on Vampire. Vampire was distracted with his attempt to stabilize himself and was unable to hold tight to Monk. Monk was falling.

No, Vampire thought as his eyes widened with fear as he witnessed Monk falling out of sight, consumed by the blackness. Vampire's Immortal blood rushed through his body and forced coordinated muscle contractions. He could not breathe.

Vampire remembered this pain. He remembered this anguish. He fought harder to breathe as his fear had turned to an overwhelming sadness, which became pain. It was a familiar feeling that he had experienced when each of Monk's eight previous lives ended and when the time after his deaths became torture for his Immortal lover. The sense of loss would only partially diminish as Vampire always knew that Monk would return to him. However, this time felt different. He did not have the same confidence regarding Monk's return. The fear became overwhelming, so much so that tears of blood formed in his eyes.

Tinker's eyes widened in panic as he saw both of Vampire's hands on the edge of the opening. He closed his eyes and tucked his chin as he flew as quickly as the fluttering mechanical wings would allow.

No, Tinker feared. He flew past Vampire at a speed that blew the Immortal's long hair and followed Monk's descent into the opening in the ground. Tinker was quick to realize the ripples in the air that signified an opening of another portal. He watched Monk fall through it. *Ileana. What have you done?*

"Monk!" Vampire yelled.

Tinker followed Monk through the opening.

"Tinker!" Vampire screamed out with the pain of his full regret. Monk had fallen into the portal and was lost to the blackness. Tinker had followed. Vampire was fighting back his emotions, his humanity. He lost control. Three tears of blood fell from his eyes, one by one into the portal before the subtle ripples in the air came together and the portal closed.

Vampire felt the presence of Ghost levitating just behind his left shoulder.

"Please," he begged as he continued to peer into the darkness.

"Not my part to play. You know that," Ghost stoically responded and blew off with a breeze.

"Come on, Tink," Vampire whispered his thoughts aloud as he stared into the darkness. "Come on."

As the crimson light in Seer's eyes diminished, he spoke in a huffed breath. "They're gone..."

CHAPTER 1
The Pit

Tinker was consumed by the blackness that surrounded him. The darkness deprived him of his usually sharp senses. Yet, he quickly became attuned to the limited light coming from Monk's back, the harsh buzzing of the wings on his own back and the rush of the cold air that slapped his exposed face with his rapid descent.

However, his need to get to Monk quickly consumed his full consciousness again. Tinker tried to pull his body into an aerodynamic posture to create a faster velocity and realized that the fluttering wings were slowing him from getting to Monk. He needed to freefall. Tinker cut the power and squeezed his body as tight as he could to make himself as streamlined as possible. He was then able to fall faster through the void towards Monk, guided only by the distant light of Monk's glowing tattoo.

Monk was becoming disoriented. He was losing consciousness but was pulled back by the pain that he was experiencing as the light of his tattoo pulsed brighter. The rush of adrenaline consumed him as he was falling through the void. His body convulsed as he began to experience a different sense of awareness and then returned back to himself. The burning increased and the changes in consciousness felt like they were occurring with every blink of his eyes.

Tinker continued his rapid freefall. He was calculating at what point to power his wings to be sure not to hit the bottom. He lost himself momentarily to the concern that he had no actual reference as to where the bottom was.

The glowing from Monk's back pulsed and then intensified to a blinding brightness. The pain that accompanied the light forced Monk to contort his body and turn his illuminated back towards Tinker.

Tinker felt another pained presence and was quick to turn his gaze left and right. He saw three small flecks illuminated by the light coming off Monk as they fell with a weighted pace. They resembled blood red fireflies. *Vampire's tears.* Tinker realized that the tears were falling faster than he was.

Tinker was close to Monk; he knew that those tears were toxic and would destroy him if he made contact with them. The first tear gained speed and turned towards Tinker's outstretched hand. He hit the ignition on the chest plate and his wings began to flutter. He veered himself out of the way of the tear and then turned the power off again to fall as fast as possible. He watched as the first tear raced past Monk and glowed like a beacon.

Tinker turned his attention to the second tear. It was close, too close to Monk. Monk let out a painful gasp and opened his eyes as if taking his final breath. The second tear pushed faster and entered Monk's left eye. He screamed out in pain; then, he fell silent and limp as his body was knocked into repeated backward somersaults in the darkness. The glow of light became more intense; it was blinding and constant.

Tinker feared the worst. He feared that Monk was gone. However, as concern rushed into him, he fought through his fear and was determined to get to Monk before his body hit the unforeseen bottom. Tinker was still unable to gauge where the bottom of the pit was. He could only see Monk glowing and the continued descent of Vampire's first tear that had rushed past them.

Monk's body was contorting in unthinkable ways. Tinker pushed on with the single purpose of rescuing Monk and stopping him before he hit the bottom of the abyss or would die trying.

CHAPTER 2
Caves of Waku

Vampire was on his knees at the edge of the opening. He was desperate for Tinker to fly out with Monk in his arms, but was losing hope. Nothing came from the openness. No breeze, no light, no sound. He felt the end. He felt Monk's loss. Vampire struggled to recapture his breath. He was able to inhale and forced himself to hold his breath.

He heard a distant whisper as Seer's words made their way to him. "They're gone."

Vampire was unable to hold his breath any longer and released it with the force of a scream. The scream was full of pain and was heard at a frequency that forced the others to cover their ears. His body began to contort into a monstrous form.

"No!" exclaimed Sorcerer to the rest of the group who were on the ridge of the valley, a distance away from Vampire. "We need to contain him!" he said to Ileana and began moving his arms, hands and fingers in an intricate pattern through the air.

Seer looked at Ghost who had floated back to the rest of the Ambassadors. Ghost maintained his levitated position with his translucent form and unwavering facial intensity. His arms remained crossed, and his sunken eyes squinted but kept their unbroken stare. A crooked smile came across his face. Cadet noticed.

A second scream came from Vampire and again shot painfully through the air. His eyes had turned completely black, and his jaw had expanded, showing the brutality of his fangs. His scream was so strong that the disturbance in the air created a forceful cyclone, which held and pushed the air itself to knock Seer out of his vision and off his feet, throwing him backwards into a boulder where Seer hit his head.

"Seer? Seer? Are you okay?" AZ ran to make sure that he was alive. Seer shook himself back to the present.

"The vision…" Seer said as if still in a dream.

"What is it? What did you see?" Cadet asked.

"They're gone," he whispered his thought, unable to elicit emotion. "Monk and Tinker. They are gone."

"What?" questioned AZ with fear. "Seer?"

"They are gone," Seer said again. "I cannot *see* them."

Sorcerer's spell had distracted Vampire from his beastly transformation. He was back to looking over the edge of the hole. He had let Monk go.

"He pulled back and let go. I lost my grip," Vampire said to himself in a whisper.

"Vampire," Sorcerer yelled. "Get back from there."

Ileana cautiously navigated the unstable surface and made her way over to Vampire. She pulled at him, but Vampire would not move. He continued to look over the edge of the black opening with pain in all his being. Ileana looked back to Sorcerer and shook her head with concern.

Monk was gone again. Vampire fought the feeling. He knew it but fought in the attempt to not believe it.

CHAPTER 3
The Pit

Tinker was losing Monk in the darkness. The light that was coming from Monk's body had dimmed and was too distant to give any details about Monk, other than offering his struggling silhouette. Tinker powered on a light on his goggles and saw Monk clearly. Tinker continued at a rapid speed with his hand on the trigger to power his mechanical wings before crashing into the bottom of the pit. He had to reach Monk. He screamed out. "Monk!"

With that, Monk's eyes shot open. They were translucent. His body continued to twist and contort. He was spinning in the air as he continued to fall.

Tinker pushed on.

Monk had rolled over in the air and was positioned with his face and the front of his body towards the unknown bottom. His robes were tattered and blowing. The markings on Monk's body began to glow brighter again. Tinker reached out to grab at the tethered robes to get a hold of Monk. Shards of fabric from Monk's robes began to slap Tinker and wrapped themselves around his outstretched hand. As he grabbed for them, they ripped away from Monk and gave Tinker nothing to secure a hold on Monk. Tinker saw Monk's arms fall behind him as if they were wings. The remainder of Monk's robes slid off his shoulders, past his elbows and wrists. They came at Tinker, who got caught up in them and was temporarily blinded. As he pulled them away from his face, he saw what he first thought was a shadow in the darkness.

The light of his goggles was focused on Monk. Tinker could now see movement in Monk's back tattoos as they began to push out and pull back into his body. The glowing appeared solid and turned to gold as something began to cut through Monk's skin, causing him to bleed. Monk screamed out in pain and spun in the air.

Tinker continued to push forth. He held his stare on Monk's eyes. Monk's expression was panicked but then a calmness came over him, as a brighter light emanated from Monk's back.

A numb feeling came over Tinker as he took in a shocked gasp. Giant bloody wings emerged from the golden light of Monk's back and surrounded him. Monk's body spun as he continued to fall but then stopped as he faced Tinker. Tinker looked into Monk's eyes and saw them turn to a brilliant bright white light. The wings fluttered and pushed Monk up to Tinker. Monk grabbed him and as soon as their hands clasped, Monk pulled him in and wrapped the huge glowing wings around Tinker. The embrace happened immediately as the first tear hit the bottom of the pit and the third tear of Vampire's blood fell onto the wings and created a rippling effect over them.

Immediately, they too hit the floor of the pit with such force that the ground broke. Fire erupted. Dust, ash and soot were thrown in all directions, polluting the air. The impact created ripples of dirt and rock as if the broken solid surface was now liquid. The walls began to shake as well, and the reaction climbed up the cavern.

The ripples pulled into the center of the opening, which darkened. Sparks shot off the encasement and lit the walls and floor of the chamber where the casing had now embedded itself. The initially golden light changed to an ominous blue, so dark that it was almost black. The reflection on the encasement dimmed. It appeared as though there was movement from the small lights as the speckles of dust held still in the lifeless air.

CHAPTER 4
Caves of Waku

"Thaddeus," Ileana pleaded. "Get back!" she yelled to the others as a rumble began to grow from within the hole in the ground. "Something is happening!"

Vampire could not move. He felt the emptiness. Monk was gone. Cadet, Axel and Aldrick grabbed hold of him by the shoulders in an attempt to pull him back from the edge.

"Thaddeus," Cadet began, trying to rationalize with him.

She was quickly halted as the ground shook. The sand became more unstable as the roofs of the caverns below fell, exposing the tunnels running under the surface. The blast from within the opening pushed them all onto their backs as dust and ash, heat, fire and soot erupted from the blackness and into the sky. Sand again began to fall as the opening Vampire was staring into widened.

"The caves are all collapsing," Sorcerer yelled.

The birth of an Immortal, Ileana feared.

The red sands at Vampire's feet began to pull again but this time they were moving faster, with added gravitational force. Sand rushed quickly into several cave openings. The far edge of the crater began to collapse. AZ and Seer were caught in the collapsing crater wall and slid into the valley as the ground beneath them crumbled.

"Everyone, get back!" Sorcerer demanded. "Get Vampire away from there."

AZ was attending to Seer who was lost to his vision as he continued searching for Monk and Tinker. Seer's eyes were closed, and he was mumbling incoherently. His facial expressions were continuously pained.

"Seer?" AZ begged and attempted to help him up.

Seer did not respond as he continued his own inner struggle. His family was gone. He was desperate to find them.

"Seer? What's happening?" AZ pleaded.

Princess was quick to assist with pulling Vampire away from the falling sands. She looked back and saw that AZ was having a difficult time with Seer.

"Go back to them," Ileana yelled back to her.

Princess nodded and ran back over to them and held Seer from the other side. She looked up to see Sorcerer still at the ridge of the crater, moving his arms and hands in an attempt to stop the falling sands.

"AZ?" she questioned.

"I don't know," he yelled in a confused panic. "I know that he was trying to find Monk and Tinker, but then he said that they were gone. He stopped speaking and then started to look terrified. I can't break the trance."

"I warned you that this would happen," Ileana said to Vampire, who had conceded to getting to safety. "We should have planned for it."

Ileana kneeled down by Seer with a look of frustration.

AZ explained to her what he had told Princess.

Ileana looked at Seer with added worry. She held her hands over his glowing eyes.

"Damn it," she said. "Someone is in his vision."

"What does that mean?" Princess asked.

"He must have been discovered on the path of another seer," Ileana told her.

"Is he lost in there?" AZ begged.

"I don't know yet," she replied with added frustration.

"Ileana!" Sorcerer screamed.

She looked up at the crater's ridge to see what was happening, as did Princess and AZ.

"We have a situation here," Sorcerer alerted as he pointed to Vampire's body seizing and Cadet attempting to hold him.

"AZ," Ileana said sternly. "Stay with Seer. Keep him calm and comfortable. And above all, keep his eyes towards the sun. As it moves, he must move. It is his beacon, his way back. There is nothing else that we can do right now."

"Ileana!" Cadet screamed out.

"Come with me," she said to Princess and the Twins. "I have a feeling that we will need you… all of you."

CHAPTER 5
Caves of Waku

"Vampire?" Sorcerer pleaded.

Vampire was lost in his thoughts. He was having flashbacks as he returned to each of Monk's previous deaths. He was lost to his fears.

Sorcerer looked at the unstable sand at the edge of the opening. "Vampire! We have to get away from here. Otherwise, we will be pulled in and buried in that pit in the ground."

"Vam-" Cadet pleaded from over his shoulder. "Thaddeus! I've been here with you in the past." She walked sideways as Axel and Aldrick pulled him in the sands. "You need to focus on Monk's scent. You need to calm yourself before you hurt someone." She pleaded in a soothing voice, uncharacteristic for the gruff, wise-cracking comments that Axel and Aldrick had become used to.

Vampire's emotional state had weakened him physically. Axel and Aldrick pulled him to his feet and threw his arms around their shoulders. Sorcerer had run down to meet them and was leading them away from the moving sands.

"Take him up there," he ordered Aldrick and Axel.

"Definitely not good," Ileana stated as the Twins walked past her and Princess. "Go with them," she told Princess.

Ileana met Sorcerer, who had stayed behind with Cadet. "Thoughts?" she asked.

"He's gonna blow," Cadet told her.

"I started to make an entrapment to contain him until it was safe, but with everything going on, it failed. I cannot do it myself," Sorcerer told her.

"Yes. I saw you," Ileana replied. "I've seen him go through this before, but this time will be more."

"As have I," Cadet told her. "And yes, he's gonna blow."

"I don't know if he's wrong," Sorcerer told her. "Monk and Tinker-"

"Gone," Cadet said as if unable to believe it.

"But we need to deal with matters at hand," Ileana reminded them.

"The Jeweled Dragon?" Cadet asked and looked to the sky. She saw no sign of the Immortal beast.

"I can't even think about the dragon right now," Ileana told them with her hands to her face. "Seer was searching for Monk and

Tinker. I felt the presence of another in his vision when I assessed him.”

“Another seer?” Cadet asked.

“It must be,” Ileana told them. “Seems as though he got caught in the Shadow Realm.” She looked at Cadet. “The path of the seers.”

“That could be dangerous,” Cadet feared.

“Extremely,” Ileana said. “AZ is watching him and moving him with the sun. We have to keep the shadows behind him. But this…” She continued and looked at Vampire in his weakened state. “We need to be prepared for what will come of this.” She looked back at Sorcerer with concern. “And Monk is not here for the usual ritual to take place.”

“For Vampire to drink?” Cadet asked.

“For Vampire to preserve the truth,” Ileana replied. “With each of Monk’s deaths, Vampire was there to take his last drops of blood… All of his memories… He was able to preserve them so that one day, he would be able to share them with him.”

“And one day, he will,” Cadet assured her with all the hope that she had.

CHAPTER 6
The Pit

On the floor and the walls of the cavern, the suspended dust began to fall. Still, no sound or movement was found from within the hardened wings that contained Monk and Tinker's bodies.

Hundreds of lights began to float through the darkness. At first, they were very dim and appeared like red embers that had been released among crimson dust particles. As they floated in the cold still air, they began to randomly strike into one another. With each point of contact, the lights shot through the air with great force and speed. And as their bonding continued, the collisions and repulsions became more intense and the brightness was transferred until there were only seven blinding lights floating in the air, each in a varied hue of fiery red. The illuminations began to grow in size and to alter their forms. They spread into larger but still solid lights and the borders began to take on monstrous forms. One by one, the brilliance of the lights began to fade, leaving behind the emerging physical forms of the seven Rulers of Hell.

Beelzebub, the Ruler of the Fourth Circle, was the first to present himself. As his crimson light transformed, he was lowered to the surface by his giant translucent wings. They continued to flutter enough to create an audible annoyance to himself, but he would never admit it. He took the form of a human-sized fly with his two eyes made up of thousands of smaller eyes that bulged from their sockets and reflected a version of whatever he was focused on, seeing it from all sides. His nose was long and constantly twitching, gathering information from any subtle changes in the environment. His grotesque body exposed his gluttony; his disheveled and stained attire bore no interest in social consciousness. He quickly moved towards the latent form on the ground and kicked at the golden surface.

"Oh, but you do smell awful," commented Mammon, the Ruler of the First Circle of Hell, who had come to form behind where Beelzebub stood. With his eyes moving to focus behind him, Beelzebub came to the awareness of Mammon's presence.

"I did not hear you arrive."

"Well, how could you with those incessant wings flapping about without purpose. I don't know what is worse," he continued as he walked towards the golden lifeless form on the ground, "the noise they make or them circulating the smell of your rotting flesh."

"As long as they keep you away, it means nothing to me," Beelzebub gargled as if needing to clear his throat. "I can't believe that you and your selfishness allowed me to get here first."

"I was busy with a pressing matter," the vulture-headed demon said nonchalantly as he leaned over to take a closer look.

"Not a single new soul has come to Hell in days. What could be more pressing than this?" Beelzebub argued back. "Did you have something to do with the fall of Gokyuzu?" He asked with the tone of a strong accusation.

Mammon did not offer a response. "Did you take anything off it? Is there anything else that may have fallen through with it?"

"I ask again. Did you have anything to do with the destruction of Gokyuzu? How do we expect souls to come through Hell if the transfer station is destroyed?" Beelzebub questioned, ignoring Mammon's attempt to call him a thief.

Mammon was looking around feverishly as Beelzebub cautiously reached out to touch his perfect human male form. His nearly naked body contracted every muscle into a retracting pose to avoid the physical contact.

"Do not touch me," Mammon cawed from his beak. The volume and tone of the scream set the walls to shake and dust to begin to fall.

Beelzebub giggled and walked to the opposite side of the lifeless form enclosed in the hardened wings. "It's a good thing that your body is so desirable. I mean that head... and that voice... Ewww."

"Says the one who smells like shit."

"Do I? I haven't noticed," Beelzebub argued and fluttered his wings faster to increase the spread of his foul scent.

Mammon retracted his position from the offense.

"I have," sounded through the darkness. "And *he's* right about the voice. Truly unforgiving."

Asmodeus, the Ruler of the Second Circle of Hell, slowly strutted her way up to the others and looked from Beelzebub to Mammon. Beelzebub quickly looked away, fearful that her flirtatious gaze would take over his ability to reason. Yet, his smaller eyes focused on her seductive form, each highlighting different attributes and curves on her body. As she looked at Mammon, her eyes moved up and down. She breathed deeply and let out a slow and audible moan before walking backwards, keeping her stare into his eyes. He returned the confident look.

Asmodeus had a striking human female form but had a deep blue tint to her skin and hair which moved as if there were a breeze. Fire surrounded her neck, creating an elegant wide collar that opened at the borders of her generous cleavage.

"But with that body, I can forgive the head," she continued to flirt with Mammon in her lustful tone. She looked down at the large casing on the ground and, as the others had done, she kicked the hardened structure. She looked back at him. "But not that screeching voice."

Mammon cawed loudly again and shook the walls. Asmodeus flickered her hand to create a fireball so hot that it was felt from where Mammon stood.

"Enough!" demanded Satan, the Ruler of the Third Circle of Hell. His anger overtook the previous argument, and both backed down. "If you are going to destroy one another, you will have to wait."

"And since when do you have anything to say about our little flirtation?" questioned Asmodeus with the tone of an adolescent girl disagreeing with her parent.

"Since we have a bigger problem," Satan pushed back. "Gokyuzu was destroyed, and I can feel life within this." He knelt down and sniffed the casing. *But how?* he thought. He turned quickly and was met by Asmodeus. His goat-like head with golden horns came right up against her face, so close that air could not even get between them. His rage was palpable and only redirected as he felt a touch on his golden horns.

He shook his head and pulled his horns to the side, throwing the offender to the ground.

"I figured it was you," Satan said as Leviathan, the Ruler of the Fifth Circle of Hell, lay tangled on the dusty ground trying to catch his breath. The sea beast used his multiple fins and tentacles to wriggle himself to sit upright and join the circle surrounding the motionless form. He slapped against the hardened structure with one of his tentacles.

"I'm a sucker for gold."

"You're a sucker for gold? Really? I think it's more like you want everything that is not yours," Mammon joked.

"Says the one who can never get enough," Leviathan insulted back with his forked tongue flickering in the open air.

Asmodeus turned her head in a query. She sniffed the air that had been stenched by Beelzebub's tortuous odor. It began to clear and fill with a familiar and lingering scent that caused her to react like a squirrel looking for a nut.

"Lucifer?"

"Lucifer," Beelzebub whispered as he stood up straighter and attempted to better his appearance.

"Did you think I would miss this?" Lucifer asked.

The strikingly handsome Ruler of the Sixth Circle of Hell moved closer to the collection of underworld demons and joined the circle.

"I figured that you were the cause of this," Leviathan spoke with a lisp through his slithering tongue.

"I would love to take credit for this, but-"

He investigated the air and then around the circle of unholy beings. "Sure! Why not? Yes. This is *my* doing." He shook his head and rolled his fiery eyes to dissuade any further discussion about him having anything to do with the arrival of this golden sarcophagus.

"Pride's getting in the way again, old friend," Satan spoke with his angered growl.

"That's such a surprise," Belphegor, the Ruler of the Seventh Circle of Hell, spoke his sarcasm through the darkness.

"Personally, I'm shocked that you were able to make it," Lucifer retorted in an offensive tone. "I mean, with your busy schedule of lying around and doing nothing."

"Fuck you, pretty boy," Belphegor quickly shot back.

"That was harsh," Asmodeus noted.

"It's all he's got, my dear," Lucifer continued in a flirtatious tone.

"It's not all I've got," the rotund imp corrected him. "I have…"

He pulled a glowing stone from the front of his pants. It was lemon yellow in color and seemed to emit a sound that resonated off the walls of the chamber. The glowing lights on the walls and ground brightened.

"A Cez stone," Satan whispered his desire aloud.

"Yes. A Cez stone." Belphegor turned his attention to Lucifer and Asmodeus. "Still think I'm useless?"

"Yes," Lucifer answered. "But the stone is not." He quickly pulled a lightning bolt from behind his back and struck the overconfident demon.

Belphegor squealed from the pain of the blast and involuntarily reacted by throwing his hands in the air, which launched the Cez stone high into the darkness. The golden glow of the stone allowed all eyes to stay peeled on its location as it soared through the air.

Beelzebub and Satan flew after it. Leviathan wound himself into a tight spring and released himself into the air. Belphegor swung himself and reached out with his arrow tipped tail. Lucifer threw another lightning bolt which hit the stone and created an explosion so bright that it blinded Beelzebub. His thousands of eyes all became disoriented, and he flew into the wall of the cavern. Satan was blown backwards from the blast. Leviathan felt the blistering scorch of the heat as the lightning bolt was rejected from the stone and sliced across the side of his cheek. Asmodeus was in the process of jumping from wall to wall and was knocked off balance as Leviathan fell back towards the ground and slammed into her. The blinding light forced Belphegor to duck for cover, and he pulled his arrow tipped tail around. His tail struck at close proximity to where Satan had found himself, perched on a wall. Belphegor was stuck. Satan was enraged at the possibility of being struck by Belphegor's tail.

The focus of the group went back to arguing and turning on each other.

"Ut hmmm."

The screams and pulling of flesh from demon to demon did not stop.

"Ut hmmm!" was again offered, but this time in a louder tone.

Still, no one stopped the fighting.

Lucifer held the Cez stone aloft in his hand and the blinding light again glowed lemon yellow and encompassed the cavern. He held it over his head until there was silence. The others all stopped their bickering and physical assaults on one another. They stood and gathered back around the still hardened and motionless form that contained the remains of Monk and Tinker. Silence prevailed as the light dimmed again.

"That's better," Lucifer whispered.

"How did you end up with the stone?" Mammon questioned.

"Well, after all I am 'The Light Bearer'. But what is a name?" Lucifer joked, tossing and catching the Cez stone.

Satan approached the lifeless form on the ground. "There is both life and death held within this," he said and kicked the hard shell. "I do not know how it got here, but it did." He looked at the others.

"We have no choice but to keep to the process of a soul's journey. Whatever comes out of there will have to go through Hell before entering Heaven and then final judgment… If that is even possible anymore."

"Whoever is in there is the first to come through in days," Asmodeus reminded them. "And very few others have moved between circles. Some of the souls have just become shadows."

"My circle is empty," Lucifer told them.

"And what is happening to the souls in the Ninth Circle?" Belphegor asked.

"Nothing," Satan replied. "They are just… gone." He looked at Lucifer. "Destroyed forever. Never to enter Heaven."

"Never to return," Lucifer added, looking hard at the lifeless form on the ground.

A collective hush came over the demons.

Lucifer stood. "The journey of *these* souls may be the only way to restore the balance and start the cycle of all souls forward again."

The demons all began to look around the cavern for they saw that there was light emanating from the bioluminescent creatures that had now been awoken by the Cez stone. They absorbed the light energy that it put out. Most of the crawling creatures stayed still, but a few began to climb around the walls and the ceiling of the cavern.

Lucifer stared each of the other Demon Rulers directly in the eyes. No one looked away. "So, it is agreed. Whoever comes out of there will journey through Hell."

"Yes."

"Yes."

"Yes."

"Yes."

"…Yes."

"No," Belphegor refused. "Not until you return my stone," he yelled at Lucifer. "The stone is mine," he demanded.

"I beg to differ," Lucifer stated, holding the stone.

A grumbling began with the other demons.

"We don't have time for this," Satan screamed in a cavern shaking volume.

"Fine. *Yes,*" Belphegor conceded. "But I'm not frightened of you."

"Yes," Lucifer concluded just to make sure that the demons knew that they were all in agreement.

Lucifer held the stone like a coin that he was about to toss. He cast the stone into the air. It landed on the backside of his left hand.

"Whoever is in there will be tested," Satan told them.

"They will all be tested…" added Beelzebub.

"More than the others," Satan shot back. "Whoever is in there came through without being processed at Gokyuzu."

"And they will all have to pass through each of the nine circles," replied Asmodeus.

"And hopefully, avoid the fate of those who are being lost forever," Lucifer added.

One by one, the Demon Rulers of Hell turned to smoke and dust, and their forms were returned to their personal circles from which they came.

"Welcome to Hell," Satan said, staring at the golden wings that held Monk and Tinker.

Lucifer threw the Cez Stone into the air and watched as the light pushed out of it and throughout the chamber. He caught it. Then, he too, the last of the demons, turned to light and exploded, leaving no form.

CHAPTER 7
Caves of Waku

"Ileana!" Axel screamed out.

"Sorcerer!" Aldrick yelled.

"Whatever it is that you were expecting to happen-" Axel continued.

"It's happening!" Aldrick concluded.

Vampire was mumbling incoherently.

"Vampire?" Princess attempted to comfort him.

"Try his real name," Axel told her.

Cadet tried to calm him and bring him back from his lost state. "Thaddeus? Please! Please, let us help you. We are all here for you."

Ileana and Sorcerer rushed over, as Ileana was also keeping a watchful eye on AZ and Seer. AZ gave her a thumb's up as Seer appeared peaceful. AZ continued to attend to moving him to continue to face the sun. The movements were very slight, but AZ would be sure to keep his word.

Ileana held her hand out towards Vampire's face. His eyes were closed, and his mouth was continuing to mumble incoherently.

"It's the Language of Vampires," Ileana told them.

"Do you understand it?" Aldrick asked her.

She gave him a disappointing shake of the head. They looked to one another for any suggestion.

"I recognize this language," Princess told them.

"Strange," said Cadet, "since there is only one vampire. Why would there be a need for a language?"

"For the written word," Ileana told her. "To keep the secrets for any future vampires."

"So, I guess you speak Vampire," Axel added to Princess in a very matter-of-fact way. "Let me guess…"

"Yes. Tinker taught it to me." Princess finished his thought with a sense of loss in her voice. "I thought that we were just speaking our own made up language," she added, holding back her sadness.

"You two really did have a strange way of playing as children," Axel said and gave her a smile to attempt to comfort his sister.

Princess focused on Vampire's mumbling. She moved in closer to hear him better. Her facial expression became confused.

"He is lost," she said, repeating his words for all to understand. "They are lost. We are lost. All is lost."

She looked back at Ileana and Sorcerer to better understand what was happening to Vampire. She understood the meaning of what he was saying. *But why in the Language of Vampires? Why with such delirium?*

Thoughts and fears were rushing through each of them as Vampire again let out the most pained scream. They all fell back with Sorcerer pulling Ileana behind him and the Twins grabbing hold of Princess as they all drew swords.

"Put those away," Ileana demanded. "They would not do any good here anyway." She turned to Sorcerer. "And you. I appreciate the chivalry, but really? You would be better to stay behind me," she told him with a grateful hand on his face.

Again, a scream came.

Princess looked back at AZ, who remained a distance away with Seer. He gestured as if to question what was happening. She motioned back that she did not know. Seer remained in his trance.

"Aldrick, Cadet," Ileana called out. "You need to get to Tinker's cart. There is a white bag with four staffs. Bring it here."

Without question, Aldrick and Cadet ran off as ordered. Aldrick had partially recovered from his injury. Cadet attempted to aid him, but his pride again took over.

Just like his father, Ileana thought. She turned to see Sorcerer staring at her.

"What?" she asked. "I came prepared. I knew the potential of what I was walking into."

He continued staring and raised an eyebrow.

"I put the bag there when I arrived at the Palace of Tebbs," she confessed.

It took longer than expected, but Aldrick and Cadet returned with the bag of rods.

"The entrance to that cave is completely blocked," Aldrick told them.

"But the roof to the entrance has fallen," Cadet added, "so there is access to Tinker's cart if we need anything else from it."

At that moment, Vampire let out a third scream and opened his eyes, which were completely red with rage.

"This is it," Ileana told them and pulled the four staff from the velvet bag.

CHAPTER 8
Hell

The Demon Rulers of Hell were gone. The bioluminescent creatures continued to slither along the walls and the ceiling of the cavern. They began to glow brighter, exposing an opening.

A breeze blew in and began to fill the chamber as dust blew onto the hard cocoon. The dust created a small cyclone, and the cocoon softened. The golden metal wings that had pulled themselves around Monk and Tinker transformed back into feathers. They were pure white in color and began to flutter gently, as if each individual feather was moving without regard to the others. And then, as if by will, the wings took control and coordinated each of the feathers into formation. They opened wide and stretched. They began to flutter with a relaxed but strong motion. Monk was still holding tightly to Tinker. The fluttering wings lifted the two men and held them hovering above the cavern floor.

Monk was conscious. He willed the wings to gently lower them to stand on the ground.

Tinker awoke. They stared at each other awaiting to hear who would address what had happened and what was currently happening. Neither had all the answers. But they were alive. Or at least they believed that they were.

The sensation of the wings grabbed Tinker's attention. He was the first to break the stare. He looked around and saw the slithering cavern creatures. More of them were moving about the walls and the ceiling. He felt as though he was looking at the night sky full of stars rearranging themselves at will.

"Monk?"

"I don't know."

"You don't know what?"

"I don't know the answer to any question that either of us can come up with right now."

"Oh good. I thought it was just me," Tinker responded, as he watched the moving lights.

Monk felt the wings moving under his control, with his thoughts. He pulled them in and out. He made them flap with enough force to lift himself into the air and then to lower him ever so gently back to the ground.

"Amazing," Tinker said as if in a dream state.

Monk concentrated on pulling the wings back into his skin. He felt them resist and vibrate in defense. He focused himself into a meditative state and then allowed the wings to calm under his control. They retreated into their tattoo outlines.

"Monk?"

"I don't even know if I am Monk," he said in a voice that was deeper and raspier than Tinker could recall.

"Well…" Tinker began after a pause. His attention was back to the wings. He was following them up and down, as far around as his point of view allowed. "Whoever you are, you may want these," Tinker told him as he held his tattered robes. "Although I'm not sure how much good they will do you."

Monk took the torn fabric and was able to assemble enough of it to cover his lower body.

"There's an opening," Tinker told him as he realized the area in the cavern walls where the light was absent.

"Yup."

"Doesn't look like we have any other choice."

Tinker followed as Monk had started moving towards the dark area on the cavern wall, where no creature illuminated the walls. He marveled at the wings but said nothing.

Monk stood in front of Tinker and exhaled slowly through his mouth as he opened his eyes.

"Can I…?" Tinker began to ask.

Monk pulled him in for a tight hug. Tinker welcomed the embrace. Monk released him, knowing that Tinker was alright.

"The Blood Moon celebration," Tinker said with a better understanding.

"The black orb," Monk added, knowing that Tinker was referencing the incident which took place on the second night of the Blood Moon on the road to Mortua when he and Seer had encountered the mysterious orb that turned into a portal and pulled Monk in.

"Well, at least we now know what happened," Tinker said.

"We do?" Monk questioned. "We have no idea where we are. This is not the Caves of Waku. Of that, I am sure."

"The future… and other side," Tinker told him. "I thought that black orb was an immature rainbow, but no. That was a true interdimensional portal." He looked around the glowing walls. "This place is not part of our dimension. You must be able to feel that."

Monk looked at Tinker with a questioning expression, still unsure as to where they found themselves.

"Then you explain it," Tinker told him.

"I can't," he admitted with a shake of the head and a still disposition. "But that would prove your theory about traveling to the future."

Tinker and Monk looked around.

"Monk?"

"Yes."

Tinker brought his eyes to look upon his friend.

"Monk. I think that you died."

Monk looked back at him.

"I do feel very much alive, Tink," he told him.

Tinker shook his head.

"I saw you die when you were falling. I felt you die," he said with a crack in his voice. "And it was my fault," Tinker said with a tear. "I shot the Dazer at the Jeweled Dragon, but she disappeared into a portal. The beam from the Dazer landed where you stood. It caused you to fall into that opening and the portal that was in it." Tinker was attempting to hold back his tears.

"Tink?" Monk replied as he walked closer to him and hugged him tight. "We're gonna get through this," he promised.

Tinker wiped his tears and forced himself to stop crying. "A tear from Vampire entered your eye," he told him. "It must have killed you."

With every other death, Vampire took my blood. This time, I took his, Monk thought to himself as Tinker kept recounting the events aloud.

Tinker continued to explain to Monk what he saw when he was falling. He told him about his eyes turning black and then white with light, and about the tattoos illuminating. He told him about the wings springing from the light.

"The last thing that I remember is that you pulled me into you. The wind was knocked from my lungs, and I passed out. Everything went black."

"And now... Here we are," Monk said, looking around the darkness.

"Here we are," Tinker repeated as he looked around them. "Wherever 'here' is."

They looked around the darkness in silence.

"Monk?"

"Yes, Tink."

"I now know for sure that when you disappeared into that black orb on that second night of the Blood Moon, the portal took you to the future," Tinker told him.

Monk looked at Tinker as the crawling blue lights illuminated him.

"I think that you were taken to the future in preparation for this very moment."

Monk continued to look at him in silence. He had already thought the same thing. Yet, he still said nothing.

"I think that you have become-" Tinker hesitated.

"Immortal," Monk finished his thought.

"But...?"

"I guess, we will be finding answers as we go," Monk told him as he pointed towards the darkness.

Monk and Tinker found themselves at the entrance to the tunnel. Tinker was turning in a circle with his hand holding something up to his face.

"This is the only one," he told Monk.

Monk turned to see Tinker looking down the dark tunnel with a pair of night vision goggles that looked similar to collapsible opera glasses, a version of the ones that he and AZ had used in the Caves of Waku. He pointed to them as if to offer them to Monk.

"I can see in the dark, Tink."

"That's right. You can," he replied as he stared through the dark at Monk's glowing eyes. After a few seconds, Tinker spoke again with concern. "I am not sure what parts of you are the same and what parts are different."

Monk looked at the goggles.

"By the way, your eyes are glowing," Tinker added with his usual matter-of-fact tone. Tinker took back the goggles and returned them to his backpack. He pulled out a clear bag that had perforations and walked past Monk.

"Disgusting," Tinker remarked with a contorted facial expression. "And these slimy glowing bugs smell too."

He motioned as if gagging as he grabbed a handful of bioluminescent creatures scurrying around the walls. He dropped them into the clear bag and grabbed for a second and third handful.

"That should do," he said gratefully and wiped his hand in the dirt on the floor of the cavern.

Tinker held the bag aloft and attached it to a retractable pole that he also pulled from his backpack. The light that they emitted lit up to twenty-five feet in any direction.

"Impressive, Tink."

"Why, thank you." He looked at Monk. "Your eyes are back to normal." Tinker motioned for Monk to lead the way.

"You have the light," Monk said as he motioned Tinker forward.

"Yeah, but you can see in the dark. And…you have the wings," he retorted with the same gesture. "I mean," he said with concern, "just in case."

Monk smiled and took the lead.

"Are we going to talk about the wings? The glowing eyes? The-" Tinker began his questions as they walked into the tunnel.

"I already told you that I don't know."

"But I'm sure that we can piece it together," Tinker continued with his inquiries as he had not started walking down the tunnel. "I mean, we should know what else you're capable of. Shouldn't we?"

"I guess. But I wouldn't even know how to figure that out. We woke up to the wings around us. The eyes turned on as I thought that I wanted to see through the dark, but I was already able to see in the dark."

"Think of something else."

"Like shutting you up?"

"You are definitely spending too much time with Vampire. You're starting to gain some of his *less* attractive qualities."

"I know," Monk agreed as he stopped walking. "I'm sorry, Tink. But I really have no answers. And I'm unsure what questions to ask."

"I do have a theory," Tinker said with caution.

"Yes. I'm sure that you do," Monk agreed, looking off into the darkness with what seemed like a heavy heart.

"*He* saved us, Monk. I mean Vampire. And *you* saved us. This," Tinker continued, "this new Monk. Wings. Glowing eyes and whatever else we will find hidden in there. This is what saved us."

Monk maintained his lost stare.

"We are alive because of you and… him." Tinker was waving his hand about acknowledging Vampire. "His tear. The tear that killed you."

"*He* sent you in —"

"He did not! I was already flying into that hole in the ground to get you out," Tinker told Monk, making it sound like it was obvious. "I shot the Dazer. It is my fault that we are here."

Monk said nothing.

Tinker sighed after confessing for the second time. He turned and took a last look at his winged backpack, trying to think of a reason to pick up the broken pieces and take it all with them into the unknown.

"Who knows," he thought aloud. "Maybe it will be useful."

"Leave it," Monk whispered and walked through the darkness.

With every other death, Vampire took your blood. This time, you took his, Tinker thought. He again sighed, but this time, it was to prepare himself for the unknown. He looked back again and moved the light in a circle to see if there was anything else that might be of use on this journey.

"Tink!"

"Coming," he yelled back as he flashed his light upwards, but missed the decayed sign above the entrance of the tunnel that read, *Abandon hope, ye who enter here.* He rushed to catch up, tripping from the uneven footing on which they trampled.

"What should I call you when you turn into the winged guy?" Tinker asked through his panting as he caught up to Monk.

"You don't have to call me anything," Monk told Tinker. "I am the only other one here. If you speak, I know that it will be to me."

"It is possible that I will be talking to myself. I do that, you know," Tinker reminded him.

"Not now, Tink. Not now."

"Fair enough."

CHAPTER 9
Caves of Waku

"Grab these," Ileana commanded as she handed each of her children a particular staff. "We need to surround Vampire."

Axel was given a copper staff that had patinated over time and held a greenish-brown appearance, like a strong tree branch. Aldrick was handed a fiery bronze staff of greater height but with a simple sleek design. Ileana looked into Princess' eyes as she presented to her the golden pole that was the tallest and thinnest, and held a reflective quality that mirrored the movement of the clouds in the sky. Ileana held her own staff made of pure amethyst. The protective and grounding nature of the crystal was felt by her children as soon as they saw the staff.

Axel looked back at Vampire's struggling. "So now what?"

"Aldrick to the north. Axel to the south. Princess," Ileana continued as they moved to where they were told, "east." She looked at Sorcerer. "You will have to take the west, and I will hold the spirit position." She looked at her children with a confident stare. "These staffs will channel your energy to and from one another. Just let the energy flow, both to you and from you. Do not fight what you feel and do not try to control it. Just let it flow. We need to contain Vampire until he recovers."

"Recovers?" Axel asked.

"With Monk gone, he has lost his purpose in aiding humankind." She looked among them. "Monk is the reason that he abandoned his original purpose... To destroy humankind. His love for Monk is the reason he looks to save and protect this dimension."

"But Monk has returned to him in the past," Princess reminded them.

"Yes," Ileana agreed. "But the Jeweled Dragon may destroy everything before Monk is able to return." She looked back at the vulnerable Immortal. "If he believes that, he has no reason to continue to save us."

"If anything goes wrong-", Sorcerer attempted to convince her to change positions. He moved his hands and created a staff that was made of ice- blue, white and transparent in places.

"Nothing will," she assured him.

Vampire was on his hands and knees. His black and white clothing was covered in the angry red sands of Waku. The redness of the sands were taking over his emotional state and compounding his sadness and fear. His screams continued. His pain was palpable.

"We need to contain him until his fear passes. Magic is the only thing that can hold him. It is the only thing that can protect him… and us," Ileana told them. "This will not be easy, and it will take all of us working together, feeling our own and each other's strengths. There is no room for fear. We must trust in ourselves and each other. You are the Three of Legend," she reminded them. "Magic is innate within you. Feel it. Allow it. Let it flow through you. On my word, you need to push all of your magic into your staff and smash it hard into the ground."

They all nodded in agreement. Princess was positioned close to where the sands had moved away. The drop would kill anyone who was to fall over.

"Brae," Ileana comforted her from just over her shoulder. "You must trust what you feel. You must trust the magic."

A sense of comfort again ran through Princess as she heard Ileana call her by her true name.

"Was it you who gave me my name?" she questioned with a smile.

Ileana winked but said nothing as she came to stand to the southeast. They positioned themselves, surrounding Vampire.

"Now," Ileana screamed, and they all dropped their staffs into the sands.

The forceful impact threw red dust into the air. A line of fire made its way from Aldrick's staff to Princess. A ripple of air flowed from her staff to Axel's, which then sent a line of red dust particles to Sorcerer. His staff responded with a line of sharp ice back to Aldrick. The ice melted on impact and a line of white light replaced all the lines. All four staffs then shot a second line of white light to Ileana's crystal staff. The barrier was up. Vampire was restrained within the magical entrapment. The white light pushed inward and struck Vampire. He screamed out in pain.

"Focus," Ileana screamed out, knowing that her children would be shocked by the scene. "Focus!"

Vampire remained on his hands and knees.

Each of the staffs began to glow. Sharp bolts of visible energy began to spark. One by one, each magical rod sparked a bolt of silver energy that connected to each of the others and pulled at the sand and dust. The electrical connection created a series of bolts that recalled a curtain. The dust clouded what was held within, including Vampire.

Each one of them felt the power coming from within, as well as being generated by the others as they connected through magic. They were feeling what Ileana had described.

Vampire looked up. The energy that surrounded him had turned white. The intensity of it reflected off Vampire's eyes, as he was able to gather the strength and the sense to look up. His eyes were black. He pulled himself to stand and was back on his feet. He rushed forward and charged the curtain of light that trapped him. He was thrown back into the center of the entrapment. The force was not felt by the others.

"Good," Ileana screamed. "Keep to the same thoughts. We are not looking to hurt him, but he needs to regain control of himself before it is safe to let him out."

"You're telling us," Aldrick said after seeing the intensity of Vampire's attack on the magical energy. He looked through the light to his brother.

Axel was already looking in his direction and nodded.

Princess held strong.

"Let me out of this, you fool!" Vampire demanded of Sorcerer.

"I am sorry that Monk is gone. We all are. But we have to stop the dragon. Otherwise, all is lost, and his death will be for nothing. It is the only way for him to come back to you, Thaddeus," Sorcerer shot back.

Vampire was panting. His rage was showing itself in his physical transformation as his eyes remained completely black and his lower jaw protruded, exposing fangs.

"You will destroy us all with your pain. Your pain is feeding your anger, and your anger is feeding your pride. You could not save him, but it is not your fault. We cannot trust you in this state of mind," he said and waved his hand to his own eyes to signify to Vampire that he was in a vial state. "Control your pain! Now!"

Vampire rushed at the magical trapping and again was pushed back by the current that surrounded him. He screamed out in frustration as the shock forced him back to his calmer physical state.

"He cannot hurt us as long as we hold," Ileana reminded them.

They trusted what she said. Princess turned to Sorcerer, and then looked at Vampire as he was back on the ground on hands and knees. He looked so broken.

"Now is not the time for pity," Ileana yelled to her. "This will end, but if we let him out in his present state, he will destroy us all."

"Monk is gone," Sorcerer added. "The Jeweled Dragon has punished Vampire and is now going to work to destroy everything. If Vampire believes that Monk is gone forever, he has no reason to save us. He feels that everything is lost. He will side with the Jeweled Dragon unless-"

"Unless we release him from his pain," Princess concluded.

"Unless he releases himself," Ileana corrected.

The ripple in the air hovered near Princess.

"It is true, my lady," Ghost confirmed to her. "And I am here to assist you if you need me."

She nodded in gratitude but said nothing. Princess held her focus on her staff. She held onto her power going to the others and their power coming into her.

Sorcerer was staring at the ripple in the air. He knew that Ghost was with his daughter. However, he also knew that Ghost had an agenda of his own in regard to Vampire's emotional plight.

Ghost took a visible form and was staring back at Sorcerer. He shook his head as if to say, No.

"You too do not have a choice," Sorcerer yelled out to him. "If things go wrong, it will affect you too."

Ghost's visible form dissolved until it had vanished back to a ripple in the air.

CHAPTER 10
Hell

Monk and Tinker made their way cautiously along the unstable path. Tinker feared looking down and discovering that the surface was made of broken skulls and bones. He was able to see through the darkness with the light that he had created, as well as with his goggles. Monk was able to see further into the darkness through his own eyes. Tinker's curiosity got the best of him, and he looked at the road ahead. *Rocks,* he thought with relief. The tunnel was becoming broader and higher. The light emitted from the slimy blue creatures was now only meeting ground and air. *Open sky,* Tinker thought.

"Monk?"

"Yes. I think that somehow, it is a night sky."

Tinker removed the goggles to look with his natural eyes. He was searching for signs of familiarity. He wanted to see recognizable constellations. He looked to see the horizon; yet, all he found without the goggles was darkness.

"At least, we seem to be out of the tunnel," he said as he found a positive point of view on their situation.

Monk shook his head as he laughed.

"Did I teach you that?"

"Teach me what?"

"Never ending optimism."

"Nah," Tinker replied. "I was born with that. Had to be or I never would have made it to you," he said with a shrug of the shoulders. "But you definitely helped me to keep it."

"I'll take it," Monk told him and put his hand on his shoulder. Monk's demeanor turned serious as he looked off into the darkness. "Tink. Like I said before, I do not have answers, but this is starting to feel familiar."

"Familiar how?" Tinker asked.

"Like I have been here before but feeling like it was not me."

"I'm trying to follow."

"So am I," Monk admitted his own confusion at his thoughts. "So, let's try to reason this out."

"For as much as reason will be able to help us," Tinker joked.

"We will have to extend our acceptance of what is reasonable."

"You seem to have come up with something."

Tinker pulled on the goggles to hang around his neck. The blue light shined on them. He pushed the pole that the bag was suspended to into the ground. It held in place as a shrieking sound emanated from the bioluminescent creatures within.

He heard a scratching noise and squinted his eyes with concern. It was not coming from the bag. The scratching stopped.

Tinker was known for talking with his hands. He needed them to be free to be able to think, theorize, and hopefully, conclude what was happening. And because his hands moved so erratically, people oftentimes thought that he was practicing magic.

"Tink?" Monk begged, questioning his silence with his hands on his face.

"Okay," Tinker began. "I am thinking and speaking at the same time, so it may feel like we are walking through a maze."

"So, like any other conversation with you," Monk again joked.

"Exactly," Tinker admitted.

Monk held his tongue.

"Okay. What do we know for sure?"

Monk motioned to talk.

"My questions are for me, Monk. Not for you," Tinker told him and began to pace on the unstable rocks.

Monk held his hands up in surrender to let Tinker work through his analytical process.

"We know that we fell… That you fell. I jumped… Flew in, actually. Gravity took its course and held to the Laws of Physics. And then, we went through a portal. But where did that portal come from? Who opened it?"

"Who or what?" Monk added to a disapproving look from Tinker.

Monk agreed to stay quiet but began organizing the information as Tinker spoke.

"We know that Vampire's blood tear entered into your eye and that after that, you transformed." He began tripping on the rocks as he paced faster and moved his hands about, as if placing his words in columns and order. "We know that your tattoo came alive and sprouted wings, but we do not know how. And we know that we do not know that... Unless you know that."

Monk said nothing.

"Do you?" Tinker asked with his hands thrown into the air.

"Can I speak?" Monk asked.

Tinker rolled his eyes.

"No. I don't know how," Monk rushed. "I just know what I feel."

"*We* don't know what *you* feel," Tinker argued. "And *we* know that *we* cannot trust *you* right now."

"Excuse me?" Monk asked with a tone of having been insulted.

"Don't get mad at me," Tinker told him. "You're the one who 'transformed' into whatever it is that you turned into."

"Yeah. I guess that's true," Monk agreed. "But *I* did save *us…*"

"*We* think," Tinker countered. "It is possible that we are dead."

"We would know if we were dead."

"Did you know when you were dead before?" Tinker asked.

"Not sure."

"So then, we don't know that," Tinker argued. "And we will accept that we are alive. Or at least that I am. I'm still under the belief that you died," he concluded with his hands on his knees as if exhausted by the logic. "And became Immortal."

Tinker was thinking. He pulled himself upright.

"Monk?"

"Yeah?"

"Vampire tears kill. They are too toxic for even a vampire. That is why they are pushed from their bodies. And there is only one thing that can form them."

"And that is?"

"Fear."

Monk looked at him for further explanation.

"Vampires don't fear anything, Monk," Tinker said cautiously.

"There is one thing that he fears," Monk said with sadness. "Losing me forever," Monk said. Monk pulled himself into a taller posture. "Tink?"

"Yes?"

"How is it that I am now even more aware of memories of my past lives? I feel as though I know more than what Vampire has told me about my past lives, more than my dreams have shown me. I have real memories, things that I do not recall from dreams, that I did not have before and from situations that Vampire and I never discussed."

"Maybe, he did tell you," Tinker said, "in that tear."

"Well then, it seems as though Vampire thinks that you and I are lost forever." Monk looked around. "I think we are in Hell."

"Oh, that is certainly not good… Not good for anybody," Tinker said and dropped his hands back to his knees.

CHAPTER 11
Caves of Waku

Vampire threw himself against the magical borders that contained him. With each push, he was thrown back. His anger was growing. His eyes remained fully black as his fangs grew. His monstrous transformation made him stronger, more primal than humane. He pushed against the humming electricity of the entrapment in an attempt to overcharge it and force it to collapse. Bolts of electricity pushed out from where he made contact, allowing him to see what was happening outside.

"Do not pull at your energies," Sorcerer yelled out. "He is restrained."

Princess looked to the sky. She was thinking about the movement of the clouds. The idea of air gave her a sense of strength.

Vampire noticed the focus in her eyes. She was not the weak one.

Axel was looking at the red sands on the ground. He stomped to feel the solid surface under his feet and felt the same surge of power.

Vampire knew that he too had found stability within his magic.

Aldrick looked to the electrical currents that reminded him of fire as they shot across the staffs and across the entrapment. He marveled at the power.

My way out, Vampire thought and pushed hard towards Aldrick.

Vampire rushed through the electrical field. Ileana reacted and focused her energy towards Aldrick. Aldrick reacted as the force of her shock reached him just in time for him to focus on Vampire's approach. He held tight to his staff and squeezed hard.

Vampire was pushed back from the magical border as fire erupted and surrounded Aldrick. Aldrick fought his fear of being consumed by the heat, but held tight to his staff.

Vampire had been thrown back and was panting hard while on his back, in the red sands. He transformed back to his human self. His fangs retreated and his eyes turned back to their calm appearance.

Outside the entrapment, AZ and Cadet continued moving Seer to face the sun. AZ was knocked backwards as Seer opened his eyes with a look of terror and sprung up. He tried to get up and run but fell back to the red sands. Cadet grabbed hold of him to try and comfort him. Seer continued his delirium as he gasped for air.

"Seer?" AZ yelled and helped to hold him down. "Seer?"

Seer yelled through his panic. "I cannot find Monk! But *they* found me!"

He was crazed and seemingly unable to comprehend what was happening.

"Who found you?" AZ demanded.

"I don't know how this happened," Seer cried out. "I cannot be held responsible."

"No one is blaming you," Cadet told him as she continued trying to comfort him. "Just please, tell us what you see."

"No. No. I did not see this. None of this was foreseeable."

AZ pulled Seer's hood and with the fabric between them, he grabbed his head in his hands, forcing him to look directly into his eyes. Seer could not hear what AZ was saying to him. All he heard was a scratching sound that seemed to be coming from all around them.

"Seer. Look at me. It's AZ."

Seer attempted to move his head or at least his eyes from AZ's vice grip. AZ held strong.

"Seer!" He screamed, demanding his attention. "Tell me what's happening," he continued with a caring voice.

"No… Not… Nothing. I see nothing when I look for them."

"Focus Seer."

He screamed as he pulled himself from AZ. Seer backed away and slapped himself in the face multiple times as if trying to wake himself. "I can't get free," he cried. "That sound. That scratching sound." Tears fell from his eyes, and he held his head in his hands.

"Who found you? Tinker? Monk? What does that mean?"

Seer forced himself to calm down. His quick, shallow breaths slowed and looked out with no particular focus.

AZ attempted to continue his inquiry, but Cadet put her hand on his arm to get his attention. She shook her head. AZ stopped himself before another word came out. Seer sat with his arms wrapped tightly around himself. He continued to slowly calm himself.

"You're okay. You're okay. You're okay," Seer repeated to himself and slowly stopped rocking. He continued to look off into nothingness, lost in the absence of his psychic vision. AZ looked at Ghost who appeared and hovered over his shoulder, overhearing the conversation.

Ghost shook his head. "We all have our own demons. Leave him to find peace with his." Ghost looked into the entrapment and saw Vampire sitting in the sand with his head dropped and his elbows on his knees. "And him to his."

"Ghost. You have to get in there," Sorcerer yelled.

"No," he refused.

"Ghost," Ileana forced. "He needs to know that we are doing this for him, not to hurt him. And he cannot hurt you."

"This is the absolute last thing that I want to do," Ghost stated.

"Maybe, this is the last thing that you have to do," Sorcerer informed him.

Ghost floated closer to the lights that surrounded Vampire. He was near Ileana.

The sun was setting. Ileana and Sorcerer showed a stronger concern in their stare.

"Without your intervention, this may take some time…" Ileana added. "Time that we do not have."

"He has to remember why he chose to fight for this dimension," Sorcerer told Ghost. "He has to believe that Monk will return to him. And the only way for that to happen is for us to stop the Jeweled Dragon from annihilating everything."

The Twins maintained focus. Princess saw her parents point to the sun as Sorcerer traced a path and pointed to the horizon. *Light magic.* She looked towards AZ, who continued to attend to Seer and his fragile mental state.

The Light Magic that came from the sun was being used to contain Vampire. He would gain power in the dark of night, regardless of the moon's brightness. Princess redirected her focus along with her brothers.

"Please Ghost," she begged.

Ghost looked at the girl and sighed. "Very well," he said, maintaining his stare on her. "Very well," he repeated as he looked into the entrapment and the magical light that bordered it. He held a sinister smile and then drew a deep breath. A gentle breeze blew in and floated him forward. Princess mired at the colors of light that were created as he made contact with the magic. The brilliance of that glow shined on her face and lit her in a way that drew AZ's attention from his present task.

"Beautiful," was all that he could say, allowing his thoughts to come to words.

CHAPTER 12
Hell

The sky had become brighter at the horizon, less black and more navy blue. It looked as if day was breaking in the place where Monk and Tinker had found themselves. The surface that they were walking upon had changed. It was less rocky and more organized into laid bricks. A rust-colored path slithered through the rolling hills.

The path less traveled, Monk thought to himself. "We will have to move on instinct more than logic."

Tinker said nothing as he took in the unfamiliar surroundings.

The hills were covered in an unnaturally illuminated green grass with a multitude of fragrant flowers that were oriented in bouquet-like patches throughout the terrain. Somehow, even in the dark, the color was visible.

"Monk? Did you ever question your faith?" Tinker asked.

"Never."

"Do you regret being a part of the Order of Naa?"

"I never chose the order. Like you, I was brought there as an orphan. I learned their ways but didn't accept them blindly." He looked off in the distance. "I agreed to the ones I felt were noble and fair, but rejected the others that seemed like senseless violence. Quahin and his forms of punishment… What happened to Seer and would have happened to you, had I not intervened. We were only children when Seer was forced out of the Order. They feared his power. They feared not being able to control him."

"Did any part of your faith come from the Order?"

"My faith?" Monk questioned. "No, Tink. My faith came from me. My faith came from you. Above all, I believe in you and the man you have become."

Tinker smiled.

"My faith is true. But so is my sin," Monk confessed.

Tinker looked at him as they continued their walk through this very curious path that they had found themselves upon.

"My rejected vow was lust," Monk confessed. "Lust for life and understanding. Lust for protecting the ones I love. I found that my values were different from those of the Order, but I needed to stay at the monastery as I searched for Seer. The Dark Sisters had taken him, and I needed to save him and remind him that he was loved… That he was part of a family."

Tinker nodded.

"It was twenty years later when I finally found him in the Desert of Xedu. But the lust to find him is what gave me the strength to keep going."

"I understand what you mean. It's like my need to seek knowledge. It feels almost gluttonous. When you left me at the Palace of Mortua, I was hidden away from people. That's when I found my sanctuary in the Royal Library. The other kids did not even know I was in the palace. Well, most of the time. On occasion, I would sneak out to see what was happening in Mortua."

"Tink," Monk interrupted. "We had to keep you hidden. Quahin would have killed you."

"I know," Tinker admitted. "But still, it was lonely. And I know that I was a bit of a strange kid." He laughed at his own memory. "Princess was my only friend."

"And a good one at that," Monk reminded him.

"The best!" he shot back in full agreement. "But still, it was lonely. Books and knowledge became my friends, and what I discovered in them became my inspiration to seek out the truth in the real world, beyond the bridges of Mortua. Remember the gryphons?" Tinker asked with a laugh and pointed at his backpack. "I have the hide in my bag."

Monk laughed.

"I would walk for hours, by myself of course, because Princess was busy being the Princess of Mortua and I didn't have any other friends. Sometimes, she would conceal her identity and walk with me... when she could. But in walking through the fields and valleys and hiking the hills outside of the city, I started to find peace in my search for knowledge."

Monk gave him a quizzical look.

"Well, not entirely. I did want to figure out a way to take off Quahin's other hand."

Monk laughed again.

"And you did when you sliced through his wrist in Bacaa," Monk reminded him.

Tinker laughed, but his emotion was lost between pride and embarrassment that he had severed Monsignor Quahin's other hand at the Purge Festival in Bacaa.

Monk looked saddened by Tinker's confession.

"It wasn't your fault," Tinker told him.

"But I wasn't there for you."

"You were 'rehabilitating' Seer from what The Dark Sisters had done to him. They convinced him that believing in their corrupt ways was his path. You had enough to deal with."

Monk said nothing.

"I started walking along the sea," Tinker said with a hint of a smile. "I would talk to the water and as silly as it sounds, at times, thought it spoke back."

Monk knew to keep quiet. He was there to listen. Tinker's confession needed no guidance, no interjection of perspective.

"I started to think of and create so many more things. Helpful things! I took that gluttony and threw it into my thirst for knowledge. Aldrick and Axel question the need for all my stuff. But all my stuff has a true purpose, potentially at least, but true. And so far, some of it has been found to be very useful. So yes," he continued, defiant. "I will continue to discover and invent. I will look to the water and see form and make it into something that is helpful and useful and can change things for the better."

"That is powerful, Tink."

"Maybe the chapter of this quest will be called 'Lost Confessions'." Tinker rummaged through his bag and pulled out the tattered journal that he had grabbed from his cart in the Caves of Waku.

Monk looked at him with concern.

"Monk," Tinker said while looking at the line at the horizon. "We are lost."

"Yes. We are." Monk looked around. "Now, let's figure out how to get back before someone else has to write our memoirs."

"Agreed."

They continued in reflective silence, until Tinker offered an observation.

"So, when you think about it, we're really not that different… any of us."

"What do you mean?"

"Well, take you and I for instance. We have been able to realize our greatest sin, which seems to be at our essence, and although not being able to get rid of it, we have been able to use it for good."

"True. But that's you and me. What about all of the others who haven't gotten themselves to the point that they can even identify or accept their sin?"

"Well, they may need a little guidance," Tinker answered with a naïve sentiment.

"Probably more than a little. Why do you think I've been back nine times so far? And you, probably the same? We have evolved our psyche with what our souls have brought from prior lives. We connect and reconnect. Our energies are drawn back to find truth. To find peace. Some of us need whole other lives to be able to see."

"Sounds pretty much like judgment to me," Tinker argued in a non-confrontational tone. "I just think that we all have the potential."

"I agree. It's just that some of us will require a lot more time and experience to rise to that potential."

Tinker walked on in a contemplative silence. Monk periodically looked to his right to see how Tinker's mind was operating through his facial expressions. It made him joyous to see his friend in his natural and most comfortable state.

"Look," Tinker told him and pointed to what looked like a village.

"We are going to need to keep our wits about us, Tink."

Tinker nodded in agreement.

"We will be tested," Monk added.

Tinker again nodded in agreement.

"We are going there whether we like it or not," Tinker said as he looked around. "This is the only road, and the only road leads there."

CHAPTER 13
The Entrapment

"Hello Vampire," Ghost said with full confidence as he came through the illuminated field and into the presence of the self-torturing Immortal.

"Go away, Ghost!" Vampire demanded.

"No," he argued without a flicker in his voice. "I was sent to talk you down from the proverbial ledge."

"I said, *Leave!*" he screamed.

"I said no," he replied, again with no interruption in his tone.

"I will destroy you if you stay."

"You already did," he told him.

Vampire seemed caught off guard. He wrinkled his brow and turned to look at the translucent spirit.

"I know you," he said, searching his memories.

Ghost gave the slightest smile on the left side of his mouth.

"I said that I am here to talk you down. Personally, I don't care if you step back or jump off. But the sooner you get down, one way or another, the sooner we can all move forward."

"Dax," Vampire said with surprise, remembering Ghost's living form.

"Do not use that name!" Ghost demanded.

Vampire held his gaze and his place.

"You struck that name from existence when you killed me in Paris. But you already know that."

"That was millennia ago. But yes. I do," Vampire admitted, yet still unable to take his eyes off the specter. "All this time?" He kept a confused expression. "All this time and you said nothing."

"What was there to say? What would it change? Would I get my life back? No, I would not. So, no," he moved in close to Vampire with venom in the stare of his hollowed eyes. "Nothing would change."

Vampire kept eye contact, but with remorse in his stare as opposed to the hatred in Ghost's hollow glare.

"You know," Ghost softened. "When I was alive, I envied you, your immortality. So, go figure," he snickered at his words. "I got what I wished for."

Ghost was moving about the entrapment with an effortless breeze guiding him as if he were out for an evening stroll. He turned towards Vampire and moved through him. The chill was palpable, even for Vampire. The cold caused shivers on contact. It was the primary weapon that a ghost had, and it could cause pain, and even death, if the specter lingered long enough in a living body.

"When I returned to this dimension in this form, I learned that to move forward you had to learn from the past. For you, that will mean revisiting Monk's previous lives. You need to remember why you veered from your path of destruction and why you chose to save this dimension. You need to remember what it feels like to have Monk return to you and to have faith that he will. Destroying the Jeweled Dragon is the only way for Monk to return to you. This is not going to be easy for you, Vampire, but it is necessary for our quest to move along. We all have our sins to overcome." He turned with an eerie grin. "Don't we?" he said over his shoulder towards where Vampire still shivered.

"Yes," Vampire forced out, overcoming the chill. "Yes. We all do." Vampire turned to face Ghost and positioned himself to take back control. "And that includes you, my old friend. It seems that 'envy' has not left your vapid soul."

"No. It seems as though it has not."

Ghost maintained his hovering presence and his direct eye contact in front of Vampire. Vampire matched his intensity. The silence became awkward.

"Who will break first?" Ghost asked as he moved in a circular pattern.

"Envy versus Pride," Vampire said as he stood in opposition to Ghost. "Which sin is stronger?" He maintained his stare. "Or rather, which sinner?"

CHAPTER 14
Caves of Waku

AZ watched the clouds that were closing in and a dust storm that was threatening from the northwest. The unspoken concern was that the impending darkness from the storm could block the sunlight that powered the Light Magic to keep Vampire contained. He looked back at Seer whose balance was still challenged but was back on his feet. He continued to appear shaken from the loss of Monk and Tinker. His expression showed concern but was not offering anything else about what he had experienced.

"What did you see?" AZ questioned cautiously, as Cadet was helping to steady him.

"Nothing," he rushed, but then relaxed into a moment of clarity and allowed himself to speak freely with them. "When Tinker followed Monk into that hole, I felt wind. I saw nothing but felt the wind. And then heat. But it all stopped, and I felt nothing... Just *nothing.*"

AZ had a look of sheer panic on his face.

"Oh shit!" Aldrick screamed.

Cadet motioned for Seer and AZ to stay by the boulders that created one of the entrances to the caves. She ran to Aldrick to see what was happening.

Seer's eyes turned red, and his body convulsed. He was down on the ground again.

"Seer!" AZ yelled out. Seer, who was holding himself tight in a fetal position, was babbling nonsense and laughing hysterically. He convulsed until he finally exhausted himself and fell unconscious. AZ checked that Seer was breathing and put his hand to his heart to feel it beating. He gave one last look to Seer and chose to go to the others to see what he could do to aid their efforts.

"AZ?" Princess questioned his presence. "Where is Seer?"

"Asleep by the boulders," he replied, observing the lights of the containment. "What can I do to help?"

"Nothing unless you can move those clouds away from the sun and stop that dust storm."

AZ looked to the clouds, which had moved closer to shrouding the sun and then observed the approaching dust storm.

"Got it," he said as he ran from her towards the cave entrance.

"Got it? Got what?" Princess yelled out.

AZ ran past Ileana, who exchanged a quick look with Sorcerer. AZ climbed down through the opening in the ceiling of the cave entrance and reached Tinker's cart. He was rummaging through Tinker's prized possessions. "It has to be here," AZ begged to the assortment of gadgets and apparatuses that were present among Tinker's things. Books were thrown throughout the cart, taking up any open space to stabilize Tinker's projects.

He flipped the pages of one of Tinker's books that had drawings of some of his inventions with names at the top of the pages.

"No. No. No," he said as he moved quickly, hoping to find something that might help. "Storm Catcher? It looks like a megaphone," he remarked.

AZ stopped and read. *PURPOSE: To limit or even stop a storm from happening. CAUTION: Needs to be activated with one or more sparks (depending on the power of the storm).*

"Yes," he said and rummaged through the cart for a device that looked like the one on the page.

"AZ!" Princess screamed. "Whatever you are planning, you better be quick."

The dust storm was getting closer and was pushing the low hanging clouds closer to the sun.

AZ quickened his pace as he continued to search. "Ah ha!" he yelled in excitement. He matched the device to the rendering. "Thank you, Tink. Thank you."

AZ pulled an unassuming copper flask from under the Storm Catcher which did look like a crank arm megaphone. *Strenium* was written across it. He searched a bit more and pulled a rifle. He checked to see if it was loaded. It was not. He grabbed a handful of bullets and forced them into his pockets. With the assortment of objects in hand, he began running again, towards the dust storm.

The bullets will explode and activate it, AZ thought.

As he climbed out of the tunnel, a breeze blew the page over and revealed the rest of the instructions for the use of the *Storm Catcher… and deposited in the receptacle before being released somewhere safe.*

"AZ!" Princess screamed with concern.

"Don't worry," he shouted back. "I got this." He kept running until he was at the outer border of the dust storm wind swirls and the edge of the cliff.

"This is it," he told himself. AZ opened the tripod that served as a stand for the device and positioned the crank arm downward to start. He dropped to his knees and pulled bullets out to load the rifle.

"They don't fit," he discovered. "They're the wrong fucking bullets."

AZ looked to the storm, which was nearly upon him. He looked back to the tunnel entrance. There was no time.

"Shit!" he screamed in further frustration. "Think AZ. Think."

He sat on his knees as the winds began to grow stronger. The dust was kicking up at his face. AZ looked at the device that he had grabbed from the cart and saw it shaking, ready to be lifted into the storm. He noticed the bullets that were scattered around him being lifted off the ground and began swirling into the air in the winds of the dust storm.

"That's it!" he exclaimed into the roaring winds and dust causing him to choke and cover his eyes.

One by one, AZ grabbed the rest of the ten bullets from his pockets and threw them into the circling winds. Each one was taken up further by the storm. He stabilized the device under his foot so that it would not blow away.

"What is he doing?" Sorcerer questioned.

"I don't know!" Princess replied.

"Oh shit!" Axel added, realizing what AZ was up to.

"He's going to catch the storm," Aldrick finished Axel's thought.

"Fucking genius!" Axel added.

"Everybody hold on as best you can! He's going to…"

AZ threw the last bullet into the air. It was pulled up and into the storm. He drew his attention to the Storm Catcher device. He turned it slightly to the northwest with the back end facing into an opening in the ground. He waited until…

"BANG!" The first bullet fired from the pressure of the storm.

"BANG!" fired the second.

"Now," he said as he took the rifle and held it like a bat. He held his foot on the Storm Catcher and took the copper flask from his pocket. He let it slowly rise into the air as more bullets were firing.

"BANG! BANG!" The bullets continued.

"Three. Four," he counted as he watched as the copper flask continued to slowly rise.

"BANG!"

"Five!"

AZ swung the rifle hitting the flask as hard as he could with the back handle. The flask flew upward with great force.

Again, he waited.

He saw the color change from within the dust storm and then heard the crash of the explosion. The flask had exploded and the strenium, a rare magical element that dissolved storms, contained within it was reacting with the storm itself. AZ started the crank on the Storm Catcher.

"Oh shit!" he exclaimed. "Where do I put the storm?" He had not gotten the storm collection receptacle. He had nowhere to put the storm as it would be pulled through the device.

"No time to panic, AZ."

He had already positioned the device with the back end towards the opening in the ground.

"Improvise. That's what Tinker would do!" he told himself and began turning the crank with all of the effort he could muster. It was as if the storm was pulling the crank back.

"Actually," he pushed through his struggling expression. "Tink would not have to improvise. He would have gotten it right the first time."

AZ pulled harder and continued to feel the storm's resistance, but the strenium was working, weakening the force of the storm. AZ began to find it easier to move the crank. He was able to pull harder and faster and saw the storm coming out the back end into the opening. As he continued to turn the device arm, he was going at a faster pace and saw the light in the sky change. The clouds that had been approaching the sun had been pulled into the storm and were now the last bits to go through the Storm Catcher, leaving the sky clear and the sunlight in full brilliance. AZ forcefully moved the crank until the entirety of the storm had gone through and he felt no resistance from the crank arm.

"He did it," Axel yelled.

"AZ! You did it," Aldrick yelled loud enough for him to hear.

They all felt their power growing stronger again.

Exhausted, AZ lay next to the Storm Catcher and turned onto his back to catch his breath. The storm swirled in the open tunnels below him, and he turned his head to see the movement of the clouds from the top of the funnel shaped destruction. AZ stood and threw his hands to the air in celebration of his achievement.

"Yes," he screamed.

"Yes AZ! Yes," yelled Princess along with her brothers.

AZ lowered his hands as he felt the ground move under him. He rolled onto his hands and knees as he heard the sound of crumbling rock. He saw the ground crack twenty feet from where he was.

"AZ," Princess screamed.

AZ made a run for it to get to the other side of the crack before the ground toppled from under him. The ground under AZ fell into the opening, and he and the Storm Catcher along with it.

"AZ," Princess screamed again and made an attempt to run to him.

"No!" demanded Sorcerer. "We cannot break our positions."

She looked panicked.

"There is nothing that you can do for him," Ileana attempted to comfort her.

Princess' pain pushed forth a greater amount of magical force into the entrapment.

Ileana looked at Sorcerer, who showed his concern on his face but then relaxed it.

"Or is there?" Ileana asked herself.

Sorcerer was still staring at Princess. He looked back to Ileana and nodded. They both cautiously released their staffs from the entrapment. It held. The 'Three of Legend' were powering the entrapment by themselves. Sorcerer and Ileana ran towards the opening in the ground. They saw that the sun was setting. Even with their strength, they would not be able to keep their powers up in the dark of night.

They came to where the new edge was and looked down to see the storm still swirling.

"The winds must have pulled the loose ground enough to break it off," Ileana deduced.

"If only Seer had half a mind right now, we could know if AZ was..."

Sorcerer's words were cut off by his amazement of AZ holding suspended in midair.

"Is she...?" he began to ask.

"Yes," Ileana replied, although not fully believing her own astonishment.

She looked back at her daughter and saw the power flying off her aura, stronger than from her brothers. Ileana turned her attention back to AZ and maneuvered her hands to cast a spell that would take him up further into the air and land safely on the surface at her feet.

Sorcerer waved his arms and hands in an intricate pattern which raised the storm collection receptacle from Tinker's cart. It flew through the air and into his grip. He cast his own spell to gather the storm into the vial. He mixed strabilium, another magical element, and sapphire dust to lighten the storm's strength. It would hold for as long as the vial stayed airtight.

"Am I dead?" AZ asked as he opened his eyes and saw the form standing above him.

"Apparently not," Ileana remarked. "And you have only one person to thank for that," she added, pointing at Princess, who continued to put out immense magical force as the air blew freely around her and bathed her in the strength of her essence.

CHAPTER 15
The Entrapment

From the inside, the entrapment was surrounded by moving lights that limited visibility from what was happening outside. Ghost looked around, expecting the confined space inside to feel smaller. But somehow, magically, it was more spacious than it appeared on the outside.

"Shall we begin?" Ghost questioned, breaking the awkward silence between himself and Vampire. He moved through Vampire and caused that unforgiving chill, as if to say that he still had the upper hand. "As I recall, you always liked a game of cat and mouse."

"Yes," Vampire said, holding back the chattering of his teeth. "You are correct. And as I recall, I have always won," he concluded, turning towards the source of his pain.

"Ah, and there it is," Ghost cracked a callous grin. "Your ego. Your pride. Your downfall." He glided effortlessly through the air and through Vampire yet again.

Vampire maintained a reactionless stance.

"And speaking of *downfall*…" Ghost continued as he maintained his back to Vampire. "Your pride is the cause of Tinker having to follow Monk into that hole in the ground, and to the demise of them both."

Ghost's words enraged Vampire, and he leapt to attack the spirit. Ghost countered with his vile chill. Vampire was held within Ghost's form.

"All is not lost, Thaddeus," Ghost whispered, even though he was enjoying torturing the Immortal.

Ghost put forth a proud smile and squeezed his cold into Vampire. Although he felt the chill, Vampire dared not acknowledge the pain. Pride would not allow it. Ghost held tight but felt his resistance.

"Now is not the time for selfishness," he confessed as he traveled forward in the air. "This will not be easy," he spoke as he looked into the dancing lights of the entrapment. "This will not be easy," he repeated as if lost in thought, "…for any of us."

CHAPTER 16
Hell

Monk and Tinker entered what felt like a regular town from the only road of rust-colored bricks. The outskirts were full of active taverns.

"Seems like home?" Monk questioned.

"Home? Really, Monk?"

"Pick a place, Tink," Monk told him. "Mortua, Dellai, wherever. Dive bars on the outer edges of the cities, filled with all the sins from greed and envy to the lazy and unreliable. Gluttonous drunks become angry and fight because of an insult to their pride."

"This doesn't sound like you, Monk," Tinker said to him with an air of caution.

Monk questioned his own words.

Fear had come into Tinker's thoughts and his nose began to twitch.

"No, Tink," Monk ordered to stop Tinker's reaction. "We are going to get through this together."

"Yes, we are," Tinker agreed with a reassured sense of optimism. "And get back to the others."

The line on the horizon that Tinker noticed earlier had not changed. Time had passed, but no added sunlight had come into the sky.

"That is odd, huh?" Tinker questioned. "Eternal night?"

"Eternal darkness," Monk told him. "And to make it worse, the false promise of hope… Hope for something that will never come to be." Monk turned in a circle and took in everything around them. "Tink? I know for sure where we are." He looked at the road ahead. "We are in Hell."

Tinker's mind swirled. He replayed everything from when he followed Monk into the pit in the ground, the portal, Vampire's tear entering Monk's eye, getting knocked out as Monk pulled him into himself, and then awakening here… in Hell.

"So, we did die," Tinker said.

Monk did not reply to Tinker's statement. "Come on, Tink," was all he said and continued to move along the rust-colored bricks.

Monk and Tinker walked among the drunken revelers and the loud parties that were taking place in the multitude of taverns in the night covered hamlet.

Monk pointed to a particular building. It was loud and had a sensual feel that emanated from the warm glow of the orange-colored lights pouring out of the windows and from the marquee above the entrance.

"We are not sure exactly where this path will lead us. So we may as well get started," Monk told Tinker.

Tinker agreed with a nod of his head but was still cautious in his stepping. As they approached the line at the entrance, Tinker followed Monk to the front where they stood confidently before the oversized creature maintaining order at the door.

The beast exhaled smoke from his nostrils. His eyes were angry and focused. He stood a good two heads taller than them. The size of his body was as wide as the two of them together.

He was staring directly at them and held the necks of four drunks between his fingers on each oversized hand.

Monk sighed from boredom.

The beast wrinkled his nose and squeezed his fingers together. The heads of the four shot off into the air like corks from champagne bottles and their bodies were thrown onto a pile of rotting flesh on the street with other limp bodies.

Monk held his unbothered expression. Tinker could not hide his horror. He knew better than to show it, but he could not contain it. His eyes were wide. His nose twitched. He did not have his multitude of gadgets to protect himself and Monk. His first thought was to run but he was with Monk, and they had to get through this. There was no running, no turning back.

"Cute trick," Monk told the beast. "But their problems are not my problem."

The beast cracked his knuckles and shook his hands as if he were warming up before boxing. Blood flew from his hands to the ground and onto Tinker's boots.

Tinker nearly vomited as Monk held his air of indifference.

Tinker hardened his expression and followed Monk's lead.

The beast moved aside and allowed them to pass. They walked up to the door in silence. Once in the tavern, they turned left into the darkness.

"Tink?"

"I know, Monk," Tinker told him. "It was just the initial shock. I'm good."

"Are you?"

"Yes."

"There is no telling what we will encounter here. So, we have to be ready for anything."

"Monk. I am good," Tinker assured him with a hand on his shoulder.

"Good," Monk said as he accepted Tinker for his word. "Tink? Do you know the story of the Nine Circles of Hell?"

"Yes," Tinker replied with caution in his voice.

"I am thinking that it is not just a story," Monk told him and pointed to the number one that had been etched into the wall behind where Tinker stood.

"Nine circles," Tinker said as he nodded his head. "Nine challenges. Seven sins plus two extra challenges. That's the only way back."

Monk's mind was racing. However, he held his tongue. They needed to focus on truth and not just theory and legend.

"Well, come on then," Tinker told him. "Let's start at the beginning."

They walked into the first room of the bar. Monk traced his hand along the number one on the wall and then slapped it as if to say, Let us begin.

"We need information, Tink. I think it's better to split up."

"Unfortunately, I agree with you. We will probably be less threatening as individuals." Tinker motioned to where he would start.

Monk nodded and pointed to the main bar. They made their way separately through the crowd and Monk was immediately welcomed into the open space at the bar. Tinker too found himself to be quite popular with the crowd.

"How 'bout I buy you a drink?" questioned the echoing deep voice from Monk's left.

Monk did not turn but stared straight ahead at the seductive barman who locked his gaze.

"Nah. I'm good," Monk replied.

"Come on. What's wrong with a bit of fun?" asked the man.

Monk sighed but kept his stare on the barman.

"What would your wife or… husband think of that?" Monk questioned back and tapped on the man's wedding ring.

"Let's just say that I've had a stressful week," he answered and was now close enough for Monk to smell whispers of cheap whiskey on his breath. "It paid off and I'm looking to reward myself."

Monk looked at the man's face and to his surprise, saw a strikingly attractive man in his mid-thirties.

"Hmmm," he thought. "Not what I expected," he added.

"Huh?" the man asked. "Couldn't hear you."

"I think that it's time to get a message to your… whoever," Monk told him with a taste of flirtation. "It's going to be a long night."

The man cocked up his best drunk sex face and agreed with a nod. He signaled to a scribe and walked away to maintain his privacy.

"He's buying," Monk told the barman, pointing to the man who had just left the barstool next to him. "But not the cheap shit."

The barman reached back to the top shelf and turned back to pour another drink for the other man and a double for Monk. The barman shook his head as he snickered.

"Judging?" Monk asked him with flirtatious humor.

"No. I don't do judgment. That's for someone else."

"How 'new world' of you," Monk said.

Monk looked around the bar and observed all the loud music and joyous merriment that was taking place among the attractive crowd.

"Do they even know where they are?" Monk asked.

"Do you?" the barman asked back.

"Do you?" Monk retorted.

"Yeah," the barman said in his most relaxed tone. "I kinda run the place."

Monk contorted his face.

"They do not," the barman added. "Not yet. And you?"

"Just passing through," Monk replied and watched the man from the barstool talking to the scribe.

"Seems like you'll be taking the long way," the barman added as he leaned in.

"Is there a short way?" Monk questioned and leaned in as well.

"For your friend," he said looking over at Tinker who had been showing off the few gadgets he had in his backpack. "He shouldn't be here anyway." He looked back at Monk.

Monk looked over to Tinker, who was still enjoying his innocence in this First Circle of Hell. "So then, Mammon, is it?" Monk asked to the surprise of the barman.

"At your service," the demon replied with a bow as his head transformed into its true, vulture appearance and then back to his disguise.

"Thanks, but I won't be needing your services," Monk confidently acknowledged and threw back his drink. "I've dealt with my demons already."

"Maybe it's not your demons that are the issue."

Monk cocked his face, looking for more information.

"Maybe it's the demons of others that you need to rely on to get you through this experience. None of you go through it alone."

Monk stared with a questioning look. "Thanks for the info. And remember, he owes you for the whole bill," Monk said and pointed to the other man who was getting his first taste of Hell while being caught in a lie as his wife entered the bar and began screaming at him.

The man looked back with a sense of desperation. Monk held the empty glass up and pointed to Mammon. Mammon made motions with his hands to show that he expected payment.

"Thanks," Monk told him and placed the empty glass on the bar.

Mammon grabbed his hand and held it with demonic force. "You can make your time in Hell easier on yourself."

"How's that?" Monk questioned.

"Just give into your sins."

Monk held his position and focus. His hand remained relaxed under Mammon's vice grip. He looked into his fiery eyes. "Nah. I already told you. Those ways are history," Monk said with a wink. "And besides, this would not be my circle anyway. I've always been…" he looked up in search of the words, "generous. Greed doesn't work for me."

"You are all meant to repeat history."

"Only until we learn from it," Monk added.

Although Mammon's grip did not lighten, Monk was easily able to remove his hand from the Demon Ruler.

"I guess I underestimated you," Mammon said with surprise at how easily Monk was able to resist.

"You wouldn't be the first."

Monk walked off towards Tinker. He felt his tattoo begin to tingle.

"Time to go," he demanded and pulled Tinker from his admirers with his now Immortal strength.

Tinker did not resist and immediately fell into step. He waved back to the crowd that he had been entertaining and turned back to

Monk who was walking in front of him. Tinker began to see movement under Monk's skin.

"Monk?"

"I know."

"Monk?"

"No. I don't know why."

Monk pushed open the door with a force that almost took it off its hinges. Night revelers were just as engaged in their joy out on the street as they were in the bar. The doorman again had his hands full of necks ready to squeeze off.

"I don't get it," Tinker offered as they stood still in observation.

"Get what?" Monk asked while he looked off in all directions without a care for the crowd of drunks and sexually charged partiers.

"Hell is awful but it doesn't seem as bad as I would have thought."

"Give it a minute," Monk told him and looked back into the bar.

The tingling and movement of Monk's back tattoos had stopped. He had rushed them out of the bar because he did not know what was going to happen if he transitioned in front of Mammon. He was unaware of the extent of his new powers and also worried if his transformation would trigger a negative response from the demon.

He looked back through the still open doors and saw the man who had flirted with him on his knees, in front of Mammon's vulture-headed form. The image of his wife turned to smoke and vanished. He was crying and begging. He handed him everything that he had. Yet, Mammon shook his head as if to say that it was not enough. The sight was deplorable. Mucus was rushing from the man's nose. His face was cherry red from the hormones and fear rushing through his system. He vomited and fell face down in it.

"Hell," Monk whispered his singular thought aloud as he stared at Mammon. "Time to go, Tink," he demanded as Tinker held a shocked expression.

Tinker saw the joy in Mammon's fiery eyes. He immediately changed his perspective of what would follow.

"Yes. This is about to happen to all of them," Monk added and grabbed Tinker by the shoulder, pulling him down an alley on the left.

Tinker stopped and tried to collect himself. His mindset went from understanding to fear.

"We cannot help them, Tink. The lives they lived already sealed their fates. We are not in the same position."

Tinker was panting with his hands on his knees.

"Did you really think that a journey through Hell was going to be that easy?" Monk questioned. "It's not."

Tinker dropped to a squat against a wall. He was so upset and crying so hard that he did not acknowledge the glow of the red-eyed rats that were running and climbing around him.

Monk shot them a look, but they did not concern him either.

"We all have our own demons to overcome, Tink," Monk told him as he watched the last of the rats move along.

"Yeah. But how many are we going to have to meet?"

"I don't know," Monk admitted. "But something that Mammon said is sitting on my mind."

"Mammon?" Tinker rushed. "The demon? That's who that was?"

"Yes."

"What did he say?"

"He said it's not only our sins but the sins of others that will have to be overcome to get us through this. Not sure what he meant with that."

"Sure, you are," Tinker told him. "Think about it, Monk. Vampire's pride. Seer's rage. The others. That's what he meant."

Monk's eyes widened in understanding.

"I'm not sure what's going on where they are, but we are all still connected. And their sins will play a part in our getting out of here," Tinker said.

"It seems they will have to overcome them to help us to get from circle to circle," Monk deduced.

"Then, hopefully, we will make a quick trip of this," Tinker said as he was back on his feet and had wiped his tears.

Monk felt an increase in the tingling in his shoulder blades again. A white light began to glow from the wings tattooed in gold. Monk dropped to his hands and knees. He was trying to figure out this sensation. It was not pain but was foreign enough to give him a sense of concern and fear.

"Monk?" Tinker yelled out as he dropped to help him up to his feet.

The glow was blinding and forced Tinker to pull back and to shield his eyes.

"Don't call me that," Tinker heard from the less familiar voice as he was still covering his eyes.

He sensed that the glowing had receded and that he would be able to look upon his friend without being blinded.

"Oh, get over it! You're in there. I know that. Even in this form, you, *Monk*, are in there," Tinker told him with a full sense of confidence.

Tinker gathered his courage and walked up to stand eye to eye.

"I can smell your scent," Tinker reported, staring him in the eyes. "Citrus and jasmine… a bit of spice. The spice is similar to my own."

Monk attempted to hold back his reaction. "Since when are you able to do that?" he asked.

"Since we woke up here," Tinker told him and relaxed his forceful tone.

The tingling stopped and the light was gone from Monk's back. Before he could ask for clarification, they heard a harrowing scream. It was violent and loud and was followed by the same scratching sound that Tinker heard earlier.

"What is that?" Tinker asked.

"Still think that Hell's not so bad?" Monk asked back with sarcasm.

Monk pulled Tinker down, out of sight. They were in a lit alley with only one foreseeable way in or out. Tinker looked up. The walls that surrounded them were high and flat. The dark sky, which had been clear but starless, was now becoming cloudy. There was a sulphur-like smell in the air.

"Do you smell that?" Tinker asked Monk.

"How could I not?" Monk replied.

The screams continued to get louder, more aggressive, and closer. The scratching sound continued as well but sounded more hostile.

"Okay. Let's go, Tink."

"Oh, Monk. I don't think so."

"Tink-"

"At least, turn into the other guy. I mean, I know that you can defend yourself, but I have a suspicion that this is going to be very different."

Monk silently agreed with Tinker's speculation. He too knew that what awaited them at the front of the alley was not going to be the joyous bar crowd that they had experienced earlier.

"We have to get to the next circle, Tink."

Tinker turned and looked at him.

"And?"

The sulphur-smelling cloud cover ignited with energy and lit a snapshot of the sight at the other end of the alley. Bodies were being attacked and devoured. Organs were being ripped out and eaten in front of the still conscious souls. Mammon's henchmen were on a rampage. They attacked with a vengeance. Their purpose was singular. Pain and suffering were their nourishment.

Another crash of thunder followed a blinding burst of lightning. The sky began to release droplets of burning rain. It was more like lava that rained down from the sky.

"Ouch!" Tinker exclaimed and grabbed a cover from the trash on the ground. He and Monk held it over their heads.

"We can't stay here," Monk told him as the lava began to make holes in the metal slab that they held over their heads. "We need cover."

"If this continues, there will be no cover, Monk. This *rain* will burn through everything it touches." He drew Monk's attention to the holes that began to form in the bricks of the alley.

"So now do you agree that we have to go?"

Tinker tightened his lips and made a frustrated growl as they stood shoulder to shoulder. Tinker had taken another slab that was leaning on the wall next to him and placed it over their heads.

"This falling lava is going to get heavier," Tinker stated.

"Yes, it is. We have to move."

The thunder crashed and the lightning lit the street. Demon attackers and victims alike were all reduced to foul smelling corpses of rotting tissue. Monk and Tinker held their position as they began to see shadows form over some of the ones that had been fully reduced to piles of gelatinous tissue. The shadows pulled away and took to the air, flying away with an audible hiss. It was the shadows that were making the scratching sound. Some of the disfigured corpses maintained their distorted physical forms and screamed out for help to stop the torture.

"Monk?"

"Shh."

The lava rain had now stopped. Tinker took the metal slabs from their heads and quietly placed them on the ground at their feet. The decayed gelatinous forms of the remaining tissue muted any sound of the metal contacting the brick.

The blackness that had been released from the bodies circled overhead. The shadows lacked direction and vibrated in a random nature. The unsynchronized vibrations oscillated at a torturous pitch, and the hissing became a more intense scratching sound. Tinker held his ears and looked at Monk, who stood in defiance.

Bright blue fireflies came into view from the sky. They created harmonious ripples of air and blew into each other, creating a glowing form.

The form grew in size and in brightness, and began to take a defined shape to lower itself to the ground. The translucence was now completely solid.

"Hello boys," Asmodeus, the Ruler of the Second Circle of Hell, greeted.

CHAPTER 17
The Entrapment

Vampire was staring at Ghost through squinted eyes. He wracked his memories to revisit every single one that Dax had been a part of. "I had no idea," Vampire admitted through a pained whisper.

"My dirty little secret," Ghost admitted.

Vampire was shaken. He seemed to still be unable to accept the concept that Ghost was his former assistant, Dax. While living in Paris in 1891, Vampire had hired Dax to find Phineas, the same name that would follow Monk through each of his lives, after catching his scent. Dax had taken an unwelcome interest in Vampire's business, so Vampire had dismissed him. However, Dax had convinced a mutual friend to intervene on his behalf. That sequence of events had led to Monk's death in that lifetime. It was only now that Vampire became aware that Dax's spirit had returned to find him in this plane of existence. Vampire had released any thought of him centuries ago.

"Why?" Vampire asked him.

"Are you fucking kidding me? Thousands of years have passed since you killed me. I have not been able to move on… I have been waiting lifetimes to get my revenge."

"You choose not to move on."

"There is something that I need to do before I go," Ghost replied in a ghastly tone.

"And what could that possibly be?" Vampire questioned with the most condescending tone. He walked towards the light of the entrapment and looked at it.

"You will find out soon enough, old friend," Ghost told him. "This will not be easy, *Thaddeus*."

"I would not expect it to be under the best of circumstances, yet alone these. I mean, with you."

Ghost let out a snicker.

"It is that pride that continues to get in your way."

"Pride? And you?"

"What of me?"

"Are you too thick in your translucent form to understand that I am not in here alone."

"But I can exit if I choose."

"Try. I dare you."

Ghost turned as if to move towards the flowing lights of the entrapment limits. He paused.

"That bitch," he whispered as he realized that he too was unable to exit through the magical borders. "Then let us get on with it."

"Yes. Let us," Vampire agreed. "Especially now that we are both aware that this is not just about me…"

Ghost paused.

CHAPTER 18
Hell, First Circle

Monk and Tinker stood in defensive postures as they surmised that Asmodeus had stopped the lava rain. The scratching sound started again. Asmodeus looked up at the swirling shadows with an unsure expression.

"How 'bout a drink?" the evil seductress asked, changing the look on her face back to her seductive glare.

"Is that all they do here?" Tinker asked.

"Allow their sins and then suffer for them over and over and-"

"Yes. Yes," Asmodeus snarled. "This is Hell. In Hell, you suffer for your sins. We all know that. Drink?"

"Is it poisoned?" Tinker asked her.

"Would you believe me if I said, 'No'?" she asked and drew her hands along the curves of her body.

"I'm good with it," Tinker replied.

Monk slowly turned his head to look at him.

"Monk, at this point no one can be trusted," Tinker reminded him. "I'm not even sure if you… or the winged you… can be trusted. But we have to get out of here and this is moving us forward."

Monk nodded and they walked towards the feminine demon who ruled of the Second Circle of Hell.

"Good," she whispered. "I feel as though I should be welcoming you back, Monk," she called out and met them in the middle of the street.

"Thank you, but no," he replied as Tinker tried not to show concern on his face. "We are just passing through."

"And this morsel," she said, reaching out with her elongated fingernails in an attempt to tickle under Tinker's chin. He pulled back. "He's got such potential."

Tinker's face shot red with embarrassment.

"But don't worry, kid," she said and took Tinker and Monk by the arms. "I'll help you through it." Her touch created a tingling sensation throughout their bodies.

Tinker again pulled away. Asmodeus giggled and lowered her gaze coyly. She looked up from her downward stare.

Monk had not even flinched. She looked back to him with a harder, more lustful, stare.

"Forget it, sister," he reminded her.

"Always worth a try," she said in concession and laughed to lighten the mood.

Asmodeus strutted between Monk and Tinker, interlocking her elbows with each of them. Her dressings were fitted and sheer. The fiery collar that outlined her full cleavage lit her beautiful face. Her curves drew the eye and with every movement, her silhouette commanded more attention. Her hair blew as if being catered to by a light breeze.

"I'm not looking to keep you here. I want you to succeed. We all want you to succeed. But you must prove yourself worthy. Think about it: what fun do we have if it all goes away? Huh? We know about the Jeweled Dragon. We know about your quest to stop her."

Tinker was lost in thought.

"We need for it to continue. But if all of time and space goes… POOF!… That means that Hell is gone. I am stuck in a void. And most likely, I will be stuck with the six of them. Forever. All of the Rulers of Hell left with only one another. That would be my torture." She ended with an inflective stare that was focused on nothing in front of her. "Or maybe, we too will be gone."

"Unacceptable," Tinker said.

Asmodeus and Monk looked at him, each surprised by his comment.

"Hell has a purpose," Tinker began. "Everything has a purpose. It is part of the evolution of every soul. If everything is gone, there is no purpose. There will be no evolution of souls."

"There would be no need for a purpose," she added.

"We cannot let this happen," he demanded. "What do we have to do?"

Asmodeus smiled and looked back at Monk. He held a stern stare back. She pulled them forward and onto her side of the street.

As they stepped onto the sidewalk, they felt the change in energy. They were about to enter the Second Circle of Hell.

CHAPTER 19
The Entrapment

Ghost floated around the inside of the entrapment. "You need to accept something."

Vampire sighed with his head down at the red sands. "What is that?" he asked, annoyed at the demand.

"Monk and Tinker were not mentioned in the prophecy," Ghost told him. "Whether you like it or not..." He paused and looked over his shoulder with a cocked grin. "They were expendable."

Vampire did not react. Ghost was disappointed.

"I have been watching you," he said, still trying to get a rise out of the Immortal. "But you have spent too much time not seeing yourself." Ghost floated as if pacing in the air.

Vampire still said nothing.

Ghost hovered over him. "Your obsession with Monk has driven you away from your purpose." He stopped in front of him. "And now, you... We, actually," he added, looking at the sparks of electricity coming off the magical entrapment. "We have no choice but to bring you back to gain clarity of the situation. Monk was the reason that you chose to fight for humankind. But he also distracted you from protecting this dimension from the rise of another Immortal… The one that you chose not to become. The one that can destroy everything."

Vampire looked up at him with a continued scowl but still said nothing.

"Even you cannot be so arrogant as to think that The Enlightenment would take your rejection lightly," Ghost lectured. "And yes," he continued. "I was obsessed with you when I exited this dimension in eighteen ninety one… Obsessed with what you had… With who you were. Only to find out when I returned in this state in the year four thousand one that somehow *you* were still the topic of conversation." He circled Vampire with increasing speed and increasing anger in his voice. "I lost centuries and still I cannot get away from you! Every major player I met was looking for you. Mavi. The Peasant King. I cannot move on until-"

"Until you choose to," Vampire said, still looking at the sand. "And until you do something for someone else." He looked up at Ghost, who was now hovering in front of him.

"What Mavi, the Peasant King and even The Dark Sisters knew is that you are still too proud to acknowledge that you would not be the last Immortal to be sent with the purpose of ending the human race. They were all looking for *you*! Mavi to warn you. The Peasant King to deliver you. And The Dark Sisters for some reason that I do not know. All I know is that they too wanted *you*!"

"We need to revisit your past choices. You need to be reminded why you chose to rebel against The Enlightenment and save humanity. You need to again choose that course. It is the only way to save this dimension. That is the only way we are getting out of this prison… And the only way to ever see Monk again," Ghost reminded him.

Vampire looked out of the entrapment and caught glimpses through the magical lights of Ileana's silhouette leading and organizing the others to maintain his imprisonment. "And this will be the fastest way to do that," Ghost told him.

"What? To go back in time and revisit my past?"

"Yes. You need to feel why you made your choice. You need to experience Monk… Phineas, again. Until then, you can not be trusted."

"Then, let us begin," Vampire agreed, matching Ghost's cold intent with his own pride.

"Excellent," Ghost replied and closed his eyes. "We already have."

His form began to expand and reflected the lights of the magical entrapment still being maintained from the other side by Sorcerer, Ileana, and the Three of Legend. The expansion of his transparent form pushed past Vampire and elicited a chill in Vampire's body. He let out a scream of angst and frustration.

Ghost's expanded ethereal self immediately pulled back with force and cocooned Vampire. The force was so strong that the energy field that surrounded the two of them was seen fluctuating from the outside.

Vampire was unable to breathe. He struggled but then lost consciousness.

CHAPTER 20
Rome, 320 A.D.

Vampire felt the softness under his body. He was lying on his back. He took in the scent of roses before he opened his eyes. It was strong and familiar, but still seemed to be such a distant memory. He was aware that he had come back into the version of himself who was present at this time.

He looked around the opulent bedchamber and mired at the red color that was most prevalent in the frescos that adorned the walls. As he looked more closely, Vampire saw mythological creatures including gods and goddesses, but standing above all of them, he saw himself painted with a glowing light surrounding him.

He shook his head, embarrassed with who he used to be, but then felt his emotional state change. He felt anger and negativity towards humanity. He knew that he had to experience the truth of what had occurred in this time but would be conflicted as he was able to also see it as an observer who traveled back to it.

"Rome," he said aloud.

Vampire stared into the sunlight that entered from the open window. He sat on the edge of the bed that he found himself lying upon. He ran his hand along the soft linen sheets. He looked up into the intense sunlight. Vampire's expression turned to sadness. He did not attempt to hide it.

"Almost midday," he said in respect to the position of the sun in the sky.

"Then you have to move fast," Ghost told him.

"The slave market," he replied while still staring directly into the sun. "The first time I saw…"

"*Him.*"

Vampire turned and looked at Ghost.

"How is this going to work?" he asked.

"We'll find out together."

Vampire stood and changed into the traditional robes that were laid out for him by the servants.

Ghost was studying Vampire's mood and behavior. This was not something that he had ever experienced with Vampire. The sadness that had overtaken his essence was new to Ghost.

"It feels as though I am not just going to be observing what happens," Vampire realized. "I will have to be who I was in this time."

Vampire looked at Ghost as he began to be consumed by that long-lost anger.

"This is going to *suck*," Vampire told him, as he began to feel more like the version of himself who was present when these events first took place.

"Says the vampire," Ghost said with a slight smile.

"But at least, *you* will get some joy out of it."

Vampire turned and walked out of his bedchamber. He walked past servants who all stopped and dropped to their knees at the sight of him. Fear was high.

During Vampire's time in ancient Rome, he had been a horrific tyrant. He was well known for the torture he laid upon any minor insurrection. Many slaves would rather die than to continue enduring his torment. Those were the ones that he would not put to death. He wanted their pain to last.

But worse than how he treated his servants was the way he treated his business dealings. He was ruthless. His greed was unparalleled even by any emperor. He was a man whose only goal was *more*.

Nearing the slave market, it was obvious that Vampire carried himself in higher regard than even the worst of the slave owners and crooked businessmen. Unlike the other patricians, Vampire was carried to the slave market on a litter by his men. The men were all beautiful and held strong physiques, which were exposed through minimal clothing. Vampire loved to make a spectacle. He gloated at his own audacity. Some of his slaves were beautiful women who he kept fit and desirable. Their role was to announce his arrival to any engagement by walking ahead and dropping rose petals. The presentation was ostentatious.

The other patricians detested him, but they also knew that for their own sake and position, they should never voice it.

This was the time of the rule of Constantine I who had come to power as Christianity had been professed throughout the land with his claim to have been driven by seeing Jesus Christ in a dream. Fear of disagreeing with the emperor led the elite to convert and follow the teachings of the Christian church… Or at least appear to follow. And it was Vampire who aided in Constantine's rise to power.

Vampire's influence went beyond his business and into the politics of ancient Rome. His business dealings, knowledge of foreign lands and adversaries, and war tactics elevated him into a position in the senate that made him irreplaceable. Yet, unbeknown to anyone, his goal was to set forth the fall of the Roman Empire and the entire human race.

As his men lowered his litter to the ground, he stood. The crowd parted with head nods and bows in respect to his unauthorized but accepted position. He followed the path of rose petals as he walked through the crowd without acknowledgement to any of the others and made his way to a platform to stand above them all.

Other patricians had similar platforms. Yet, his was higher and at a more prestigious location, directly in front of the auction platform.

Vampire's inner thoughts were in turmoil. He was familiar with this version of himself, but he had evolved into someone else. Regardless of his inner battle, this version of himself felt primal. This was his original purpose. He could see himself giving in and returning to who he was at this time in his existence.

But then he smelled the most intoxicating aroma, the scent of crisp citrus. A gentle breeze blew in the scent of jasmine to mix with that citrus and a touch of spice. Vampire snapped back to himself. He realized it and smiled. This scent was what started him on his path. The scent woke him to his own potential, a choice of his own making. It was *him*.

His obvious distraction was caught by the other slave bidders who always kept one eye on him. He realized it immediately and wondered if this was what happened in the original playing of this scene. Vampire calmed himself and got back into character. He waited.

The scent lingered in the air as the slave auction began. Vampire knew what he was there for. Or at least part of him did. He was there to revisit his first meeting with Phineas and to learn what went wrong. He had to accept and release himself from the greed that he put into this world when he first came to destroy it.

Slave traders were marketing and selling their product to the other patricians. Vampire did nothing.

He waited.

And waited.

And waited.

And then, it was time. He knew what was about to happen but had to allow himself to relive it without altering the outcome.

Slaves were brought onto the platform and there he stood. Phineas was among four others being auctioned in front of the crowd. All were male. All were young. All rivaled the beauty of the accompanying slaves. Yet, Vampire's focus was on him, the second from the left.

Phineas stood at least six inches shorter than the others who all looked like giants. He was younger but held himself with an air of strength. He showed no fear, no anger. He showed nothing at all as his gaze was directed solely into Vampire's eyes.

Vampire first realized that his face was unscarred. This would be the last day that he would ever see Phineas without the scar across his face.

All five men stood bare in front of the crowd. Vampire also noticed the markings on the side of his body were not yet present. He knew that they were coming and that his anger would be the cause of them.

The bidding started with the young man on the left, the tallest and most muscular. The price for the striking slave continued to rise.

"Full price," Vampire yelled out, "plus twenty percent," he continued.

The crowd gasped.

"For the second man," he added to the continued surprise of the crowd.

The man maintained his direct gaze at him and to Vampire's surprise, he continued to show no emotion. Most surprising was that he showed no fear.

Vampire had broken protocol, which was what he often did when these events originally took place. No one would stand in his way. His bid was acknowledged and agreed upon, *plus twenty percent,* and the man who stood second from the left was removed from the platform.

Vampire stepped down from his bidding platform and returned to his litter. The eight slaves lifted it in unison and carried him back to his villa. The auction continued.

Vampire was outside watching the sunset when a pair of guards presented his recent purchase.

"Signiore?" a guard questioned.

"Bring him here," Vampire said without turning from the setting sun.

The newly purchased slave was brought to him.

"Leave us," he told the men who had brought the slave.

They departed without question.

The slave stood in the golden orange of the setting sunlight. Vampire was in two heads as he played the sequence of events that would follow this moment. He knew that he could not intervene to change things; only learn, only heal.

"Do you know who I am?" he asked the slave.

"No," the slave answered after a pause.

"Good," he told him and then turned to see him bathed in the light. The rays of the setting sun caught him from the side and changed his eyes to the color of caramel. "That's when I truly knew I needed you," Vampire said aloud. That had not happened at this original meeting.

The slave did not understand the comment but knew that he best not say anything. The side of Vampire that was experiencing this moment for the first time did not understand the comment either nor why he said it.

Vampire walked up to the slave and stood directly in front of him. He realized that the slave was taller than he appeared to be when next to the giants on the platform.

"Do you fear me?" Vampire asked him.

"No," the slave answered.

"Why not?" he asked.

"I have nothing," he answered, "nothing to live for and nothing to die for. So, you cannot hurt me more than I have already been hurt."

Vampire stepped back.

"But you feel that hurting me will make you... *more*," the man continued.

Vampire was reacting out of both versions of himself. The version that came back to experience this realized that the slave was right. He questioned how but did not have time to linger. The version of himself that was experiencing this for the first time stuck to his pride and gave the man a cocky grin. He turned to walk away.

"You will be bathed and presented to me again," Vampire told the slave.

Vampire entered his villa and walked with heavy steps towards his chambers. His inner turmoil erupted again. Both versions of himself were battling: one was aware of his desire and the feeling that it created within him; the other version knew how this night's events would go and was afraid that he would not allow the outcome to occur. He needed to accept what he had done.

This battle forced his hands to his head as he slid down the wall on which he now leaned and found himself seated on the floor. This was the first time in his recollection that he had been knocked from his sense of control. Both sides came to the same understanding. They both understood that what moved forward from this moment moved in the direction of love.

Vampire picked himself up and walked over to a door that opened to the outside. He stepped out and again stared at the now sunless sky. The intensity of the colors that lingered comforted him. He felt the array of life in those colors. He allowed himself to understand that he was experiencing a life changing moment.

An hour had passed when the knock came to the door.

"Enter," he demanded.

The door opened and the slave entered alone.

"Shut the door," he demanded.

The slave did as instructed.

"Come here," he said and was again obliged.

The man came to stop in front of Vampire.

Vampire undid the silk rope that surrounded the man's waist and held his dressings in place. The dressings opened and left the man's defined body exposed. Vampire pushed the dressings from his shoulders and let them fall freely to the floor.

Vampire took his own robes and let them fall to the floor. Both men stood naked in front of one another. They stared deeply into each other's eyes.

The slave's stare went unchanged. A slight flicker came across his stare as he realized from both sides that this moment would happen as it had.

Vampire took the man and lifted him with minimal effort. He threw him across the room and onto the bed.

The slave was now reacting. His surprise at Vampire's immense strength forced an understanding that the man who had control of his future was beyond what he had anticipated.

As he lifted his head to see where Vampire was, he was again surprised to find that Vampire was already atop him, pinning him to the bed.

"What is your name?" Vampire demanded.

The man resisted.

"I asked you a question," he demanded and pulled at his arms with force enough to cause pain.

"Phineas," the man replied, hoping that the pain would stop.

Vampire did release him, but only momentarily as the version who was experiencing this for the first time still needed to go through with the full experience. He pulled again and caused Phineas pain.

Phineas squirmed under Vampire. He begged for him to release him.

"I am the master here," Vampire argued. "You make no requests," he continued with venom and annoyance at the man's begging. "And you are Phineas no more," he told him and reached for the poker that was burning red hot in the fireplace.

Vampire brought the scorching metal onto the slave's forearm.

"You, like all things, are mine," he told him as the sweet smell of burning flesh whiffed into his nostrils. He pulled back as he realized that the scent was followed by citrus and jasmine. An earthy spice followed and lingered in the air. He immediately pulled himself from the man who he had just branded as his property.

Phineas collected himself. He knew that he could not win and accepted the pain. The look in his eyes calmed and he sat up.

"Then, so it is," Phineas replied.

Vampire was shaken.

"You are always where you are supposed to be," Phineas said. "If this is what is meant to be, then let it be."

With these words, Vampire stood at the edge of the bed. His surprise was almost to the point of shock. He just stared. Both versions of himself were battling within but his fear was rising.

Phineas sat at the edge of the bed. He reached out for Vampire.

"You long to destroy everything in your grasp," Phineas told him. "Regardless of your marking me, I am and will always be Phineas."

Vampire reacted as his inner battle became more intense. His form began to change as his eyes became black and his teeth grew to fangs.

Phineas did nothing. He held his hand in the same outstretched position.

Vampire reacted by pushing Phineas' hand and attacking him. He bit hard into his neck and tasted the sweet balance of his blood.

Phineas still did not react.

Vampire released him and morphed back to his human form.

Phineas panted for air as the blood continued to flow freely out of his neck.

"I am sorry," Vampire told him.

Phineas kept his gaze upon Vampire's eyes.

Vampire, in an attempt to avoid the dying look in the man's eyes, changed his form again, and he sliced Phineas' face, scarring him. He took the last essence of life from his blood.

Vampire changed again back to his human form and spit the blood into a vial.

Phineas was gone.

Vampire was full of sorrow and regret, as he realized that he had pushed away the one thing that could have saved him from his own path of destruction. He realized that he had lost love. He made a promise to himself to find it again. And because of that single moment, he did not destroy humanity like he was sent to do. The memories of that one day would torture him until he found love again.

But how will I find this love again? Fear came with the thought.

Hours passed as Vampire held Phineas. He looked to the night sky and watched the stars begin to show themselves. *Dracu*, the ancient dragon constellation, shined bright in its position in the center of the darkness above. They were some of the first stars to arrive in the night sky.

I will find you again, he thought as he looked between Phineas and the stars.

Vampire closed his eyes and stretched out his hand.

The eight stars that made up the constellation all began to shine brighter. Each of them, one by one, began to stream across the sky and fall across the land. As they fell, part of their energy transferred into Vampire's hand, which was glowing. He forced his hand hard against Phineas' left side and held it there as the energy was absorbed. The mark of the constellation of Dracu was left on Phineas' body and transpired to his soul.

"We are one," Vampire said to his lifeless body, hoping that his spirit would understand. "Two parts of the whole."

He looked back to the sky and saw that the space where Dracu had shined bright was now dark with the night sky, never to be seen again.

The world around Vampire faded away.

"Am I to expect them all to be that intense?" Vampire asked Ghost back in the entrapment.

"Yes," Ghost replied. "Possibly even more so."

Vampire nodded his head.

"I am ready."

CHAPTER 21
Caves of Waku

Aided by Princess and her Air magic, AZ was safely back on solid ground and the sky was cleared of the dust storm. Cadet helped Seer back to his feet as he too had fully recovered. AZ, Cadet and Seer stood close to the entrapment and were mesmerized by the energy that was being emitted. Cadet reached her hand out.

"Do not touch it," Sorcerer commanded. "You would not survive."

She heeded his words, and each of the three stepped back in unison.

"I'm not used to Vampire being so out of control," Cadet told Seer and AZ.

Axel looked at Aldrick and smiled.

"You sure you don't want to try to get in, AZ?" Aldrick yelled out in jest.

"I'm trusting your father on this one," he answered.

AZ turned to look at Princess, who was staring back with a sweet smile. He blushed.

"Good for you," Seer told him. "What you feel for her truly did set your path in motion."

AZ blushed deeper. He looked at the position of the sun in the sky. He tapped Seer and pointed. His concern about the sun's lower position became shared.

"Why do I feel like we should be worried about this?" AZ yelled while still pointing.

"We should," Ileana replied. "But I can take care of that."

Ileana looked at Sorcerer.

"Seems quiet in there, right now," he told her and nodded.

Ileana closed her eyes and lowered her head. She began to speak an enchantment in a language that AZ did not understand.

"The language of Witches?" AZ asked Seer.

"No," Cadet replied. "The language of the Elements."

AZ looked but allowed himself to understand nothing and to simply accept what was happening.

"With everything we've experienced so far, how can I question that the Elements have their own language?" he asked while shaking his head.

"Good step, AZ," Seer told him. "Anything is possible."

AZ nodded and watched the position of the sun rise higher into the sky, as if time had moved backwards.

"An hour," Ileana told them. "That is the most that they would agree to."

"They, *the Elements?*" AZ asked her.

"They, the Elements," she confirmed as she took her position back at the entrapment.

CHAPTER 22
Oberndorf, Austria
December 24, 1818

The snow fell outside the well-maintained St. Nikola church. The smell of incense and the aura of joy filled the wooden hall. The candlelight illuminated the grand space with a soft kindness that reflected the season. Neighbors greeted each other with double kisses and fine holiday greetings. It was Christmas Eve.

"Why has the organist not started?" were the words repeated throughout the pre-gathering of Midnight Mass.

"The organ is broken," was the sad response that followed.

"What a shame. On Christmas Eve..." was then put forth as if scripted each time.

"You have no idea how much I appreciate your assistance with this, Herr...?" The monsignor rushed while preparing for the celebration in the sacristy.

"Thaddeus. Call me Thaddeus."

"Thaddeus," the nervous priest agreed and came closer to shake Thaddeus' hand.

He placed his left hand atop their already shaking right hands, a move that Thaddeus did not care for.

"With the organ in disrepair, we were simply in the worst bind as you could imagine. And this poem was put to music, but without the organ, the guitar will just have to do. Not that I will have anything to do with it. Father Mohr and the schoolmaster… What is his name?"

"Franz Gruber," Thaddeus informed him.

The monsignor looked at him with a ruffled brow.

"You're welcome for the guitar," Thaddeus offered his statement without a hint of sarcasm, although he heard it in his thoughts.

The monsignor gave him a second look with an even more ruffled brow.

Regardless, in this transaction, it would mean nothing. The stressed priest would be bled dry before morning. This was a regular routine for Thaddeus on Christmas Eve, a gift to himself. He would assist a church in need and get an invite by a pious hypocrite posing as a pillar to a community through the workings of his church, and then feast upon his sanctimonious neck.

"What is the name of this poem?" Thaddeus questioned.

"It is called…" The priest looked around for the papers. "It is called *Stille Nacht*. I must admit, it made me very reflective when I first heard it."

Thaddeus had no issues with the church. As a matter of fact, he had no issues with any religious belief. Throughout time, he had been in the confidence of some true characters of historical events and turning points for religions. Yet, he did have issues with the men who hid their hate behind the good teachings of those prophets and writings. Every year, on what he considered the most holy night, he paid those prophets homage by ridding their teachings of a hypocrite. This was his yearly gift to faith; a tithing per say.

The monsignor had finished his preparation with the slew of altar boys and younger priests attending to his barked orders. He demanded their exit and placed his final gold ring on his left ring finger. The gemstones in that ring alone could have fed the whole county through the winter.

"Good choice," Thaddeus spoke softly aloud.

"I'm sorry. You said something, Herr… Thaddeus?" the priest asked, still marveling at the eight jeweled rings on his fingers.

"No. No," Thaddeus demanded. "I'm just happy that I was able to help, even though there was no time for the organ to be repaired."

"No. It will not be the same. A guitar is not an organ. But it will be a lesson in pride, to not attempt to reach higher than one should. What better homily for Midnight Mass?"

"Hmmm… Note to self," Thaddeus said jokingly.

The pious priest maintained his condescending tone as he adjusted his robes in the mirror. He did not pay any attention to the fact that Thaddeus cast no reflection in the mirror. The monsignor turned and nodded to him as he exited to get in place for the entrance procession.

Thaddeus snarled his face and shook his head. He turned, walked out of the preparatory vestibule and entered the main hall of the church.

Thaddeus had always liked Christmas Eve. As a matter of fact, it was his favorite day of the year, full of joy and anticipation and love. Hope and magic were prevalent, and that reminded him that anything was possible.

Thaddeus made his way past the local townspeople, nodding to the smiling faces and the pleasant greetings. After all, he was a stranger in this town, but on Christmas Eve, that did not matter. He would be offered an invitation that would also serve as an alibi.

Thaddeus stopped. He felt the excitement and knew the aroma from before. He knew what it was. Better yet, he knew *who* it was. He attributed this feeling to what mortals referred to as 'a rush of adrenaline'. It had happened before, but not for over a hundred years. Thaddeus found himself looking frantically around the crowded church. He began to pace nervously up and down the main aisle and began to draw attention to himself through this inappropriate behavior. He was aware of the crowd but did not pay any mind to the stares.

He stopped midway up the aisle, facing the altar. He began to smile as he took a deeper inhale. The aromas of jasmine and crisp citrus mixed with an earthy familiarity and a tantalizing peppery spice. He felt a light breeze and again the familiar scent of... *him*. Thaddeus closed his eyes and inhaled deeply, taking him in and unlocking every memory from every lifetime before. He held that breath until it was all revealed to his memory. He slowly exhaled as he turned.

Walking up the center aisle was Phineas Devereaux with the mayor and his family. Phineas Devereaux was a French entrepreneur who had come to the region to expand his family's shipping and transporting empire. Oberndorf was a profitable hamlet due to its location on the river Salzach, a very profitable salt transport route.

Monsieur Devereaux had been invited to the mass and had agreed to come as a guest of the mayor for the Christmas holidays. They were being escorted to the prestigious seating in the front of the church.

Thaddeus could not keep his eyes off him. Phineas had met his stare at the exact moment that Thaddeus had come into view. Devereaux seemed as though he was also unable to break the visual embrace. As he approached where Thaddeus stood, he stopped. His group had continued forward, unaware of his pause.

"Do I know you?" Phineas asked, not being able to place exactly who Thaddeus was.

"Yes. Yes, you do." Thaddeus showed his most charming smile.

"You seem nervous," Phineas added with a chuckle, calling out the obvious.

"I was never able to hide that from you," Vampire admitted with added joy. "As a matter of fact, you are the only person that-"

"Monsieur Devereaux?" the usher offered. "You are seated up here." The usher looked cautiously as he stared at Thaddeus.

"Yes. Of course," he replied to the usher. The eye contact kept up between Thaddeus and himself.

The usher cleared his throat as if to attempt to move Phineas along.

"Is there room for my friend?" Phineas questioned.

"Ummm," the usher attempted an excuse.

"No. No. That's all right. I am seated already. Just came to say 'hello' to a business associate." Thaddeus freed the usher from his embarrassment.

The sound of a guitar began, signaling the parishioners to be seated and to begin the Midnight Mass celebration.

Phineas walked off with the usher but continued to look back with a flirtatious smile and a nod. Thaddeus stood frozen in place in the middle of the aisle, as he watched the image of Phineas, recalling him from all their previous lives together.

"Herr?" questioned a staunch older woman in all black who was seated in the pew next to where Vampire stood.

Thaddeus was forced back to the present. He shook his head and looked at her.

"Please *do* take your seat," she demanded.

Thaddeus nodded and looked around. He motioned towards the back of the church.

"Lovely outfit," he sarcastically remarked. "Very… festive."

He walked to the back of the church.

Phineas, who was seated on the aisle, continued to watch him. Thaddeus turned and caught him. Phineas did not attempt to hide his attention. Thaddeus smiled back and motioned as if he were tipping his brow.

"Always the same," Vampire whispered. "Love at first sight."

Ghost was in the direct line of sight when Vampire opened his eyes. They were back in the entrapment. Vampire was smiling.

"That did not seem so hard," Ghost told him with a sense of disappointment.

"Lust was never my sin," Vampire told him. "It was Monk's."

He paused and smiled bigger.

Ghost did not allow Vampire's playfulness.

"The rest will not be so easy."

"I am not concerned," Vampire told him.

"For now," Ghost quickly shot back with a blank stare.

"But I am not understanding the order of these past lives. Monk and I shared four of his lives between Rome and Austria."

"I do not make the rules," Ghost said and launched back at Vampire.

CHAPTER 23
Hell, Second Circle

"Who knows?" Asmodeus said to Monk with a shrug of the shoulders. "Maybe you'll give into your old ways and decide to stay here."

"We're needed elsewhere. And there won't even be a *here* if the Jeweled Dragon destroys everything," Monk reminded her.

"I had to offer," she told him as she led them to a tower.

Tinker was looking at Monk with concern.

Monk turned and looked back. "Round two," he said with a comforting wink at Tinker.

Asmodeus walked them into an opening between two pillars that extended upwards and out of view. Tinker looked to see where the top was but only found it to be lost in the darkness.

"No wonder there are no doors," he joked under his breath.

Within the rectangular opening, Monk and Tinker found themselves wondering if the structure was solid or if it was an optical illusion. They walked down the long and well-lit hallway that appeared to morph in shape and became triangular. The presence of a ceiling became apparent, and the walkway seemed to slope down at the far side with blue lights better defining the shorter but still towering walls.

Tinker looked around with a bit of confusion. He thought that he heard running water but saw no source. The sound was welcomed but the lack of its origin was concerning.

Monk did not appear to have any concerns as he continued to walk arm-in-arm with Asmodeus. Her seductive nature continued to be quite apparent in her strut and the sound that her heels made on the hard ground. Each step created a ripple of light.

Tinker realized that the floor was made of light and water. His mind began to wander and to question how they were able to walk on such a surface. But he had found his source of water. It made him smile.

A dark figure was visible a good distance ahead. As they moved closer, Asmodeus smiled bigger.

"This is for you," she told Monk.

Asmodeus stopped walking and extended her hand for Monk to continue. She looked back to Tinker and held her arm in front of him to stop him from proceeding.

"Let's see what happens first," she said to the nervous young man.

With her touch, an electrical surge shot through Tinker's body. The nervousness and the adrenaline rush were ecstatic to her.

Tinker thought to yell out to Monk, but held himself back. Tinker looked up and dropped his shoulders in frustration.

Challenging your demons in Hell, he thought. "How in the world did this happen?"

Monk continued his slow progression towards the dark figure. As he got closer, he moved in what appeared to be a choreographed pattern that was matched by the other.

Tinker put his goggles on and squinted to make out the form of the dark figure. It was masculine and somewhat familiar.

Vampire, he thought.

"Yes," Asmodeus said to him.

"Can you please not do that?" he yelled at her, angered that she entered his mind.

Tinker's mind was his and his alone. He mustered up the confidence to challenge the demon for she had crossed a line that he would not accept. His protection of his mind was greater than his fear.

Asmodeus looked at him with a sense of shock and then anger. She looked behind him and noticed movement in the water that made up the floor. She softened her expression and turned back to watch what happened with Monk.

Monk and the dark figure were now moving in a circle that appeared like a very passionate tango.

Asmodeus was challenging Monk's lust. Other figures came out of the darkness and joined the dance. Monk was pushed and pulled against them. Hands moved across his body and his hands across theirs. Soft touches of fingers ignited his flesh. Lips came close and the pressure of the exhalations caused him to sweat and then to shiver.

Monk stopped. Slowly, the others began to dissolve into black mist and dissipate until only the original form was left standing. *Vampire*, Monk thought. He reached out for Vampire's figure as it too dissolved into black mist and blew away into the air.

Monk turned back to Asmodeus and Tinker. He bowed to her and then walked back to them.

Tinker's nervousness returned as he watched Monk. He looked down and was comforted by the movement of the water. He smiled and gave nod of the head. His action went unnoticed.

"Monk," Asmodeus said as she and Tinker reached the other side of the hallway. "You have proven yourself, but you must continue to do so to get beyond this point."

He nodded in agreement of understanding the added layer to the quest.

"Thank you," he told her and kissed her hand.

"The others may not be as helpful," she confessed. "You and I had already come to an agreement," she reminded him. "I released you lifetimes ago." She turned to Tinker. "And as for you," she said to his concern. "You have a greater journey ahead. You have a much bigger role than you have ever allowed yourself. Step into it. You have everything you need," she told him. "I cannot tell you more than this."

She stepped hard and the ripple effect moved away and seemed to soften the surface. Tinker felt his feet begin to sink.

"Monk?" he yelled out with concern. "Not good."

"Move, Tink," Monk demanded as they reached out for the opening at the far side of the open space. It had moved further away.

They continued to lower deeper into the fluid flooring. Moving became harder as the color changed from blue to violet. The fluid went from water to something thicker, which slowed their movements. They now had no stable surface and were swimming and fighting to stay afloat. Monk realized that the color had changed again to a deep crimson red that resembled blood.

"Tink!" Monk yelled as he felt himself sinking.

"Monk!" Tinker attempted to yell back but was choking as waves that were now crashing over them.

The surface calmed and became solid again. It was white. Monk and Tinker were gone.

CHAPTER 24
The Entrapment

Vampire felt a shift. His eyes grew black.

The left side of Ghost's mouth curled upwards into an unconvinced half smile. He immediately saw that Vampire was about to fight. He had studied him for years and knew his patterns. Ghost laughed at his failure to show restraint in this moment.

"I would pity you, but what good would that do?" Ghost asked him as he continued to mock him.

Ghost's laughter caused the release of more venom into Vampire's bloodstream. His anger grew. He lifted his head and slowly released his anger in a controlled exhale that pushed outward against the entrapment.

Ghost hovered, unaffected by Vampire's acting out.

"Yes," he told him. "Let the rage build. Anger. Wrath. Hate. Choose your word," he lectured as he floated around where Vampire was. "I am already aware of your next experience."

With those words, he was immediately on Vampire and suffocated him within his form. Vampire struggled for air, but the distraction of his rage had left him unguarded, and Ghost was able to take control.

CHAPTER 25
Caves of Waku

"Hold tight," Sorcerer yelled as the entrapment pushed outward.

"Here we go again," Aldrick said as he squeezed firmly onto his reddish copper staff.

"Aldrick," Ileana yelled to him. "Be careful with your energy right now. You are born of fire, as was Vampire. The electrical current is attracted to you more than the rest of us."

Aldrick nodded in understanding. He looked at Axel, who nodded support. He looked at Princess, who did the same.

"You are safe, Aldrick," she told him. "We are all in this together."

"Just like in the womb," Axel joked. "Seems cozy enough."

Aldrick smiled, hiding his concern. Axel was not fooled. This was new to him, new to the three of them. Aldrick was used to being in control. It aided him in battle, in negotiation and in life. But now, to be tapped into an essence much stronger than he had ever encountered threw off his confidence. He did not know what it would do or how he would be able to control himself.

Sorcerer was staring at him with visible concern. Ileana pulled his attention and shook her head.

"Remember," Ileana told him. "They are the Three of Legend. They are part of the prophecy," she reminded Sorcerer.

The entrapment began to vibrate. The top began to pull itself upwards into a point that began to work its way in Aldrick's direction. Aldrick continued to hold tight to his copper staff, but he could not focus his energy. He was distracted by the movement of the entrapment towards him.

Out of concern for their own safety, AZ and Cadet backed away. They each pulled on Seer's sleeves.

"Aldrick," Princess yelled. "Focus. We are here with you."

He turned to look at Axel, who gave him a wink.

"She knows things, brother," he told him. "Tinker taught her," he added playfully to add a sense of normalcy into their banter.

Aldrick smiled and focused his energy. The entrapment stopped moving and slowly returned to its stable form. The energy that it contained was strong, but it was evenly dispersed.

"That was Vampire's rage," Sorcerer yelled. "It was seeking an outside host."

Princess, Axel, and Aldrick felt a sense of pride at how they were able to work with Ileana and Sorcerer to maintain the entrapment.

AZ was quick to acknowledge the sound in the distance. The sound of breaking earth grew louder. He and Cadet looked at one another and then at Seer who continued to not react.

The entrapment bulged outward again with added force.

It pushed out and pushed the air with enough force to knock Princess backwards. Princess was closest to an opening in the ground.

The ground below her feet became unstable, but she did not let up. She began to lose her footing.

It will take care of itself, she assured herself and slowly released a breath.

The ground was now like liquid under her. She had no stable surface and fell through.

"Princess!" AZ screamed as he ran closer to her.

"No, you fool. You will be lost too," Seer yelled as he came out of his trance and pulled at AZ's pant leg, holding him back. "We need to get away from this edge."

The adrenaline pushed through AZ and fueled his fear. But then, the tingling in his body began to dissipate as he noticed that a light was emanating from the hole in the ground. It was the light of Princess' staff and the intensity had not dimmed.

The ground beneath her feet began to stabilize. Princess maintained her focus on keeping the entrapment. However, Axel was down on a knee with his left hand on his patina staff and his right hand dug into the sands. His eyes had turned forest green and then back to their normal color as the ground stopped breaking.

"You may want to step to your left," he said to his sister, playfully.

She did as he instructed and saw the ground fall as he removed his touch from the sand and stood with both hands back on his staff.

"That's my boy," Ileana whispered to the air.

"What the-" Aldrick began.

"Earth," Sorcerer told them, keeping his eyes on his son. "Like we told you. Your powers are innate."

"Earth," Axel whispered.

"He is commanding the ground," Aldrick said.

"More like working with Earth. Element and champion… together," Ileana added. "Earth is your Element," Ileana reminded him. "Your destiny is now confirmed."

"Meaning?" Axel asked.

"Meaning that each of you, 'The Three of Legend', will come to a point when your particular Element will be called forth by your bonds to work with you to keep you safe," Sorcerer explained further.

Ileana and Sorcerer looked at one another with pride.

CHAPTER 26
Hell, Third Circle

Monk and Tinker found themselves face down in red sands. Monk rolled over and looked up into the hot sun. The scene was familiar, but it was not what they thought it to be. The sky was red and orange in color, not blue.

Are we back at the Caves of Waku? Monk thought, questioning himself as he thought it.

Monk turned his head and looked at Tinker, who was rocking back and forth in an attempt to calm himself.

"Tink?" Monk questioned.

"This is becoming too much, Monk," Tinker sobbed. "I can't figure any of it out. I don't understand anything," he yelled. "Can you please just turn into the other guy and fly us out of here? I don't even understand that. I'm trying but can't figure it out."

"Well, I haven't exactly established a true working relationship with him," Monk replied with jest, in an attempt to give Tinker a sense of familiarity.

"Don't be funny, Monk."

"Sorry, Tink," Monk said as he cautiously walked to where Tinker sat. "I understand the stress of all of this."

"Do you?" Tinker begged. "Do you, really?"

"I do, Tink. Remember, I'm going through this too," he reminded him.

"Yeah, but you have him, the one with the wings," Tinker yelled. "And you have Vampire. If it comes down to it, he will help you out before he helps me," Tinker cried in his fear.

"You know that that would never happen," Monk assured him and came to sit next to him. "I would never allow it," he told him and put his arm around his shoulder to comfort him.

Tinker was shaking from his fear and anger - anger at the situation, at always thinking himself second in everyone else's life.

"Tink?" Monk questioned with kindness in his voice. "You know what is happening here, don't you?"

Tinker turned to him. "This trial is not yours, Tink," Monk reminded him. "It is close to us, but it is not ours."

Tinker's expression softened. His anger dissipated and he became concerned.

"Seer," he said.

"I immediately thought that we were possibly back at the caves," Monk said. "But now I think that we are in the Desert of Xedu.

It looks different from when I found Seer here. But it is the Desert of Xedu."

"Well, that was faster than I had hoped," spoke a voice with such force that the sky appeared to ripple and shake. "I anticipated a longer period of fun."

"You mean, torture," Monk said as he looked over his shoulder and saw Satan come into form.

The outline of his horns and hooves was the first thing to appear from the red sky and sand. Then, the rest of him, from head to toe, came into view.

"You are frightening," Tinker told him in a nonchalant tone.

"Aren't you the little tough guy?" Satan shot back with sarcasm.

"No," Tinker apologized. "I mean it. You are frightening." He lifted himself from the sands and walked over to where Satan stood, towering into the sky. His physical form was ablaze. Satan rushed his head down just inches from Tinker's face. The heat was so intense that Tinker was forced to shut his eyes. The smoke that came off the burning demon forced Tinker to cough from the fumes. He attempted to hold his breath but continued to cough. Satan pulled himself back to walk over to Monk who was sitting, unaffected. Satan's hoofed feet stomped forcefully with every step that he took.

"How do we get out of here?"

"You know better, old friend," Satan told him. "Just because the two of you do not have a place in my realm, doesn't mean that you are free of me."

"Seer," Tinker added. "We know. His wrath."

"This was where I found him. I rescued him from here when he was taken by The Dark Sisters," Monk added.

"Not only him," Satan reminded them. "There is another that has to get beyond his own rage, his own pain."

Satan looked to Monk and lifted his eyebrow.

"Vampire," Monk realized. "He has to get past all of them… Seven sins."

"Yes. But not just beyond them," Satan explained to them. "He has to relive them and then decide whether or not he wants to get past them. Remember, Monk, he unleashed each of them upon you. Each of your lives was ended because of his sins."

Monk squinted his eyes as he attempted to hide his anger at the demon's words.

"You cannot hide rage from me, fool," Satan laughed. "Allow it and put it where it belongs. Use it. Focus it on its cause and allow it to show its truth."

Tinker was looking at Monk and watching as his expression hardened.

"Monk. Don't," Tinker told him with a softness in his voice.

Monk's eyes turned black. He dropped his head to his hands and fell to his knees. Tinker watched as the light began to glow from Monk's back. Satan let out a hardy laugh.

"Yes, Monk. Yes," he yelled and continued to laugh. "Release him. Release Archangel."

Monk's body was aglow. The light retreated and he began to vibrate. His eyes shot open and glowed white. The white light shot out and up to the red sky. The vibrations became more intense until they became a sonic explosion that knocked both Tinker and Satan off their feet.

"Monk?" Tinker yelled out.

Satan continued to laugh as he laid on his back in the red sands.

Tinker ran up to Monk and attempted to put his hand on his back.

"I told you not to call me that," Archangel yelled with his eyes still aglow.

The shock of the anger in his eyes forced Tinker to lose his balance again and he fell onto the red sands.

Archangel took flight and was lost in the red sky.

Satan continued his laughter at Monk's transformation. Rage had taken over Monk and allowed Archangel to regain his form.

Tinker looked to the sky but saw no sight of him. He was enraged by Satan's continued laughter and ran to him in an attempt to attack.

Satan flicked Tinker away with a finger.

The distraction was enough to give Archangel the opportunity to pull Satan by the chain around his neck into the air.

Satan struggled against Archangel's choking. Archangel allowed all his rage to come to his grip and gave the chain a hard tug. Satan raised his oversized arms and dropped his heavy fists onto Archangel's back and wings, which forced him to release his grip, sending him toppling downward to the surface.

"Archangel!" Tinker yelled and ran to where he lay motionless in the desert. His impact had sent the red sands into the air and left him in a small crater.

Satan casually landed on his hoofed feet and walked over to where Tinker was trying to revive Archangel.

"When he wakes," Satan said to Tinker, "remind him that I am a Demon Ruler of Hell. He cannot kill me," he said and then walked away. "You will remain here until *he* and the others work through their wrath," Satan told Tinker as he left hoofprints in the sand. "Whether you want to believe it or not, we are on the same side, Tinker. But the longer you stay here, the more your wrath will take over."

Tinker heard his words but was processing the transformation of Archangel. His form had returned to Monk.

"His *gifts*," Satan's voice echoed but paused for the right words, "were agreed upon by opposing parties."

"What parties?" Tinker yelled out in anger.

"Remember Tinker," Satan said. "We are on the same side."

He continued to walk with a confident stride as the color of his form began to blend with the landscape and was absorbed into the redness of the sands and the sky of the Third Circle of Hell.

"The same side as Hell?" Tinker said to himself. "I think not."

Tinker attempted to wake Monk. He checked to make sure that he was breathing and had a pulse. He was alive. Tinker closed his eyes and lowered his head as he held tight to Monk.

CHAPTER 27
Shadow Realm

Seer looked off into the distance as he heard the scratching increase in volume and intensity. It sounded like it was growing closer. He saw only a misty blackness that surrounded him.

"There you are."

Seer heard the collective haunting voice and immediately felt his essence shiver.

"You knew that we would find you again," a singular voice told him.

"He could not keep us from you forever," a second voice added.

Monk, he thought.

"And now, he is not there to stop you from coming back to us," a third voice said with a harrowing laugh.

"Welcome," the three voices said in unison. "He is gone. But we are here for you. Come back to us."

Seer's eyes turned bright red. He saw AZ and Cadet attempting to wake him. Seer was in a vision and not able to physically move.

In his vision, he opened his eyes and returned his consciousness to the Shadow Realm. In the Shadow Realm, his eyes were not glowing. The misty blackness defined itself into three forms as the scratching became more intense. He saw the shadows with full clarity as they flew erratically around him. He saw The Dark Sisters.

Chapter 28
Caves of Waku

Seer inhaled as if it was his first breath. He began coughing and turned to his side to vomit.

"Seer," Cadet demanded as she noticed his eyes returning to normal. "I really need you to hold it together."

"Cadet," Seer said with a shake of the head. "I've been searching."

"For?" she asked him.

"I'm looking for Monk and Tinker," he told her through gritted teeth. "I'm trying everything." Seer's frustration was obvious in his tone.

Cadet held him by the shoulders. "They are gone." She attempted to get him to understand. AZ approached, catching himself up on the conversation.

Seer pushed her off. He stood on his own and took in a deep sigh. "I've been following others through the Shadow Realm."

"The Shadow Realm?" AZ asked.

"Where we seer's go in our visions," he replied. "The place where I look into someone's future."

"It's not just that," Cadet argued. "It's a dark place."

Seer ignored Cadet's comment. "It's where I went to see the vision of your path, AZ… When I told you that you could be with the princess if you chose to move in the right direction," Seer continued, reminding AZ that his vision helped him to secure his own way. He turned back to Cadet. "That's why I've been so-". He slowed himself and paused to collect his words.

"Concerned?" AZ gave him the word.

"Yes. Monk and Tinker are my family," Seer reminded them.

AZ understood what Seer had said. In the past, they had discussed the process of how someone with such a gift sees. He was aware that Seer following others was a dangerous undertaking. But Seer would do whatever he could to find Monk and Tinker, even if the cause was hopeless. Seer was still not able to accept their passing.

"The Shadow Realm is more active than I have ever seen it. I have made a deal with a group of shadows," Seer told him. "They will keep searching. Just in case." He knew to keep his answer vague.

AZ looked at him with empathy while Cadet showed her concern.

"Seer?"

"No," he said with a shake of the head. "They cannot be gone."

AZ motioned to speak, but decided it was better to hold back. He put his hand on Seer's shoulder to show his support.

"Then, keep searching," he told him. "We'll handle things here."

Seer softened to AZ's kindness. He turned with a grateful smile.

"If these shadows find anything, they will get the information to me," Seer said. "I will be here with you in the meantime… My friend."

AZ smiled. Cadet hid her continued worry.

"Not sure what we can do right now," AZ admitted as he watched the others maintain the entrapment.

"Nothing." Seer looked around, agreeing that there was nothing they could do. "But there must be a way in so that we can report Vampire's progress back to the others."

"Ghost is in there, but has not come out," AZ reminded him.

"He probably cannot," Seer replied. "I'm sure that Ileana and Sorcerer made it so that he would not be able to transfer out until they wanted him to."

"Or at least until the sun goes down," Cadet added with understanding. "The entrapment is powered by Light Magic. Only the sun can produce enough of it to hold Vampire."

"And unless Vampire settles himself, I expect that all Hell will break loose," AZ said without thinking.

Seer squinted his eyes as he thought about what they could do to speed up the progress. He stared at the electrical nature of the entrapment and watched as the particles danced in perfect chaos. There was no set pattern to their movement.

After a moment of silence, AZ questioned, "Seer?"

Seer turned to him still deep in thought.

"Who, or rather, what are these shadows?"

Seer hesitated. He looked back to the entrapment and sighed. He wondered if he should respond. He knew that the dark forces with whom he was working would call for questioning from the team, especially Ileana.

"Jigglers," he confessed with an exhale of the breath he had been holding.

"Jigglers?" Cadet yelled with fear. "You don't understand the seriousness of this," Cadet yelled. "You said 'shadows', not Jigglers!"

"What are Jigglers?" AZ asked.

"A Jiggler is the shadow of a shadow," Cadet replied. "I can't believe this," Cadet spoke through gritted teeth. She turned to AZ. "Jigglers are the things that you are told do not exist. They are the things that you know to be afraid of as a child. The Dark."

AZ was now concerned.

"Remember as a child when you were afraid of the dark, of what was under your bed or in the closet. Those were Jigglers. And they are real. *Very* real." She looked back at Seer with disappointment.

"I had no choice," Seer told them with sadness in his voice. "But I think I can convince them to show us what is happening inside the Entrapment… So that we can know when it is safe to let Vampire out." He looked at the fading sun in the western sky.

"The only things in there are an Immortal and a spirit," Cadet reminded him. "You cannot *see* either of them."

"No. But the Jigglers are no longer connected to a living being. They are able to watch our dimension through the shadows. As long as Vampire is casting a shadow, they can enter and report back to me what is happening," Seer explained. "For Monk," he added, "and Tinker," he concluded with a tear.

AZ softened to Seer's sorrow. "Then, I guess, it is time to take a walk on the dark side. Come on," AZ demanded and began to run towards the entrapment.

Seer was by his side.

"Ileana," AZ yelled out. "We think that we might have something that can help."

Seer pulled him back.

"It doesn't matter who gets pissed off. What matters is that we get in there and find out what is happening," AZ told Seer. "The sun is going down, and we will have no defense against Vampire."

"I'm listening," Ileana told them and nodded to Sorcerer to listen in.

"You tell them," AZ told Seer. "I won't know all of the answers."

Seer hesitated again. He feared judgement but believed that his rationale was sound and that they needed the aid of any ally.

"I have been searching for Monk and Tinker," Seer began.

"Seer. They are gone," Sorcerer interrupted. "You said that you lost sight of them."

"Which could mean that they are… dead, but could mean other things too," he added with confidence. "They could just… somehow… be off our grid." He turned to AZ. "I lost them to darkness. I did not see their end."

"Continue," Ileana commanded.

Cadet had walked up from behind them, shaking her head. Seer looked at AZ who nodded and winked to show his support. He wanted him to know that it was safe to admit what he had been doing.

"I was searching for them, or at least any clue as to what happened to them," he confessed.

Aldrick, Axel, and Princess were all trying to listen in as well.

"And I employed some… darker… associates from my past," he continued.

"Darker?" Princess asked, as she was able to overhear clearly.

"Jigglers," AZ told them.

Sorcerer looked to Ileana, who did not match his stare. Princess was taken back. Aldrick and Axel could only hear parts of what was being said but saw the full reactions of the others.

"What are Jigglers?" Aldrick asked.

"Shadows," AZ rushed.

"More than shadows," Cadet argued. "They are what is left when a soul is destroyed. When it is gone. Jigglers are dark and evil creatures. Full of rage and hate. They are what remains when a soul is destroyed."

Sorcerer spoke through his concern. "Jigglers are very dangerous and uncontrollable. Jigglers are those dark shadows that hang over your shoulder and cause you to turn in fear; the things that make you feel that you are being watched, the cold chill that causes you to shiver for no reason." He looked at Seer through squinted eyes. "They are souls that have been destroyed, never to fulfill their journey back to The Enlightenment. They are used for torture by dark forces. The Dark Sisters created and employed them in the past."

Ileana looked at Sorcerer with an unsure expression.

"I may be able to convince them to show us what is happening inside the Entrapment," Seer repeated to the whole group.

No one spoke.

"Look," AZ commanded. "The sun is setting, and you have already convinced the Elements to give us more time. But they will not do it again… Your words. The strength of this entrapment will not hold without the sun's energy. We need another plan, and we need it fast. There is no telling what emotional state Vampire is in, and if Ghost has made any progress with calming him down."

"This is very dangerous," Sorcerer told them. "Are you sure that your deal is safe?" he asked Seer.

Cadet maintained her disapproval.

"I have spent a lifetime in study and practice to do exactly this," Seer told her with confidence.

Silent concern continued to linger in the air.

"Well then," AZ said, breaking the silence. "I guess, we have a plan."

Ileana agreed with Cadet's unspoken concerns. Monk and Tinker were gone, but Seer could not accept it. He was employing darkness in an attempt to find them and bring them back.

So where are you heading? Ileana wondered about Seer's future.

CHAPTER 29
Anfa – Cornwall, 1650

The rough seas rocked the ship from side to side. They pushed hard from bow to stern. The salty water rushed over the deck and through the floorboards into the areas below. The soaked monks that boarded the ship in Cornwall held to their faith.

Their white robes were a stark contrast to dark dressings of the crew aboard the ship. The crew held tight to the ropes as they continued to stabilize the ship through the overpowering waves.

The Monks of Cornwall were taking their mission to northern Africa in hopes to lead the "lost people of those lands to find God". Among them was Brother Phineas.

Brother Phineas was on deck aiding to steady the ship through the storm. His face was scarred and his hands were bleeding from the ropes cutting through his skin. On any given day, Brother Phineas preferred being part of the action instead of quietly praying, as was the common practice of the rest of his brothers.

This type of unauthorized behavior was the primary reason that Brother Phineas was a concern to some of his superiors. His conviction was strong, yet, the heads of the monastery did not care for his independent thinking and rogue tendencies. Although the other brothers would not follow his logic publicly, there had been rumblings of understanding and possible agreement with his views and actions.

The abbot in charge of leading the brothers to establish a foundation near the city of Anfa was named Trace. He knew that he was going to be challenged by the resistance of the Berbers, Arabs, and tribesmen whom he looked to reform. He was already challenged by the thoughts of the Barbary pirates that would most likely look to take their ship and kill or enslave those on board. The abbot was consumed by his worry about the fear of the men with whom he was entrusted, but mostly, the one that he considered to be a fallen brother, who he knew he needed to get on his side.

He needed Brother Phineas because the young monk had repeatedly proven himself in battle for the cross. Phineas was admired and respected by the other brothers and would prove himself again, if countered by the pirates. His innate charm drew an empathetic perspective to his side.

Brother Phineas' views, although within the teachings of the church, did at times steer off the straight line that the order aimed to shoot. He questioned and voiced his questions. And he allowed for other questions.

Abbot Trace permitted him his moments because he knew that the strong hand of the church would pull back on the other brothers. Abbot Trace was still adjusting the length of the leash that he allowed Phineas, as Brother Phineas required a different approach.

The open seas had proved difficult for most. The up and down movements of the ship along with the intermittent side to side tipping caused many on board to suffer. Vomiting was common throughout the ship. The crew had grown weary of the monks not being able to hold themselves and resorted to handing them the mops to clean up their own messes.

Brother Phineas seemed untouched by the nausea and vomiting. This added to the other brothers recognizing him as a beacon to turn to for strength.

"The wine is always good," he told them simply.

Abbot Trace continued to find it difficult to get him under any sense of his authority. He had grown envious of Brother Phineas' ability to bring the crew members to God. However, he had to remind himself that this was why Brother Phineas was brought on this mission, that this ability would prove helpful with the "pagans" of Africa and if encountered, with the pirates.

It was late. The seas had calmed enough for the exhausted crew and weary monks to sleep under the cover of the night. The ship was navigating under the dark starry sky.

"I figure that we will arrive on shore by daylight," Captain Seamus told Brother Phineas.

"Thank you, Captain," the respectful monk said as he continued to look up, hoping to find a break in the clouds and locate familiar constellations.

Brother Phineas made his way through the series of ropes that tended to the sails. The waves were still a bit rough, but more like a rocking which granted sleep to the others. Brother Phineas held the ropes to stabilize himself.

"Abbot?" Brother Phineas questioned the shadowed figure.

"What were you discussing with the captain?" Abbot Trace questioned with an annoyed tone.

"He expects that we will reach port by daylight," Brother Phineas replied without agenda.

"And why did he tell you and not me?" he demanded.

"I suspect because I was the one standing there," he answered with a touch of sarcasm.

"I am rethinking our need for you as we continue," Abbot Trace admitted.

"Meaning?"

"*Meaning* that you will be remaining with this ship and head back to Cornwall while the rest of us continue the good Lord's work," the abbot told him with an air of superiority. The leash was being pulled back.

"If that is God's will," Brother Phineas replied without resistance.

The lack of begging added to Abbot Trace's displeasure. This would have given the abbot the leverage that he wanted to keep Brother Phineas in line. However, Brother Phineas did not give him what he wanted. Abbot Trace saw this as if he had stolen that leverage and therefore required punishment.

Brother Phineas was looking at the stars, over the edge of the boat. Trace grabbed hold of a wooden mallet and hit Brother Phineas in the back of the head, knocking him out. He looked around to be sure that no one saw what had happened.

A life raft was suspended in front of him. He took this as a sign from God that he was doing the right thing. He loaded Brother Phineas' body into the small boat and struggled to lower it slowly to the water. He wanted to avoid drawing attention.

The strain to control the boat was intense. His hands bloodied as he controlled the ropes.

But then, that was it. The life raft with Brother Phineas was in the water. Abbot Trace released the ropes. He had done what God had asked of him: he had gotten rid of the evil that Brother Phineas would have brought with him in his teachings.

Abbot Trace turned and walked back to his private quarters. He entered, washed the blood from his hands, wrapped them and went to sleep with a clear conscience.

Morning broke. Abbot Trace was awakened to the excited sounds of "Land Hoo!"

He rushed to get up and was momentarily slowed by the pressure he put on his wounded hands. He unwrapped the bandages that he used to stop the bleeding and grabbed a pair of emerald-colored gloves. He pulled them up to his elbows.

He pushed open the door of his cabin and saw the scurry of activity. He continued to feel vindicated by his actions of the previous night. God was pleased with him. The serpent had been cast from the garden and reaching land safely was his reward.

He heard yelling from the other side of the ship. The tone was not that of excitement at seeing land. He stepped out from his cabin to the pounding release of the first cannonball.

"Pirates!" a white-robed brother told him and made the sign of the cross.

Abbot Trace saw the pirate charging his way with a sword drawn. He quickly pulled the praying monk in front of himself and saw the painful surprise as the pirate pushed his blade deep into the man's midback.

"Abbot?" the brother begged.

Abbot Trace stepped back and kicked the dying man backwards to knock the assailant off balance. He retreated into his cabin and locked the door. Abbot Trace looked around in panic, as he was unable to see a way out.

In his moment of prayer, a cannonball burst through the wall and offered him an escape. As the dust cleared, he saw a life raft rocking back and forth in the wake of the cannon fire. One of the ropes had been cut through; however, the boat was still intact.

Abbot Trace needed to get to it and cut the other rope. He would escape in it and row to shore while the onslaught continued.

"The Lord will provide," he told himself.

Abbot Trace walked over the debris of his cabin and attempted to not draw attention from the chaos that was raging outside. The locked door was being shaken as the marauders continued their attempt to break in and either capture or kill him. Neither of those options were acceptable to him. He would escape.

"The Lord will protect me," he told himself. "I am with him," he said aloud. "And he is with me."

"But I don't think that he heard you," answered the angered voice of the man standing in the opening in the wall.

The forceful shaking of the door caused him to turn. He looked back and was blindsided by the handle of the sword to his head. As he lost consciousness, he saw the second man enter. He thought that he saw a red light surrounding him before blacking out.

Abbot Trace was choking on the water that had been thrown onto his unconscious self. It forced him back to the present where he found himself bound with his hands behind his back and tied to the mast of the ship. As he opened his eyes, Abbot Trace saw the other monks on their knees, also with their hands tied behind their backs. The ship's crew had been killed.

Abbot Trace thought that his present state of confusion and the sun in his eyes were tricking him. He thought that he was seeing Brother Phineas standing with the pirates. He blinked several times and squinted.

"Yes, Abbott," Phineas said. "It is I."

"Phineas?" he questioned. "How?"

"You mean, after you tried to kill me?" Phineas shot back without any sense of anger.

"Phineas," Abbot Trace attempted to recover as he saw some of the monks looking towards him with shock and anger.

"So, you invited these savages to our ship to destroy us?" Abbot Trace asked. "Kill the crew? We are here to do God's work!"

he yelled out, still attempting to take the attention off of his *alleged* actions.

"I think that God has a different agenda than you, Trace," Phineas yelled and rushed towards the abbot.

Abbot Trace closed his eyes in fear of the attack. Nothing came. When he opened his eyes, he saw the rage in Brother Phineas' face. His eyes were focused and full of wrath. The lines in his face told of the years of torture that he had endured under the strong hand of Abbot Trace. But this time, the tables were turned, and Trace could do nothing but cower in fear.

"Where is your God now?" asked the pirate captain.

He was holding Phineas back.

"I could let him go," he said. "I could let him kill you," he continued to Trace's growing fear.

"I'm sure that you deserve his rage, but I don't think that you deserve his sorrow. If he were to kill you, he would have a moment of relief but a lifetime of regret. I will not allow it. He deserves better."

Phineas knew the pirate's words to be true and softened the intent of his attack. The pirate lightened his control over him but continued to hold tight to his hand.

"You deserve better," he told Phineas.

Phineas met eyes with the pirate captain and saw him nod in respect. He returned the gesture.

"You deserve better," he repeated, "but he doesn't." The marauder drew his jade-colored sword and pushed it deeply into Abbot Trace's heart. He twisted it so that the sharp edges were positioned horizontally.

Phineas looked on in shock. He rushed the captain's hand with his free hand and attempted to pull the sword out. It did not move. Phineas lost sight of logic. His rage had subsided, but his faith did not. He did not believe that God wanted this. The pirate captain would not release the abbot. Blood was spilling from Trace's mouth. He was coughing blood onto Phineas' soiled white robes.

Phineas could think of only one thing that might force the pirate to release his sword. He stared at the glowing green blade. He pushed himself onto the length of the sharp edge that was facing him. It sliced into his skin.

The pirate's eyes widened in shock. He withdrew his sword, but Phineas' body was already leaning hard into it. It sliced deeper.

"No!" the pirate screamed out. "Why did you do that?" he begged in angst.

"That is not the Lord's way," Phineas told him.

"Phineas," the pirate called out as Phineas closed his eyes and his heart slowed. "Phineas," he called out again.

"Thaddeus," Brother Phineas whispered his final word to the pirate captain.

Thaddeus, the pirate captain, was able to hear the slowing of Phineas' heart. He looked up to Trace and saw that he was already gone. He looked back at Phineas and lowered his face to his neck.

Vampire sat silent.

"The Sword of Sansit," Ghost remarked. "You had it."

"Apparently, I did," Vampire replied with controlled emotion.

"And then lost it," Ghost continued.

Vampire looked at Ghost with a sense of disgust. Ghost floated around him. "Earlier," he confessed, "I was floating above the pit when you and Monk lost your grip. I saw what was happening."

"But you did nothing," Vampire added and looked back at the ground and into his own thoughts. "Interesting," he said after a moment of silence in a surprisingly calm tone.

"What is?" Ghost asked.

"I understand that I have acted out in rage due to insecurity," he replied.

"I'm not looking to analyze you."

"Actually, you are," Vampire told him with a bit of a jest. He stood and walked around the limited space of the entrapment.

He held his hand up to attract the electrical charge of the light that contained him and Ghost. The tingle of the charge was welcomed.

However, he knew that to take it further would cause overwhelming pain.

"I was birthed from fire. I was born to rage. But then with the repeated loss of Phineas, I learned fear."

"You were created to bring fear," Ghost countered.

"But then I brought it to myself," Vampire further challenged. "Fear of losing him."

Every part of Vampire's essence was focused on Monk.

"I can still feel him." He spoke his thoughts aloud. "I can still smell him." Vampire said and wiped a drop of sweat from his cheek. "He is not gone."

He played with the wetness on his fingertips as he was thinking. He looked at the electrical current that swarmed around them. He tried to see through it but was unable to make out any forms. He focused on Monk and envisioned him following a path of water. He breathed into the daydream and smiled as he felt himself become a place of refuge.

"There is only one way out of here," he said and turned to stare at Ghost. "Let's get out of here."

CHAPTER 30
Hell, Fourth Circle

Tinker opened his eyes as he felt the cold solid surface form under him. He was immediately astounded by the vast library in which he found himself and Monk. Tinker was still holding tight to Monk's unconscious body. He checked to be sure that Monk was breathing and his heart was beating strongly. Yet, Tinker's curiosity got the best of him. He gently lowered Monk's head and laid it upon two books on the stone floor. He stood wide-eyed with a true sense of amazement.

The books were endless. The knowledge was endless. Everything that anyone could ever want to know was housed inside this room.

Even more than the library at the monastery, he thought.

Tinker was astonished by what he was seeing. He walked a few steps from Monk to get a full perspective of the vast space. He stood in the center of the space and spun slowly, taking in the grandeur of it all.

The amber flames that illuminated the room were soft and comforting. They invited a quiet read. They invited an eternity of quiet reads.

Tinker knew that they were in Hell, but to him, this could have been Heaven. He could stay in this room forever and learn. He could read and learn and think and read and learn and think for eternity.

"Gluttony," Monk said to him from his dazed state. He was sidelying and propped up on his elbow.

Tinker returned to him and helped him to stand.

"This one is yours," Monk informed him.

"Gluttony?" Tinker questioned as he looked at his lean body. "I'm not…"

"For knowledge," Monk said, acknowledging the room with an arm gesture.

"Ah," Tinker allowed. "I guess I can see that." He had a reflective look. "And to be honest, I do like to eat."

"A lot," Monk added.

A distant buzzing sounded through the air.

Monk looked up to the endless shelves of books that stretched beyond his sight. Tinker too looked up with more excitement and astonishment that all this knowledge could be his.

The buzzing grew louder, the pitch grew higher and became irritating.

"Beelzebub," Monk said with a shake of the head.

Tinker had his hands over his ears.

The buzzing had grown painful as the demon came into sight.

Monk stood unaffected. Tinker looked at him with confusion. "I think I'm getting the hang of this," he yelled to Tinker over the loud buzzing.

"What?" Tinker yelled.

Beelzebub hovered in front of them, and the high pitch of his flapping wings brought Tinker to his knees in pain. The giant fly-like demon cocked his head to the side and focused his thousands of eyes.

The light shot intensely from Monk's back and temporarily blinded Beelzebub.

"Yup," Monk said. "Definitely getting the hang of this."

Beelzebub fell back as one by one his eyes came back into focus. When his vision was restored, Tinker was on his feet, standing next to Archangel. The buzzing of his wings had stopped.

"Nice trick," Beelzebub admitted. "*Phineas*," he added with distaste.

"I am not Phineas," Archangel told him.

"You are and always will be... Phineas. Time after time, life after life, you have been and will continue to be Phineas... The slave, the monk, the doctor, businessman, whatever else you have been. Your essence is always the same."

Archangel maintained the intensity in his stare and the strength in his stance. Tinker looked back and forth between them. He caught a whiff of a foul scent and could not help but cover his nose with his pale-yellow scarf.

"That's what comes from playing in shit," Archangel told him. "The curse of being a demon trapped in the form of a fly."

"A demon god!" Beelzebub rushed back, demanding respect.

"Giant fly." Archangel looked the Ruler of the Fourth Circle of Hell over with distaste. "That's what I see."

Tinker started to see aspects of Monk in Archangel's banter.

Archangel looked around and let out a frustrated sigh. "What do we have to do to get out of here?" he asked.

Beelzebub flapped his wings faster and spread the intensity of his foul stench.

"Get out of here quickly," Tinker added under his breath.

"That is up to you," the giant insect said. "And by you," he looked at Tinker, "I mean, you."

Tinker's eyes widened.

"Told ya," Archangel said.

Beelzebub lowered himself close to Tinker. "You are welcome to stay here forever and learn everything that you could ever want to learn, or..."

"Or get through this quickly and use all the knowledge that you already have and will ever gain after we leave," Archangel countered.

"It's really not a hard choice," Tinker told Beelzebub apologetically.

"You say that now." He walked to an oversized book that hovered above a golden flame. "Go ahead, ask one question. You will find the answer in this book."

"Tinker?" Archangel interfered.

"No," Tinker replied as a bead of sweat fell from his forehead. "I'm good, thank you."

He resisted, but lifted his chin to attempt a better look at the book.

"Then, just think of one," Beelzebub tempted. "You don't even have to say it aloud. Your *chaperone* will not be able to stop that," the demon enticed with a confident stare at Archangel.

Archangel closed his eyes and focused his energy. The light from his back filled the room as he transformed back to Monk.

Beelzebub had anticipated this move. He recovered quicker as he had brought the book up to block the light.

"Your trick is getting old," he told Monk. "And I do believe that it was not enough," the demon laughed and pointed at Monk.

"Tink?" Monk asked with concern that his trick was not enough of a distraction to stop Tinker from thinking of a question. "Tink?"

"Sorry, Monk," Tinker apologized, embarrassed that he was unable to resist. "I couldn't help it. Knowledge is all I have. Questions and answers."

"That's not true, Tink," Monk argued.

"What? What else do I have?"

"You have me," Monk told him. "You have Seer and Princess. You have all of us, even Vampire."

Beelzebub let out a loud, "Ha!"

"He thinks the world of you," Monk continued to counter.

"Because of you," Tinker told him.

"That's not true," Monk attempted to make his case. "We are a family."

Tinker was silent.

"And there it is," Beelzebub spoke with a snarled confidence that Tinker had thought of a question. "Family."

Tinker walked towards him. The pages of the golden book turned back and forth as if blowing in the breeze. They stopped at the answer to Tinker's question. He began to look onto the glowing pages. He reached to touch the words on those pages, but instead, he closed the book.

"What?" Beelzebub questioned. "That is not how this works."

"Answering that question is not going to change who I am," Tinker told him. "It's not going to offer me any solace."

Tinker looked back at Monk.

"Like Monk said, I have a family," Tinker agreed and smiled. He turned back to Beelzebub, "But thank you for the opportunity."

Beelzebub was shocked. His thousands of eyes were focusing on all sides of Tinker. They were not able to focus on an understanding of Tinker and his character. His action was not expected. It was not seen as an option. Yet, it was what happened. This was Tinker's truth.

Beelzebub's eyes continued to move without any coordination. He became frustrated and took flight. He grabbed the golden text and he began hitting into the shelves of books. The shelves shook just enough for the books to come free and fall from their varied heights. Volume after volume fell; hundreds, thousands toppled down towards Tinker and Monk.

"We're gonna get trapped under all of these books, Monk," Tinker yelled as he was being pummeled by the falling texts.

"Maybe, we can find the one that can help us get out of here," Monk yelled.

"I think that he's holding it," Tinker argued. "Ouch!"

Beelzebub continued to fly erratically and knocked more and more of the heavy volumes towards them.

Tinker and Monk had found a temporary shelter against a wall that was covered by the thin walkway of the floor above.

"Do you smell that?" Tinker asked Monk.

"Paper?"

"No," Tinker replied. "Rain. Snow…"

"Tink?"

Tinker walked out from the narrow overhang. The books continued to pile up as the demon continued his disoriented attack on the volumes that lined the walls.

Tinker looked down at the floor. He saw a thin trail of water flowing. It disappeared under the books on the floor and reappeared in the areas where books had not yet covered the stone tiles.

"Monk," Tinker yelled and pointed to the thin line of water.

"Follow it," Monk told him.

Tinker dodged falling books as he followed the path of the flowing water. He kicked volumes out of his way to see where the water led. Monk assisted in blocking the falling books so that they could follow the fluid trail as it flowed to what they hoped was a way out.

CHAPTER 31
Firenze, Italy, 1347

Vampire again found himself surrounded by familiar and welcomed luxuries from his past. He was being attended to by obedient and loyal servants. He was given constant and repeated flirtations from both women and men that made up the court of Firenze. It was the eve of The Renaissance, and the energy in high society was beginning to explode with artistic excitement and scientific experimentation.

However, matters at hand demanded attention. The Black Plague had also made its way to Firenze. Illness was spreading quickly throughout the poorer streets and neighborhoods and had begun to find its way to the homes of the aristocracy. Those in the court had experienced the loss of servants and vendors. Their concern for their own safety took over their thinking and they turned to the only one who they felt could help protect them. In doing so, they had no choice but to place themselves at the mercy of Don Vampiro.

Somehow, the 'Great Death' had not made its way to his home, nor to those who were in his employment and lived on the grounds of his vast estate. The main villa itself housed many of his more important business acquaintances. Others had been given residence in temporary structures throughout his gardens and pools.

"There is a…" Don Vampiro's personal butler searched for the right word. "*Man*… at the main gate."

Without turning from his stare out the window, Vampiro snarled. "Send him away."

"He will not leave," the butler whispered into his ear. "He seeks an audience with… *Thaddeus*."

Don Vampiro looked at his servant with annoyance.

"*He* called you by name," the butler told him and maintained his position.

Vampire paused in thought as he looked around the room of drunken aristocrats.

"I will meet him at the gate," Vampire told him. "Make sure that they keep drinking," he ordered as he got up and walked away.

Vampire called for the guards at the gate to be temporarily relieved. Once the guards were far enough away, he walked towards the locked gates with a powerful stride.

"Who dares come here and demand an audience?" he yelled out but did not see anyone.

"I dare," he heard but was still unable to see anyone.

Vampire heard a whistle. He looked around in haste.

"Down here, big boy." The rough voice came from the edge of the road beyond the gates. The flowering bushes concealed the miniscule man.

"I must remind myself to reinforce the lower parts of the gates to keep out unwanted vermin," Vampire said with an annoyed tone. "Why are you here, Sansit?"

"You have something of mine," Sansit told him and walked to stand directly in front of him, with his hands on his hips.

"I should kick you through that gate and into a tree," Vampire said with the same annoyed tone.

"I'd be back," Sansit replied. "But I won't knock next time. I'll burrow into your people's brains and take your control away. You and your fortune would crumble, and all of your gluttonous acts would be no more."

Vampire wound his leg to kick Sansit, but Sansit was faster on the draw. He had jumped to Vampire's other leg and climbed up his body to his neck. Sansit pulled the emerald sword from the scabbard at his hip and drew it upon Vampire's neck. Vampire stopped his motion and felt the power that seemed to hum off the green blade.

"Ah," Sansit said with a sense of lightness. "You know what this is."

"The legendary Sword of Sansit," Vampire replied.

"And you know *whose* it is," Sansit added through gritted teeth and held it just off Vampire's skin.

Vampire said nothing.

"It takes an Immortal to destroy an Immortal," Sansit reminded him. He withdrew his blade and leapt down to the ground. "One slice of this would pass right through you and you would be done for," Sansit told him.

"Why are you here?"

"I told you," Sansit told him. "You have something of mine."

"She is not yours," Vampire told him. "Gnim is not interested in being part of your life any longer."

"Did you ask her?"

"Why would I do that?" Vampire asked with a shake of the head. "She came to me."

"To you," Sansit told him. "Not for you."

"Regardless of that, she is free to go if she chooses."

Sansit laughed. "No kidding."

Vampire was shaking his head. "What are you offering?" Vampire asked.

"The city," he replied.

Vampire looked at him with a judgmental snarl of the mouth.

"I don't think that that is yours to give."

"Or is it?" Sansit argued back. "The 'Black Plague', as they are calling it, is my contribution to ridding this place of the sewage that is humanity."

Vampire's eyes squinted with an angered stare.

"Oh, come on," Sansit laughed as he drew a line in the dirt road. "What did you think? That I was just here for my charm?" He let out a true hardy laugh. "I have lingered here because of your failure. So has Gnim. The Enlightenment is very disappointed with you and wants me to fix what you have broken."

Vampire knew that what he was saying was true. He knew that he had failed in his purpose to destroy humanity. He had made a choice not to. Vampire knew that although he found much of mankind intolerable, he did have a true purpose in not wanting to rid it out of existence. He knew that another had been sent to complete the task. However, he also knew that having the Immortal warrior, Gnim, on his side challenged her partner, the Immortal warrior, Sansit. Vampire knew that Sansit's true hope was to win Gnim back and not to destroy humankind.

"And it seems that your suggestive nature has Gnim turning away from her purpose as well," Sansit told him with a condescending shaking of his finger. "You're a bad influence."

"So I've been told," Vampire replied. "But again, she is not mine to give or take. Gnim will make her own decision."

Sansit rolled his eyes and threw his blade over his shoulder as he made his way down the dirt road. Vampire followed with a slower stride as his step length was the same as three of Sansit's steps.

"You could offer me a lift," Sansit told him.

"Not going to happen."

CHAPTER 32
Hell, Fourth Circle

"Keep running, Tink," Monk yelled out as he dodged and knocked away volumes upon volumes of books falling on them.

"As if there is another choice," Tinker shot back in frustration as Beelzebub continued knocking into the endless height of tightly packed shelves.

"Well, you're the one who needs to know everything," Monk yelled.

"Not now, Monk," Tinker argued. "You're starting to sound like Vampire again. Is that an Immortal thing?"

"Not now, Tink," Monk retorted.

"Oh good," Tinker told him as they found a momentary refuge in what seemed like a giant fireplace.

Monk turned and looked at Tinker as the multitude of books continued to fall and began to block their path.

"Water led us to safety," Tinker told him through his panting.

Monk too was breathing heavily. He smiled through his exhaustion. He looked down and saw what he thought was a large rodent.

"Sansit?" Tinker questioned.

The creature that was crawling on the floor turned its head and looked up at Tinker. He stood on his hind legs and reached the height of Tinker's knees.

"Do I know you?" Sansit asked.

"No sir," Tinker answered. "I do not believe that you do," he told him."You are the Immortal warrior, Sansit, and owner of the Sword of Sansit." Tinker gave a subtle bow in respect.

Sansit responded with the same.

"Do you know how to get out of here?" Monk asked him as the crashing books were now knee high and sliding into their temporary refuge.

"You, I do know," Sansit said to Monk with a hint of distaste and a quiver of his upper lip.

"Your legend is greater than mine," Monk told him.

"Not according to what I've been reading in here," he replied and turned his back to Monk with his arms folded tight across his chest and his nose to the air.

"What did you do to him?" Tinker begged Monk with embarrassment.

"Nothing," Monk replied. "Sansit," he argued as Sansit held himself uninterested in Monk's words. "We have never met…"

"Why would I want to meet you?" Sansit yelled. "This is all your fault."

Monk and Tinker looked in astonishment at the loudness that came from the miniature character that stood at their knees.

"I have been down here for what feels like an eternity," Sansit explained, "and I have never read about anyone who has caused as much destruction as you." He moved closer to Monk. "It was you that caused that vermin, Vampire, to sway from his task of destroying humanity. It was you who kept going back for him to discover again rather than lose hope and just finish the job."

Monk said nothing as Tinker stared open-mouthed at the minuscule Immortal.

"I keep thinking that I have read most everything in this dungeon of knowledge," he continued to Tinker's excitement. "But forget it, kid. It never ends. Knowledge keeps growing and if you give into it like I did, you sacrifice everything else about yourself in the pursuit of theory."

"Theory without application," Monk said as if speaking a familiar thought.

Sansit looked at Monk with such rage in his eyes that they looked red. Monk was unsure why.

"Are you a seer?" Tinker asked.

"No," Sansit replied. "Just a glutton for knowledge."

"I can understand that," Tinker admitted.

Sansit dropped his head and was shaking it.

"I lost everything. I was lied to and lured into this place by those evil Witches," he told them. "I was tricked because of what I thought I wanted most. I have learned everything that I thought I wanted to learn about but it was all useless knowledge. The cost was never being able to use it."

The books had piled to waist height as they continued to slide into the floor of the fireplace.

Tinker was busy in his backpack.

"What are you doing, boy?" Sansit asked as he continued to climb atop the piles of books.

"Putting theory into practice," Tinker told him as he pulled out rope and gloves. "The chimney," he told them. "We can climb up."

"To where?" Sansit asked.

"Don't know," Tinker replied. "But it will give us an opportunity that we are not going to get if we just stay here and think about it."

Sansit's face lit up with a wide grin that then opened to show several missing teeth.

"Finally," Sansit said. "I am finally getting out of here."

"You couldn't figure this out?" Monk asked.

"I didn't have rope, smartass," Sansit shot back. He turned to Tinker. "And he wonders why I don't like him."

Tinker smiled. "Don't worry," he told him. "He'll grow on you."

"Like a plague," Sansit replied with a snarl at Monk.

"Monk?" Tinker asked. "You know what you have to do."

Monk nodded and closed his eyes. The glow came from his back.

"Holy…" Sansit began but could not find the right word to finish what he was seeing.

"Not sure about it being *Holy*," Tinker said, as they watched in awe.

Monk showed less pain and angst as he controlled his transformation into Archangel. As the wings protruded and spread, they took up the entire opening at the front of the oversized fireplace. His wingspan blocked the books from continuing to slide towards them.

Tinker looked up the chimney and then back to Archangel.

"How's he gonna flap those things in there?" Sansit asked.

"He won't have to," Tinker replied. He turned to Archangel. "You're going to have to get a good jump and take the rope. Put these gloves on just in case you need to grab hold of the sides of the chimney."

Archangel looked up the chimney but was unable to see an opening.

"What is it with this place?" he questioned. "What do demons have against showing where things end?"

"For them, it's all about the journey, not the destination. The end is not always the same," Sansit answered. "Hell is different for every soul."

Archangel looked at him with a curious expression.

Sansit realized that without thinking he had answered Archangel's question. He turned to Tinker.

"This is Hell. Everyone's personal Hell is different. Even if the path is the same, the distance traveled may not be. Hell shows no ending. It is up to the individual to overcome what it is that they are here for and find their own end point."

"Sounds like life," Tinker said. "And then?"

"And then, judgement begins," Sansit told him.

"Can you lecture us later?" Archangel asked. "The weight of these books will crush you once my wings move away."

Sansit's upper lip began to quiver again in disgust for Archangel talking to him.

"Okay," Tinker told them. "Sansit. I'm going to tie this rope around your waist," he explained and assisted Sansit to be held firmly at the middle of the rope. "And I will tie the end around my waist." He turned his attention to Archangel. "Once you take off with the rope, you will be pulling us up with you."

Archangel nodded.

"Just realize that we…" Tinker told him and looked at Sansit and then back to Archangel, "or at least I, am not Immortal. If you pull too hard, you will crush my bones." He looked back to Sansit. "That's why I am at the end."

"I like you, kid," Sansit said.

"Thank you," Tinker replied. "I like you too."

Archangel cleared his throat. Sansit rolled his eyes. Tinker giggled.

"Looks like he'll fit right in," Tinker told Archangel.

"Ready?" Archangel asked as he squatted down and quickly retracted his wings. He pushed off and ascended up the chimney.

Sansit and Tinker were pulled up as they too took to a squatted position. They jumped up as the rope became taut. Archangel was using his hands to push off the inner walls of the chimney and make haste to reach the unknown endpoint. Sansit was pulled up, as was Tinker. Tinker looked down through the chimney for a second as the books flowed into the fireplace and filled where they had stood. He was pulled into the blackness of the flue and was holding himself tightly to avoid contact with the walls. His arms were around his head and his eyes were now closed as he gritted his teeth.

CHAPTER 33
The Entrapment

Vampire found himself back in the entrapment.

"Firenze feels different," Vampire said as he reminisced about the last experience and the Duomo of the Cathedral of Santa Maria del Fiore. "That vermin, Sansit, was sent to do what I had not done." He looked at Ghost. "Sansit was sent to destroy humankind because I chose not to." Vampire stood and walked around the confined space, staring out at the peeks of life beyond the electrical force containing him. "I started the Renaissance to make up for Sansit starting the Black Plague. So, I felt that I should be there while it was in full effect and to keep Sansit from destroying what I protected. The Renaissance kept him distracted from his task and entertained. He was always a glutton for knowledge and beauty."

"Such a name dropper," Ghost told Vampire with a shake of the head.

Vampire also shook his head, more so at himself for agreeing with Ghost's remark. "I had been in Firenze for decades," he told

Ghost as he traced through the sand with his foot. "I could not leave. But that was a darker time."

"And you had a different take on life," Ghost added, as if he had been there.

Vampire looked at him quizzically.

"You speak as if you were there," Vampire countered.

"There?" Ghost laughed. "Not at the time. But yes, I have traveled through your timeline. I have seen the things that we are experiencing."

Vampire continued with his disapproving stare.

"I am a ghost. I have the ability to move between dimensions," he explained and floated to be next to him. "And that includes time. Yet, even with that ability, I cannot make any worthwhile contact with anyone when I go." He kept his focus on the etching that Vampire had drawn in the sand. "I cannot feel. I cannot love. I must admit that, yes, I am envious of the living. I am envious of you… Of what you have always had with Phineas."

Vampire said nothing. It was time to listen.

"What you share has gone on for thousands of years. Nine of his lifetimes."

"Nine deaths," Vampire was looking down at the drawing.

"All is not lost, Thaddeus," Ghost told him. "The Jeweled Dragon will not veer from her course. She will destroy humankind and with it, all of time and space. But it is up to you to keep going or to stop here and lose more than just him."

"Just him? There is nothing without him," Vampire argued through his pain. "I came to understand that eight times before." He turned and looked at Ghost. "You have no idea what it is like to be in this pain."

Ghost said nothing.

"And you envy this?" Vampire questioned. "I never wanted this. And I certainly never wanted to feel what I am feeling… You're better off not being able to feel or love," Vampire told him.

"Then, what was your plan?" Ghost asked with growing agitation. "Did you expect to find Phineas, save all of time and space and then to live happily ever after? Everything should have bent to your design? It did not, and here we are."

Ghost was face to face with Vampire. Both began to demonstrate increased frustration.

"He was mortal," Ghost reminded Vampire. "You are not. There is no other way. He, like all mortals, will die with each lifetime…"

"And then, come back," Vampire shouted.

"Only if we succeed. Only if *you* destroy the Jeweled Dragon," Ghost shouted back.

As his frustration built, Vampire's physical form began to show signs of transforming into the savage version of himself.

"And this is how you want to leave his legacy?" Ghost asked in a calmer voice.

Vampire's transformation halted and he returned to his human looking form.

"No," Vampire admitted. "No. It's not," he added as he turned and walked to the edge of the entrapment.

Vampire held his hand at the border of the electric energy and allowed himself to suffer the current flowing through him. He allowed himself to be punished as he felt Monk.

"Monk and Tinker are not mentioned in the prophecy," Ghost reminded him, but this time, with a softer tone in his voice.

Vampire attempted to argue.

"The eight stones are mentioned. They fell for Monk, but it is AZ who can find them… not Monk," he added.

Vampire looked at the lights of the entrapment. "This is my fault," he said.

"Pride," Ghost said flatly. "Pride has always gotten the worst of you."

"Don't you mean *best?*"

"No… Worst," he told him as his vaporous form engulfed Vampire and squeezed until Vampire conceded.

CHAPTER 34
Hell

Archangel had pulled Sansit and Tinker through the top of the chimney. They found themselves in a field.

Sansit pulled a blade from within his robes. "Hey kid," he yelled. "I think you should recognize this."

Tinker's eyes widened in excitement as he reached to touch the pointed tip of the broken emerald blade. He inhaled as his eyes widened.

"We were told that it was at the Palace of Tebbs, but we did not find it," Tinker told him.

"It was," Sansit told him. "The Witch, Baltaan, was gifted it by her hack of a king husband."

"You trusted Baltaan?" Monk asked.

"No." He snickered but said nothing more.

"How is it that you now possess it?" Monk asked Sansit. "Part of it," Monk added, noting the fractured emerald blade.

Sansit snarled at the question.

"I became careless and lost it in battle when I was grieving over Gnim. It was discovered by Lexter, who was the King of Tebbs at the time, and was handed down through his family for centuries. I read that Dubair, the reigning King of Tebbs, gave it to Baltaan as a wedding gift," Sansit told them. "And then, Baltaan used it to kill the Queen of Witches in an underwater battle."

Tinker's eyes widened as his stare moved back and forth from Monk to Sansit.

"You may want to reread that chapter," Monk joked. "Ileana is alive."

"Then, she must have the other part of the blade," Sansit deduced. "It was broken by magic in that battle between Baltaan and Ileana. Baltaan then handed the hilt and the lower part of the blade over to The Dark Sisters as a testament to her loyalty. I read that they had come to Hell. So, I went and stole it from them as they were being sentenced here for eternity."

"Do you know for sure that Ileana has the other part of the blade?" Monk turned to look at Tinker and shook his head.

"No. I only think that she does," Sansit snarled.

"So, you did not read anything about it? That she has it?" Monk examined further.

"No! I told you," Sansit barked.

"We have been traveling with her. She mentioned nothing about having your sword… Only knowing where to find the Ring of Gnim," Tinker told him and pointed at Monk's wrist.

Sansit's eyes widened. He rushed at Monk and pulled back the sleeve, exposing the portion of the ring that had attached itself to Monk.

"Gnim," he whispered.

Monk was kind as he spoke. "Ileana had hidden the ring in the ancient city of Istanbul. We retrieved the ring but do not know where the center of the shield is."

"The ruby," Sansit again whispered. He looked at Tinker who was awaiting explanation. "The ring is the frame of the shield. The ruby is the center."

"The ring is in four pieces," Monk explained. "The other parts are with Vampire, Ileana, and one of Ileana's sons, Axel."

Sansit was not listening.

"Do you know where the ruby, the center of the shield, is?" Tinker asked.

"No," Sansit told him after a pause.

"When was the last time you used your sword?"

"The last time that I used it was when I lost it in battle against that foul creature," he replied with a snarl.

"Which foul creature?" Monk asked.

"*Your* foul creature," Sansit replied with added facial contortions. "I stabbed him with it, but he escaped from me. Guess I didn't destroy him." Sansit spit in disgust.

"Vampire," Tinker deduced.

Sansit paused for a moment to calm himself at the thought of Vampire consorting with Ileana and possibly having the other part of the blade. He looked up at Monk as if to tell him some hidden information. "Vampire let go," Sansit said, nodding towards Monk's wrist.

"Why would you say that?" Tinker asked.

Sansit pointed to the chimney that was sticking out of the ground.

"It was all written in those books, my boy," he told him with a relaxed smile. "Written, rewritten, waiting to be written, but all in there. That's one of the stories that I kept coming back to."

Monk looked down with sadness.

"But you did not read about the other part of your sword? Or the ruby center of the shield?" Tinker asked. "Or about Ileana being alive?"

"Nope."

"Well, reread that story too," Monk told him, defensively. "He did not *intentionally* let go."

An uncomfortable silence followed.

"Why do they keep them in Hell?" Tinker asked, breaking from his own tension. "Those books with all the knowledge," Tinker continued his question as Monk peeked down the chimney to see if there was any sign of Beelzebub.

"They don't," Sansit told him. "You do… Or rather, you did. As did I. Our own personal *Hell*."

Tinker looked at him as if he did not understand.

"Hell is not a physical place. Hell is a state of mind. You are your own Hell. You create it for yourself. That library would have been a trap for you like it was for me." He looked to Monk who was paying attention to his logic. "And you had to break free from it." Sansit turned back to Tinker. "That would have been your Hell. Your sin. Your gluttony," he continued. "That was *your* challenge. But you took control and realized that something was greater than the sin. You decided to get us out of there."

Tinker understood the logic but remained silent. He began to shake his head.

"No," Tinker argued. "You are always where you are supposed to be."

"No truer words were ever spoken," Sansit agreed, rescinding his previous statement. "We share more than the same sin, my boy."

Silence followed.

"But who writes all those books?" Tinker asked.

"The Enlightenment," Sansit told him. "They keep the records... Or at least the records that they want to keep." He turned to Monk. "That's why I can't find the rest of my sword or the ruby in Gnim's shield. And that's why I did not know that Ileana was alive."

Monk looked back to see Tinker staring at the chimney top.

"Tempted?" he asked.

"To jump back into that? No. Definitely not," Tinker replied with a giggle. "I am all about the pursuit of knowledge but not at that expense."

"And now, we're a team," Sansit told him. "And you too," he said to Monk.

"Oh, thanks," Monk replied. "I wasn't sure if you were going to come around to liking me."

"Who said that I like you? I just said that you are part of the team," Sansit told him. "But you can give me a ride so that I can see where we are going."

Tinker laughed and Monk followed suit, as he squatted and allowed Sansit onto his shoulders.

"So, you and Vampire have history?" Tinker asked Sansit.

"Yes," he answered. "I was sent to destroy him. My failure to do so landed me here after a final falling out with Gnim."

Sansit paused and looked off in silence. He turned his head in all directions and tapped Monk on the shoulder to tell him to turn so that he could get a full view of the landscape.

"You know where we are?" Sansit asked.

"I can only assume the next circle," Tinker deduced.

"Nope," Sansit told them.

"Then where?" Monk asked. "Did we get a pass and move on to six?"

Sansit laughed.

"That doesn't happen," he said through his laughter. "We're in a sort of *waiting room*."

Monk and Tinker looked at each other. Tinker shrugged his shoulders. "I'm becoming frighteningly comfortable with not understanding things in Hell."

Sansit kept his gaze off into the distance.

"So…?" Tinker began.

"Your journey is… unusual," Sansit told Tinker. "You see, you're not the expected type of traveler through Hell." Tinker's mind was reeling as he was trying to understand. He leaned in and whispered. "I read it. You're still alive. And because of that, someone else needs to work something out for us to be able to move forward."

Monk and Tinker looked at one another again. Monk's eyes widened as they said "Vampire" at the same time.

"Until he works his stuff out regarding his own gluttony, we are stuck here," Sansit told them.

"We?" Monk asked. "So, you really are part of our team."

"Like it or not, I'm stuck with you," Sansit told them without taking his eyes off the distance. "Our personal Hells crossed paths and now we continue to travel together until it is time to part."

"And when will that be?" Monk asked.

"Careful," Sansit told him and looked down at him. "Remember, I only just started to tolerate you."

CHAPTER 35
Firenze, Italy, 1348

The Black Plague had raged throughout Europe for over a year. Tens of millions had already died and more continued to suffer as society was collapsing. Social interactions had been minimized and high society events were fewer and fewer.

"Signore?" questioned the cautious servant.

His master did not respond.

"Don Vampiro?" he continued with the same hesitancy.

The fear in saying the name was enough, but a negative response from its bearer would be even worse. The glistening began to form on the man's forehead while he dared to not attempt another questioning. The nervous servant stood at full attention and anxiously waited. He knew that he was pushing his limit with the second request for attention. A third would cost him.

Don Vampiro stood from his high-backed, gold-leafed chair and walked past the young man. Once he was out of the room, the servant exhaled. Don Vampiro was met by his head butler in the hallway.

"An invitation arrived for you, signore," the head butler informed his master and handed him the envelope.

"I'm not going," he told him.

"You may want to see who sent it," his servant advised.

Don Vampiro stopped and turned to the butler. His head attendant did not fear him like the others.

"You will most likely find the *dinner* to be to your satisfaction," he concluded and left him with the envelope unopened in hand.

Don Vampiro held and tapped the envelope against his other hand as he thought to himself. He did not want to admit that he would want to go to the event. It would give him a chance to hear the gossip about properties and businesses that had become available due to the deaths of the owners.

Don Vampiro had become obsessed with *more*. More money. More status. More than everyone else. Even though he was in opposition to what Sansit had created, the Black Plague had offered him the opportunity to take things at a bargain.

He dropped the unopened invitation on the small table near where he stood and walked off. His staff would take care of the details. Don Vampiro would attend, but would not respond that he was coming. He did enjoy watching hosts scramble to accommodate his unannounced presence. And besides, the blood of these nobles was still unaffected by disease at this point.

The Black Plague had spread through other houses of noblemen and in the poorer areas where he usually fed. No one questioned the deaths of the poor, but the taste of the blood had soured from the disease.

He would attend.

Four white horses pulled with force as Don Vampiro's coach made its way along the single road to the elaborate villa. One driver and two coachmen accompanied the carriage as the torches lighting the way reflected off the gold detailing. All three men were masked with ornate variations of "beak masks", usually seen on doctors treating those afflicted with the Black Plague.

The staff at the villa all panicked as the coach approached. They immediately recognized the markings and knew that Don Vampiro was not expected. They were all wide eyed and rushing about in an attempt to remedy a situation before it actually occurred.

The carriage came to a stop. The coachmen stepped down and looked at the house staff. The servants were scurrying about. They looked at one another and then back to the coach. They all paused.

A timid man came out of the villa. He looked at the staff, who did not give him any information regarding what was happening. He slowly approached and nodded to the coachmen. The driver sat in position and did not look at the staff.

The man bowed to the two coachmen, who turned and faced one another. With his hand shaking, the man reached for the golden handle and opened the door of the coach.

It burst open and the man retracted with a nervous yell. Don Vampiro emerged and walked past the man and the house staff, who all immediately moved out of his way.

The air around him felt tense. The attractive man servant heard his own voice crack as he was about to announce the arrival of 'Don Vampiro'. He threw a quick side glance at the enchanting signore who had arrived fashionably late.

All eyes were turned as he entered. Cautious nods and flirtatious smiles came his way inside the elaborate ballroom. Gasps and surprised rumblings were overheard. It made him smile. The crowd was as hungry for a taste of him as he was for a taste of them; a different kind of tasting, but a tasting nevertheless.

Don Vampiro had come to the home of a count who had been housing high ranking politicians and business associates. Vampiro knew that some of the attendees were business rivals who had sided with the host over him. He had come to show his strength and teach them a lesson.

Don Vampiro hid his surprise as he caught an unexpected but welcomed aroma. He looked to the servant who was trying not to stare. It was not coming from him. He began to look at the other guests but already knew that it was not coming from them. The scent was coming from behind him.

Don Vampiro turned and saw the two men entering. Had he not caught the scent, he would have been furious that someone would have had the audacity to enter after him. He was always the last to enter and the first to leave. He was always to be the most alluring, the most elusive, the most desired, and the most celebrated. Not being the last to enter an event was not an option.

However, tonight was different. The familiar scent of citrus, jasmine, and the touch of earthy spice had been absent for one thousand years. He recognized it immediately. And he knew why. He welcomed it in a way that he forgot everything else.

Don Vampiro turned to see the two men entering the ballroom. They were well dressed and obviously of the highest class, but there was something different about them. They entered with a different purpose than the other guests. They were not there to show themselves off and to be impressed by the frivolities of the dons and doñas who were in attendance.

"Buona serata," Don Vampiro said to the men, who were engaged in casual conversation.

"Buona serata, signore," replied the taller and slimmer man.

The other man gave a nod and a slight smile. He failed at his attempt to show disinterest. Vampiro immediately knew that the aroma was coming from this man. He knew him immediately, as the man knew him. He looked at the scar that blemished his otherwise beautiful face.

"A deranged patient," the grinning man told him with a shrug of the shoulders as he realized that Vampire was staring at the scar. "To be fair, he was taken by the plague and not in his right mind," he said without any self-pity. "But I was not infected," he added to ease the usual concern.

"Patient?" Don Vampiro questioned. "Are you a doctor?"

"We," the man motioned between himself and his friend, "are doctors. We have been working in the poorer areas of the city."

Don Vampiro looked confused. The people at these parties were not partial to helping the poor. They only said that they look to help the poor.

"This is Simone," he said as Simone extended his hand.

"God hears," Vampiro said to the acknowledgment of Simone knowing that he understood the origin of his name. "And you are?"

"Phineas," the man replied as Vampiro said the name in his own head at the same time.

"So much stays the same," Vampiro said as if in a reverie.

"Excuse me?" Phineas asked as he looked to Simone to see if he understood what the curious man in front of them was talking about.

"Nothing," Vampiro said, realizing that he was talking out loud. "Why are you here?"

Phineas chuckled and again looked to his friend to see if he was following the line of questioning.

"What I mean is, you do not seem to have the same agenda as the other guests in the room."

"Ah," Simone replied. "We do not."

"We are here on a mission to get funds to help those who have been taken by the Black Plague," Phineas explained.

"It's an ongoing battle," Simone added. "The church keeps referring to it as a curse, which only heightens their sense of superiority."

"But we," Phineas again motioned between himself and Simone, "are easily able to guilt them into aiding us."

"How is that?" Don Vampiro extended his hand for them to walk with him down the stairs, into the eager crowd.

"Well," Phineas began. "Through family fortunes, we are richer than most of them. Therefore, by their logic, we are more important, and they will do anything that we ask to gain favor with us and our families."

"Sounds manipulative enough," Vampiro joked.

"We are not saints," Phineas told him.

"We are doctors," Simone added.

Vampiro took a deep inhale through his nose. The scent was intoxicating. *Phineas has returned.*

"Quarantine is the only thing that will stop the spread," Simone told Vampiro. "But the people will need sanitary living conditions and provisions in the meantime."

"Do you not fear the plague?" he asked them. "Do they not fear that you may have contracted it and may spread it here?"

Phineas and Simone looked at one another and smiled.

"Fear? Yes, they fear. However, they would rather die within our presence than have us shun them." Phineas paused. "And besides, my mentor here has come up with a filtration system and a suit that allows us to be protected from the disease and the poisoned air that surrounds it."

"Mentor?" Vampiro questioned. "I never realized-"

He looked at Simone and felt as though the air had been pulled from his lungs.

"Are you okay?" Phineas grabbed hold of him to steady him.

His touch knocked them both off balance. Vampiro dropped his glass, which Phineas swiped from midair without a single drop being spilled. He took a swig of the bubbly alcohol.

Vampiro was astonished. *The earthy spice*, he thought. The realization that Simone was actually an earlier life version of *Tinker* had caught him off guard.

"Pardon my observation, but he seems…"

"Younger than me," Phineas said, finishing Vampiro's statement. "He is. And much smarter." He looked at Simone. "And that's why he is the mentor."

This moment had not occurred when this meeting originally took place. Vampire's realization that Tinker and Monk had shared at least this lifetime together was unknown to him when he originally experienced it. He could not help but to react to this new understanding.

"I mean, yes," Simone began to break the awkward moment. "It is impressive… My filtration system. But it's not that complex. It's all in the water."

"Water?" Vampiro questioned with a smile. "It is you."

Simone and Phineas were looking at one another with a mutual thought that Vampiro may need some medical assistance. Phineas gave Simone a look that told him that he was going to investigate further.

"I think that I am going to secure some funding," Simone told them and nodded as he excused himself.

"Would you like to get some air, Don Vampiro?" Phineas asked and extended his hand towards the open door that allowed in the welcomed night breeze.

Vampiro obliged and walked out into the starry night.

"How do you know who I am?" Vampiro asked. "I did not introduce myself."

Phineas laughed.

"You do not have to introduce yourself," he said through a wide smile as the cool night air blew Don Vampiro's long locks of grey, white, and black. "Everyone knows who you are. You have been the talk of society since your arrival."

"I guess that is true," he agreed with a sense of pride.

The two men walked into the gardens. They walked in a comfortable silence.

"You seem familiar to me," Phineas told him. "Yet, we have never met."

"No?" Vampiro said nothing more.

Phineas felt like he should be given more of an explanation, but Vampiro just looked off into the night sky.

"There used to be a constellation there," Don Vampiro told him as he pointed to the starless area of the sky.

"A dragon. Yes?" Phineas said as he too was staring into the open darkness.

Vampiro nodded his head. "It is you," he whispered.

Vampiro turned to Phineas. He reached out and touched his side. Phineas did not pull away as he felt the warmth of Vampiro's touch. His hand was held strong to the markings on Phineas' side. His eyes were closed as visions rushed through him.

"That constellation is on your left side," Vampiro told him.

"How do you know that?" Phineas asked through forced breath.

Vampire was aware that throughout this exercise of being pulled back into these moments in time, he was experiencing life from the perspective of both living them for the first time, and also from the perspective of reliving them with a purpose to learn from them.

"Because I'm the one who put it there," he said and leaned forward to kiss Phineas.

Again, Phineas did not pull away and welcomed the gesture. The adrenaline rush was stronger.

"You seem like you are doing better," Phineas joked as they stood with their foreheads touching and their eyes closed.

"I have never been better," Vampiro told him. "Would you like to accompany me home?"

"Yes… But I will not."

Vampiro pulled back.

Phineas laughed. "I bet you never get that, huh?"

"No, actually," he replied and thought that he should enchant him to his will.

"I have work to do," Phineas added.

Vampiro held a disapproving look.

"I have to guilt rich people out of money to help the poor."

Vampiro laughed.

"You think that will help your cause?" Vampiro questioned with an air of arrogance.

"Why not?"

"This plague was sent to remove humankind from this place."

"Now you sound like them," Phineas told him.

"Yes. But not only the poor and the sinners."

"You say that with such commitment."

Vampiro turned to Phineas and made a facial expression to acknowledge a sense of truth in that statement. Vampiro sighed and pointed to the starless area in the sky. "Long before that constellation was taken and put on your side, humanity was destroyed."

"Then how is it that we are having this conversation?"

"Because man is the worst plague that has ever existed."

Phineas waited in silence for further explanation.

"Humankind is strong. It crawled itself back to where you are now," Vampiro explained.

"Well then," Phineas said as he raised the champagne flute that he had rescued from Vampiro's lost grip, "cheers to us."

Vampiro laughed.

"Yes. Cheers," he said with an empty hand that he raised. "But then, that is why I am here." He walked closer and took the glass from Phineas. He lightly brushed against his finger, and they again felt the rush of adrenaline.

Phineas quickly regained his composure. "To destroy?"

"Yes."

"I guess that will mean destroying me as well," Phineas stood eye to eye with Don Vampiro.

Vampiro stood quiet. He was thinking out of two minds now.

"Destroying you would be the last thing that I wanted to do," he said. "And besides, you have your filtration system."

Phineas did not appreciate his attempt at humor.

For the first time, Vampiro stepped back from his pride. He did not question why. He knew why. He did not want to lose Phineas forever. He was now battling himself. He knew what he had been sent to do, but he did not want to do it. He thought of Sansit and his visit to his estate a year ago.

Phineas watched in patient silence as Vampiro's face battled. After what was now an awkward silence, Phineas spoke.

"So, if you were sent to destroy mankind," he began, "then why is it that you haven't already done it?"

Vampiro cocked his face into a half smile.

"Because of you."

The next morning, a messenger arrived at the villa of Phineas' family. With the invitation was a note offering a sizable donation to Phineas and Simone's cause.

Phineas smiled and scribbled a 'Thank you' onto the invitation. He handed it back to the messenger.

"My master asked that you take him with you as you do your work," the messenger stated.

Phineas looked at the man curiously.

"May I have that back?" he asked of the invitation.

The messenger obliged.

"The address is here." Phineas wrote on the invitation. "We will be gathering provisions all day and then starting there at six o'clock. This is where he should meet us at that time."

The messenger nodded and walked towards the coach.

"Doctore?" he begged.

Phineas paused.

"Grazie," he said with concern at overstepping. "My family lives in that area. I pray for them."

Phineas nodded and held his hand to his heart.

It was six o'clock. Phineas and Simone were pulling a cart full of food and clean water through the dark streets of the tortured city.

They donned full protective dressings, including the golden bird-like face masks with Simone's water filtration system to keep the air that they were breathing safe. Strands of black metal tubing came off the back of the masks and the ear coverings. Intermittent steam puffed out of the contraption after each segment of gurgling sounds. The filtration system was working.

The sun had already gone. The cart was lit with torches. It was weighted and difficult to pull through the labyrinth of uneven streets. Phineas and Simone were heading into an area of the city that had become overwhelmed by the Black Plague. They wanted to minimize exposure to anyone and anything, and they had decided to not expose a horse to the area to avoid a continued spread. This made their task more arduous, but they were committed to the safest plan.

Standing in the darkness ahead was Don Vampiro. He wore no protection other than a cloth around his nose and mouth.

"You will need more than that." Simone's voice was muffled under the mask.

Vampire did not fear the plague. However, he needed to blend in to avoid looking conspicuous. Don Vampiro stared deep into Phineas' concealed eyes as he took the protective gear and put it on.

Phineas met his stare from behind his mask as Simone finished preparing Vampiro.

"Just breathe normally," Simone instructed.

They went door to door. They left food and clean water as they educated the inhabitants about staying indoors. They moved dead bodies from inside the homes to stack them in the middle of the street.

Vampiro was not making any attempt to assist Simone and Phineas. He was again in two heads. He saw that what Sansit had set out to do was in effect but knew that he could not allow it. Phineas was providing a reason to not destroy humanity; he was the reason to allow mankind to flourish.

"So, why is he here?" Simone asked Phineas.

Phineas shook his head as he watched Vampiro's curiosity with the poor, sick, and dying. He could not make out any facial expressions through the mask, but he watched as Vampiro cocked his head into positions that told Phineas that he was working through something.

The last of the provisions had been distributed. Don Vampiro turned and saw the lines of soiled white sheets covering the dead bodies in the street. They would be carted away and buried in a mass grave.

As the sun was rising, the lines of white became visceral. Don Vampiro was experiencing the pain that he was sent to cause. He was also seeing the humanity of Phineas and Simone in their attempts to stop the pain, in the aid and kindness that he had witnessed throughout the night.

"Where's mine?" asked a man on the street.

"Sorry, sir," Simone apologized. "We are out. We will be back tomorrow so that everyone gets provisions."

"I'm hungry now," he screamed.

"I am sure that you are." Phineas stepped between the man and Simone.

"Now," he demanded.

Phineas looked at him through the bird-like mask. He squinted his eyes, attempting to find scarring from the plague on the man's face.

"Sir, excuse me, but you do not appear to be affected," he told him. "You should stay in your home or find lodgings in another area of the city to avoid possible infection."

"I'm here for the food," the man continued to argue.

"Sir," Phineas continued. "I beg of you. Please return home."

Vampiro watched the exchange but kept his distance. He had to allow the scene to play itself out without intervening. However, he was growing concerned as he knew what was about to happen.

The man pulled a knife. He stepped up to Phineas and attacked him. He pulled the mask from his head and sliced him deeply across his healed facial scars.

The commotion was loud enough to draw the attention of the neighbors. The residents opened their doors and windows to see what was happening. Many were infected, weak and coughing. Someone stepped in to help to get the man off Phineas. As Simone was attending to Phineas, Vampiro ran over and pulled off his own mask. His face showed his pained expression. He knew what was going to happen.

Within three days, the infection began to show itself. Within three more days, Phineas would be dead.

No one was allowed to be present due to isolation precautions; not even Simone. Don Vampiro was at his bedside. Upon his last breath, Don Vampiro sank his teeth into Phineas' neck and tasted his tainted blood. But beyond the stench of the poisoned blood, he tasted the kindness, the joy, the love that had again been Phineas.

As he sat back with Phineas' lifeless body in his arms, he vowed to himself to again wait for Phineas, and to change his own course. He vowed to save mankind.

CHAPTER 36
Caves of Waku

There was an eerie calmness in the cool air. The sun was going down, and the worry that had taken a collective hold earlier was still apparent. Ileana watched the entrapment and saw through it. It was becoming thinner with the setting sun. She knew that moving the sun higher in the sky again was not an option. The Elements would not agree to it a second time.

Sorcerer looked over as he and their children maintained their posts surrounding the magical structure that kept Vampire and Ghost contained. He too was thinking of alternative actions and did not want to admit that Seer working with Jigglers might be the only way to understand what was happening inside the Entrapment.

CHAPTER 37
Hell, Fifth Circle

Monk attempted to question Sansit again. Sansit was quick to throw his hand forward and grab Monk's face to squeeze it tight. He pulled at his lips and held them together to keep him from talking about Gnim.

"What's that?" Tinker asked as he saw what looked like lines of lights coming on in the distance. "The lights seem like they are in the air." He put his binoculars to his eyes.

"Maybe they are," Sansit told him. He took his hand away from Monk's mouth, slapped him and pointed directly at his face. "Not another word," he demanded and jumped to the ground.

Monk held his hands up as if in surrender and shook his head.

Tinker was already on the move. He was walking through the tall grasses towards the lights. Sansit was slicing through with his blade.

"I can make it easier if you would like," Monk told him.

Sansit stopped and put his hands on his hips. He looked aggravated.

"I would like," he replied.

"You don't look like you would like."

"What? This is my happy face," Sansit replied.

"Good thing that your Hell wasn't a room full of mirrors," Monk said and squatted to let Sansit onto his shoulders.

"Just move," he demanded. "And catch up to the kid. I'm sure he's talking to himself about something, and I don't want to miss what he's thinking. I like that kid."

Monk sped up until they were listening to Tinker's stream of consciousness ramblings.

"Carnival lights," he said. "Carnival lights."

"Careful, boy," Sansit told him. "Remember, Five is worse than the others."

"But doesn't that depend on whether or not it's your sin?" Tinker deduced from earlier conversations. "What is the sin of Five? Envy."

"Envy," Sansit agreed.

"Well, Monk's was lust and both yours and mine were gluttony. So, we should be fine."

"Keep in mind, there are other forces working here too," Sansit reminded them. "Your friend has to get through his sins as well. That's why we had that little pause before these lights came on. *You know who* was slower than we were to get through his gluttony."

"Good point," Tinker said.

They walked closer in silence.

"I bet I can guess how this is going to work-"

"This is not a game," Sansit reminded him. "Not to be taken lightly."

"I'm sorry, Sansit," Tinker apologized. "I am terrified. We are in Hell. But if I don't hold onto my usual processing, I will have a true panic attack and be of no use. I do not mean any disrespect, but this is how I deal with my fear."

Sansit nodded in understanding. "Okay, kid. Do it your way. But just remember, you cannot make friends in Hell."

"We met you in Hell, and you're our friend," Tinker reminded Sansit with all the innocence of a schoolboy.

Sansit sighed and tapped Monk on the head.

"Is he for real?"

"Yes," Monk told him. "Yes, he is."

CHAPTER 38
The Entrapment

"That hadn't happened before," Vampire said to Ghost, who lingered close to the electrical border.

"Yes, it did." Ghost looked out and watched the movement of the others through the thinning boundary.

"What I mean is that I never realized that I saw Tinker in one of Monk's previous lives."

"Tinker. Yes. So then, I'm not the only one to come back into *your* world."

Vampire thought back. "Simone," he said aloud.

"Who is Simone?" Ghost asked.

"*Simone* is Tinker's real name."

"*Was…* That was Tinker's real name," Ghost said. "It was a previous life."

"Phineas has always been Phineas," Vampire argued. "Coincidence?"

Ghost said nothing.

"The kid has always wanted to know something about his family. It's something," Vampire argued with kindness in his voice.

"Even if it is from a previous life?"

"Even if it is from a previous life," he answered with a slight smile.

Ghost was quiet again.

"What?" Vampire asked in a now agitated tone.

"Name or no name, he always had someone on his side," Ghost replied as he watched Sorcerer and his family working together to maintain the entrapment.

"Envious?" Vampire asked.

"Yes, actually." Ghost was lost in his own memories. "But not just because of that. I have been envious of so much for so long that I don't know how to be anything else."

"Seems like it's your turn, then." Vampire stood, awaiting Ghost's form pressing into him until he was transported to another one of Monk's lifetimes.

"Whether it is my turn or not, these lessons are all for you," Ghost reminded him.

He floated over and gently engulfed Vampire. Vampire relaxed into it.

CHAPTER 39
Paris, 1891

The avant-garde revellers packed the Chat Noir cabaret in Montmartre. The music was loud. The drinks were strong. The crowd was a mix of social classes, fashionable customers in search of a good time… Except for one.

"How can you still live there, Hugo?"

"Where?" Hugo asked over the lively music and the dancing.

"In the Marais! That rat infested ghetto that you call home."

"It is my home. It inspires me," Hugo replied, without lifting his head from his writing.

"It inspires *me* to avoid it," his classically handsome friend countered with a snarled expression.

"Oh, Dax… So much bigger than you really are."

Dax ignored Hugo's remark as he looked out with his lips pulled tense and peered through the drunken cabaret crowd of Paris fashionistas.

"Hugo? Who is that man?" Dax sipped champagne and waved his hand aggressively in the air signaling the waiter to bring another bottle.

"Which?" Hugo asked without looking to see the man under discussion.

"The interesting one," Dax replied, physically lifting Hugo's face and turning his attention to the table on the left side of the performance stage.

"Oh." Hugo lifted his glasses and squinted. "No idea." He returned to his writing. "But *interesting* is definitely appropriate."

The waiter returned with the bottle and presented it to Dax and Hugo, who took no interest in it.

"No worries," Dax quickly said to the gracious waiter. "I'll take that." He grabbed the bottle from the waiter before it was able to be uncorked. "Hugo?"

"Mmmm…"

"Be right back."

"Mmmm…" Hugo continued writing.

Dax was a striking man. His good looks and his ability to know just enough about popular subjects had given him somewhat of a charmed life. Dax spent his youth in a modest household, but always thought of himself as deserving better.

Dax longed for the fancy clothes and the carriages that carried the elite through Paris. He wanted to be one of those people who walked into a fancy hotel and had the door held open for him. Instead, he had chores and not enough food. He shared a bed and the stench of not bathing.

It was without a word to his family that he left his childhood home in the Fifth Arrondissement in the middle of the night. He walked with his head forced high over the Petit Pont and never looked back. His envy for what he did not have had become insatiable.

Dax was slick and resourceful. He was the first prostitute who Marcel Proust, the novelist and literary critic, had come to as a teen. Dax further used these charms to blackmail Proust's family into getting him invitations to the innermost circles of high society, in return for him keeping his mouth shut. Marcel was obsessed with Dax and with each encounter, Dax gained access to more influential circles, even those far beyond the iron-fenced mansions of the Seventh and Sixteenth Arrondissements.

He also gained comrades in the progressive artists and writers of the time. Associating with them gave Dax an opportunity to mingle with the elite of Paris. Dax was able to persuade one of them to take him on as a companion and found himself living quite comfortably in a lavish apartment along the river in the Seventh Arrondissement. Unfortunately, it was not enough. Dax's constant desire for more found him regularly arguing with his supporter until he had finally crossed the line and his most recent patron had pulled out of their *agreement.* Dax was now looking for a new and more "appreciative" individual to sponsor him.

He made his way through the maze of tables and partygoers of the notorious nightclub. He dodged being pushed and knocked off balance by intoxicated night owls.

Dax made it to the right side of the stage, which seemed impossible to get around due to the hoard of gentlemen smoking cigars and tipping their top hats. Dax kept an eye on the man at the table.

Still there, Dax thought as he continued to look for a route blocked by the elite of Paris and their playthings. Dax saw that the man was gathering his things on the table and began to stand. "No!" he yelled. His demand was lost in the music and revelry. Dax looked at the stage and decided that it would be the quickest way to reach the man.

"Mesdames et messieurs," began the emcee dressed in Bohemian drag.

"Pardon." Dax pushed past him as he rushed across the stage and slid off the other end, landing just hard enough to slam the bottle on the table and to put himself face to face with the man of interest.

"Dax," he introduced himself as he extended his hand.

The gentleman seemed taken back by his abruptness but was quickly distracted by something alluring. Dax sniffed the air but only took in the whiffs of cigar smoke, floral perfumes, and body odor. He was immediately confused by the man's reaction.

"I said, 'Dax'! My name is Dax."

"I heard you." The man looked at Dax. "You know that your name more or less means 'weasel'."

"I was told it means 'leader'," Dax shot back and raised a hand triumphantly.

"You were lied to," the man stood as if to leave.

"No. Wait!" Dax demanded. "I got this for you," Dax added, raising the champagne bottle. "I mean, for us," he concluded with a seductive smile.

The man cocked a side grin and returned to his seat, scanning the crowd.

"Okay, Weasel. I am, after all, a bit… thirsty. Let's see what you're made of."

"Leader," Dax reminded the man as he popped the cork. The champagne began rushing out since Dax had been jostling the bottle his way over.

Dax quickly put his mouth over the opening of the bottle to swallow the champagne as it rushed out. He kept a seductive glance on the other man and once the bottle stopped running over, he handed it to him.

The man's glass sat empty in front of him. But this was now a chess game, a battle to see who the last king on the board would be. Dax had made the first strike but now, it was the other man's turn.

He took the bottle from Dax and seductively put it to his lips. Check. He took a gulp, licked the rim of the bottle, and handed it back. Dax took the bottle and was sure to feel for the man's hand, expecting that he would nervously pull away. The man did not pull back. Check. Dax was now unsure of his next move and realized that this interaction was not keeping Dax in the power position.

"Well then… I guess you win."

"I always win," the man informed Dax. "Thaddeus. My name is Thaddeus. Why did you come over here?" Thaddeus asked.

"I am looking for a job-"

"I'm not looking to keep a prostitute."

"I'm not…" Dax was thrown off by Thaddeus' straightforward response. He slowed his approach to choose his words carefully. "I'm not looking for that type of employment."

"Then what?"

"I'm looking for something with more growth potential."

"And what makes you think that I can help you?"

Thaddeus had a complete sense of control. Dax was immediately jealous. He wanted to be him.

Dax chuckled.

"I've been observing you. I can learn from you." He took another swig from the champagne bottle. "And obviously," he continued, giving Thaddeus' appearance an impressed glance, "you can afford my services."

"What exactly are your services?"

"Anything you want…"

Thaddeus cracked a sensual smile. "I already told you that I am not looking to hire or keep a prostitute."

"Then you tell me what it is that you need, and I'll do it," Dax replied, feeling more confident with himself again.

Thaddeus sat in thought, although he maintained eye contact with Dax. Dax was back on a familiar playing field and was able to match him look for look. Thaddeus was mildly intrigued with Dax and his approach to getting through life.

"All right."

Dax leaned in.

"I need a valet who knows not to ask questions and to do what is asked, when it is asked."

"Seems easy enough."

"I need a valet who will not go looking into my affairs," Thaddeus added with a curious squint to his eyes.

"Okay."

Thaddeus leaned in to deliver the last condition. "And knows not to overstep."

Dax paused but maintained eye contact.

"And what I need is a sizable personal cash flow that allows me to maintain my present lifestyle, and as previously mentioned…" Dax also leaned in and again kept eye contact, "with room to grow. Eventually, I will elevate my position in society."

"Your future is up to you. Do you accept my conditions?"

Dax looked at Thaddeus' outstretched hand and for a second, he thought that this was a bad idea. *A deal with the devil*, he thought. However, his envy for all that he did not yet have drove him to extend his own hand and shake. "Yes."

Check mate.

"Go and say 'good night' to Hugo. It's time to leave."

Dax looked back at Hugo who was still focused on his journal. With his back to Thaddeus, he wrinkled his face in surprise. Hugo had said that he did not know him.

"How do you know…"

"Hugo? Personally, I don't. But I am in the business of knowing things about people."

Dax contorted his mouth to say, *I'm impressed.*

"Now, let's go."

Thaddeus made his way out of Le Chat Noir. He tipped his hat to the emcee as Dax walked over to Hugo as instructed.

"Hugo?"

"Mmmm?" Hugo replied with disinterest.

"Hugo. I am leaving…"

"Au revoir."

Dax grabbed Hugo's face and pointed it towards the final glimpse of Thaddeus as he exited.

"Do you see that man?"

"How can I not?"

"Do you know him?"

"No."

"Are you sure?"

"Absolutely sure. I would know if I knew that man."

"This is going to be interesting." He was off. "Bye, Hugo."

"Bye," Hugo echoed as he stared at the empty space that Thaddeus had just exited.

Outside Le Chat Noir, the street was bustling with a mix of drunken debauchery and scandalous excitement. Dax saw Thaddeus entering a coach and rushed to join him. Thaddeus forced his walking stick across the coach entrance to block him.

"You said that we were leaving."

"We are. You've accepted the terms and are now in my employment."

"Yes, so-"

"So you now have to go and find whoever it was, expectedly a man, who emitted that scent," he concluded looking through Dax's eyes to his very soul.

"I don't smell anything… not anything good," he added as his nostrils took in the stench of the Paris streets.

"It was in Le Chat Noir."

"Cigar smoke? That was most everyone," he giggled.

"No. Not cigar smoke. Find whoever left just before you arrived at my table. One of those people is of a particular interest to me, and you need to find said individual by this time tomorrow."

"How am I supposed to do that?"

"You made it seem that you are a man of many talents. I already got you started. The rest is up to you."

Dax tried to contain his anger. He had anticipated that he was going to entertain clients and usher them in and out of a well-manicured office with a view of the Seine River. Chasing down an invisible person was not what he wanted.

"You shook my hand and gave me your word," Thaddeus reminded him. "Or is it too much for you?"

Dax's ego would not allow him to admit, *Yes*. But that was more because he was not interested in finding this person. And regardless, it would be too much for anyone.

"I already gave you some clues. I expect you are looking for a man. Always has been a man. He entered and exited at the time you came to interrupt me."

Dax's anger was beginning to surface in his facial tension.

"Oh, yes," Thaddeus rushed. "He'll be a kind person. He will not have been too drunk…" Thaddeus drifted off into a reverie. "And probably smiles and laughs a lot. That should be enough." He looked out from the coach. "Most of these people look inebriated."

Thaddeus tapped the silver tip of his walking stick on the roof of the coach to signal the driver to go.

"Oh! And one last thing," he added as the coach began to move on. "He will most likely come from a charitable, yet humble, family."

A twinkle lit in Dax's eye.

"I will expect to have my needs met by tomorrow evening… In time for supper."

Dax heard him as if it were secondary in his mind. He had begun working through his mental database of potentials. Tomorrow was the inaugural dinner of the *Bazar de la Charité;* if this man was going to be anywhere by dinner tomorrow, he would be there. Dax relaxed his mind and gained an immediate sense of pride. He turned his attention to a different gentleman staring out of the curtained window of his coach.

The following evening, the setting sun was lighting up the Paris sky in an array of pink, orange and gold. It was the perfect backdrop for the inaugural dinner of the *Bazar de la Charité.* The evening had brought good weather, a gentle breeze, and those amazing colors in the sky.

"Stunning evening, isn't it?" Dax questioned his new employer as he extended a hand to help him down from the coach that had just arrived at the event.

"Yes. Why yes, it is," Thaddeus retorted with a refreshing lightness about him.

Dax was confused by this change in personality but welcomed it. Dax noted that Thaddeus was taking silent but very deep breaths. He mimicked him to try and understand what he was smelling.

Late spring in 1891 Paris brought about many aromas; some welcomed, like the scent of blooming roses, and some undesirable, like the drunks urinating in the alleys of Le Marais. But this event would bring together the welcomed air of the French Catholic aristocracy to raise money for their charitable organizations. Dax followed Thaddeus' lead and tipped his top hat to the other charitable benefactors. Dax offered him a glass of champagne, which he accepted, but did not sip. Thaddeus definitely seemed to be in a more agreeable mood tonight.

I guess, Dax thought to himself, *whoever he is looking for might be worth looking into.*

Dax leisurely ushered Thaddeus from charitable booth to charitable booth. "So, I thought that we could…"

He turned to see that Thaddeus had stopped and was staring at a young man in a dunking booth. Dax's interest was piqued.

"The things that I will do for charity," he heard the man yell out. "Come on! Three chances to dunk me. If I go in, you also get a glass of champagne. But if I don't, I get the glass and the champagne in it." He laughed as he delivered his line and was joined in laughter by the crowd. "And so far, I'm still dry... On the outside."

The crowd riled in laughter. The man looked up and saw Thaddeus. His bright smile turned coy. Thaddeus was taken by the subtle scar that ran diagonally across his face.

"I'll give it a try," Thaddeus yelled out.

"That will be-" the attendant began.

Thaddeus handed him a roll of bills that would be more than sufficient.

The attendant's eyes widened, and his mouth gaped. Dax mirrored his reaction; he looked at Thaddeus, then at the money and finally, to the man in the booth.

So, this is who we've been looking for, Dax said to himself.

A second attendant attempted to hand Thaddeus the three balls. Thaddeus held out his walking stick and continued to stare at the man in the booth.

Dax was slow to understand that the walking stick was for him to take.

Thaddeus looked over to him with a disapproving glare.

Dax quickly corrected his blunder, taking the stick from his employer.

Thaddeus removed his top hat and his overcoat that appeared black, until the light of the setting sun hit it just right to reveal a deep purple.

"Good luck," the man in the dunking booth told him with his full smile returning. "It is a bit warm out this evening."

"And I expect that it is going to be getting hotter," Thaddeus followed.

The crowd laughed and cheered.

The first ball flew.

The man in the booth watched as it missed the target, but noted the force with which it was thrown. He quickly turned back to Thaddeus as a hush came across the crowd.

"I think that they're thinking what I'm thinking," he yelled to Thaddeus.

"And what is that?" Thaddeus asked with a jest in his voice.

"I'm glad I'm not the target."

The crowd laughed again in agreement.

The second ball flew through the air, but again, missed the target.

Screams of disapproval came from the crowd and the man in the booth shrugged his shoulders and continued to smile.

"I do have one more," Thaddeus reminded him.

The man in the booth held his hands up as if to signal surrender.

The third ball made its way through the spring air, slicing until it hit dead center on the target. The sound of the bell went off as the platform opened and the man fell into the water, splashing those who stood near. Laughter and cheers erupted as Thaddeus threw his arms up in the air in victory. The man in the booth came up from below the water and continued to smile in good fun. The soaked, smiling man playfully spit water out of his pursed lips. Thaddeus laughed as he stepped back to avoid getting wet.

The man in the booth splashed water at him and extended his hand to shake it. They immediately locked eyes at first touch. The man in the booth jokingly attempted to pull Thaddeus into the water, which added to the joyous response of the crowd. Both men seemed to lose their breath a bit but quickly recovered.

"This is for you," Thaddeus handed him the celebratory glass of champagne from the side of the booth where the ladder created an exit from the tank.

"No. No, my friend. That is for you. You earned it."

Thaddeus and the other man maintained a lingering stare that did not go unnoticed by Dax.

"Do I know you?" the man asked Thaddeus.

"In a sense."

The man looked confused. "My name is Phineas," he said.

"Yes, I know," Thaddeus replied.

Phineas searched his mind but could not place him.

"My name is Thaddeus. Let me help you," he offered to give him a hand to assist him out of the tank.

"Actually, some friends jokingly took my clothes, and I really should not be this exposed in public."

Thaddeus laughed and motioned to sneak a glance under the water.

"Not funny." Phineas laughed and jokingly splashed water at him. He referred to the sheerness of his garments as they were now soaked.

"Very funny."

"I guess, it is. Truth is-"

"You never minded being naked," Thaddeus told him.

"No. But considering-" He cut himself off. "How do you know that?"

"Hold on, my valet has my overcoat. This should help." Thaddeus avoided answering the question. He signaled for Dax to come. "After all, it's the least I can do. I'm the one who got you all wet," he said with a playful flirtation in his tone.

"Yes," Phineas agreed. He maintained eye contact.

Dax arrived and forced a smile, unsure as to why he was called over.

"Thank you, Dax," Thaddeus said with a kindness that Dax had not expected. "I'll take that from you."

Thaddeus held his overcoat to shield Phineas' exposure and assisted him into the coat for Phineas to button up. He took his top hat and walking stick.

"Thank you, Dax. That will be all for tonight."

Dax was taken back as Thaddeus put his arm around Phineas' shoulder and guided him away from the dunking booth.

How dare he leave with him, Dax thought as his fists balled up. He charged up to the target and hit it with all his might, which caused the platform to split and have the spectacled gentleman drop hard into the tank. Dax continued into the night without a look back.

The weeks that followed the *Bazar de la Charité* found Dax's days filled with communications from Thaddeus via notes left for him. He had not seen Thaddeus since the event. Dax was the only one to enter the large home on a daily basis. Thaddeus did not keep a regular staff. The written instructions included him letting in workers and watching their progress on renovations and cleaning. Dax began to think of himself as the "man of the house".

He had quickly gotten used to putting his feet up and drinking his tea from the imported porcelain cups. Rooms that were not being renovated were locked. He did find it odd that even the areas of the house that he did see seemed to be a bit empty. He would have thought Thaddeus to have a more extravagant taste considering his financial state. Thaddeus had become even more interesting to Dax: a puzzle that he would have to solve.

"Why are you here?" The question came with irritation through the air in a stern voice that made Dax shake and spill his tea on the coffee table.

"I- I- Where have you been?" Dax ordered back.

"Excuse me?" Thaddeus questioned with authority.

"What I mean is… I'm sorry… I didn't know that you were going to be here. I just showed the workers out and needed a minute."

Dax spied Phineas accompanying Thaddeus but standing in the shadows to allow their exchange.

"What I meant was," Dax began again with a bit of familiar flirtation. "I haven't seen you in weeks and have been worried sick."

"So, you figured that you'd make yourself at home with a cup of tea and your feet up in my parlor?"

"I figured that I would wait," he rushed. "I didn't know what else to do," he said, expressing a great deal of concern. "Hello?" he said to Phineas to take the conversation away from his pending punishment. "I'm sorry. I did not see you there. Can I get you something?"

"No. You can go," Thaddeus demanded.

"I am Dax. Thaddeus' valet," he greeted with an extended hand.

"You used to be *Thaddeus'* valet," Thaddeus interjected. "I think that it's time we had another arrangement."

Dax's eyes opened wide in anticipation of his new role.

"I've been hearing rumors about your inquiries, and I told you from the beginning that you need to stay out of my business."

"Maybe, we should talk about this privately," Dax whispered.

"I have no secrets from Phineas. He is welcome to know everything about me and my dealings," Thaddeus admitted.

"I was just… I was just inquiring to make sure that you were okay! Excuse me for being concerned!"

"You weren't concerned," Phineas snickered and offered with a wrinkled brow. "You were poking around for information."

"I'm sorry. Who the hell are you again?"

"You know very well who I am. Your inquiries did not stop with your concern for Thaddeus, but also into my business and attempting to scandalize my name."

Dax looked at him with confusion. "My dear man, you are sorely mistaken."

"He is surely not," Thaddeus shielded.

"Society people talk. Something that I'm sure you are aware of since you were trying to use that to the benefit of running both of our names through the mud. But they also know very well which side to stand on in a duel."

"And which side is that?" Dax asked with disgust.

"The winning side," Phineas offered back. "You are not able to offer them anything that would put you in a position to have them side with your coup. And why? Why would you attempt to damage our reputations with your lies and deceit? Thaddeus is a good man, and you don't even know me."

"Because you have what I want! And even worse, you just fell into the water and took everything that I was working so hard for!" Dax's anger was surmounting.

"As you were under my employment, you embarrassed me with what you attempted to do. Get out," Thaddeus held a large number of bills out to Dax.

Dax looked at them and puckered his lips, pausing a minute to take in a deep breath to allow his head to stay high.

"I embarrassed you? You who stand here holding out a payoff to your 'houseboy' in front of your sodomite lover," he screamed over the silence. "You embarrass yourself." Dax walked past and forced his shoulder into Thaddeus as he walked by him. Thaddeus did not budge. But he did turn to allow Dax a false sense of success.

The front door closed with a slam. Thaddeus did not flinch. Phineas walked over to Thaddeus and dropped his head forward to the side of his shoulder.

"Are you okay?" he questioned with his face embedded in the rich violet silk of Thaddeus' overcoat.

"Yes. Just disappointed." He turned and stood facing Phineas.

Phineas stayed quiet but motioned his face into a look of kindness.

"But we always have to realize that that is the way things are supposed to play out. Some of us are in for the long haul and others… Temporarily in our lives," Thaddeus said with a soft smile.

"But with purpose," Phineas added. "After all, he's the one who told you to go to the Bazar."

"Yes. Yes, he did." Thaddeus lightened his mood a bit with Phineas' words.

"Hugo?" Dax questioned with angered confusion.

"No. I will not do this for you. You got yourself fired from a very good position. And all because you cannot get over wanting everything that belongs to someone else. Face it, Dax, even if he did take you in and offer you everything, in a short time, you would have fancied the next step up."

"Oh, I'm sorry, Hugo. I'm sorry that I want more than to keep my nose in paper writing all about the poor and downtrodden of our time. I *am* the poor and downtrodden and it sucks! I want more!"

"That's your problem. All you want is more. It will never be enough because all you want is *more*."

Dax sat in silence for a minute and although he was processing what his friend had analyzed, he would not allow his face to give any resemblance to accepting that it was true.

"Well, thank you for your free advice, Hugo. I do believe that we are done here."

"Dax? Come back," Hugo attempted but Dax had already grabbed his silk emerald-colored coat and had made for the door.

Hugo shook his head but did not follow.

Dax found himself wandering through the warm breeze that graciously blew through the Paris streets. The crowds of drunks and prostitutes blended seamlessly with the elite of Paris. In the Belle Epoque era, your looks and charms were able to take you far. Unfortunately for Dax, he made the mistake of testing just how far.

"Dax?" Someone yelled out from the darkness. "Is that you?"

The elegantly attired couple were making their way into the grand opening of *La Cuisine Blanche,* with what promised to be the must have invitation for the season. "Dax! You must join us!"

Dax lightened his mood and graciously accepted the offer.

As it should be, he thought to himself and walked arm in arm with Gaston Worth, son of designer Charles Worth, and his wife, Julia. The initial introduction had been made when Dax brought business paperwork from Thaddeus for Gaston to sign.

The night continued with Dax pretending he was in attendance as Thaddeus' representative. He also made it a point to give just enough information regarding the "explicit nature" of the relationship between Thaddeus and Phineas. His goal was to get that information back to Phineas' family so that they would demand that he not have anything to do with Thaddeus.

The summer had gone by, and the autumn air cooled in the evening. Dax had found himself employed as the assistant to the painter, Pierre-Auguste Renoir. Dax maintained a suitable lifestyle, and he longed to join his new employer in the growing Bohemian movement taking place in Montmartre. However, Dax had moved to Le Marais. He found that living among the commoners held potential for great influence. The artists had a cultural way into society; however, the servants knew the secrets of their employers. He would be able to use this information to continue to elevate himself if necessary.

"Yes, Hugo. I know," he continued as they rushed down Rue Saint Honoré.

"It's not going to be that easy, Dax," Hugo nervously replied.

"What's so difficult?" He stopped and pulled Hugo by the lapels of his jacket to look him dead in the eyes. "All you have to do is meet me at Pont Louis Philippe at midnight. Is that so hard? Really Hugo! I just don't understand why you can't just do this one thing for me."

"One thing? I'm constantly doing things for you."

"Oh, so that's what we're doing? A pissing contest to see who's a better friend? Okay! Fine! You win. You are a better friend. Just forget it. I'll… I'll try to find someone to help me."

Victor Hugo was a kind man and a good friend. His guilt was immediate. "Fine. Dax. I'll be there. But after this… Please-"

"Oh, thank you, Hugo! Thank you! I promise! This is it! I will never ask you for another thing for as long as you live!" Dax pulled him in for a tight hug.

"Okay. Okay," Hugo laughed. "That's enough. Really. You are so emotional."

Dax smiled and shrugged his shoulders.

"I'll see you at midnight," Hugo said as he walked away.

Thaddeus had left his evening in the bustling *Moulin de la Galette* in Montmartre. Phineas was not available due to work commitments. He had been enjoying the time with some artist friends but excused himself from Señor Picasso and Monsieur Toulouse after being given a letter by a contemporary of theirs, Pierre-Auguste Renoir.

The letter was sealed. As he read it, he was immediately disgusted. In the letter, Dax begged for forgiveness and promised to never contact him again. However, he asked that Thaddeus allow him the decency to apologize in person. The letter offered a time and place: *Midnight tonight on the Pont Louis Philippe*. He also asked that Thaddeus come alone, which caused some suspicion. However, Thaddeus had no concern about outwitting or overpowering Dax, and therefore, decided to go and conclude this chapter of mistakes.

Thaddeus had left his good company of artists with a chilled bottle of champagne and another of absinthe.

"Go easy on that one, Toulouse," he joked.

"Oh yes, Thaddeus. It will be easy," Toulouse joked back as he took immediately to the bottle of green spirit.

Thaddeus met his coach a short distance from the Moulin de la Galette because of the heavy crowd.

The coach made its way through the streets, turning left and right as there was no direct route to Ile Saint Louis and to Pont Louis Philippe. Thaddeus had a coy smile as he thought not about Dax and what dramatic event was about to unfold, but rather of Phineas. He thought of the lifetimes that he had known him and how he was lost after each of Phineas' deaths. He thought of his own part in each of them. His ego would never let him stop believing that Phineas would come back, but each time, he thought, *When?*

Either way, he did not have to succumb to that pain right now. He decided to focus on joy and to allow for that joy to exist to the fullest. After this meeting with Dax, he would go to meet Phineas and tell him about their past. He knew that the idea of living multiple lifetimes was not the accepted philosophy of a mortal Catholic mind but Thaddeus knew that Phineas would be open to the truth and hoped that he would continue to embrace their connection for eternity. He smiled as he knew that Phineas would understand.

After all these lifetimes, he finally felt as though he was strong enough to discuss the entirety of their existence with his true love. Phineas was the reason that Thaddeus was able to love. He was the reason that Thaddeus was able to turn his Immortal focus from destroying life to helping to protect and preserve it.

It had taken over an hour due to the bustling Paris streets, but the coach finally arrived. Thaddeus sent the driver away, since Phineas' work engagement was near, and he was going to see him after this meeting with Dax.

"Thaddeus?" Victor Hugo called out as if he were trying to pull the name back as he was saying it.

"Victor. Good evening."

"Yes. Yes. Good evening," Hugo replied with a quiver in his voice.

"What's wrong, Victor?"

"Oh… Oh… Nothing… It's just that I am supposed to meet…"

"Dax," Thaddeus finished his sentence with a shaking of his head. "What game are you playing now, Dax?" he asked his thoughts aloud.

"I did not know that you were going to be here. I swear," Hugo continued nervously.

Thaddeus said nothing but looked around spying for trouble. This was Dax's doing. Trouble was the only way that this could now go.

"Don't move, Victor."

Hugo found himself gripping hard on the railing of the bridge. Thaddeus began to search the crowd using the night and heat vision that were among his Immortal gifts. To his surprise, he smelled that familiar aroma that usually brought a smile to his face. This time, it brought panic.

"Phineas?" he whispered with fear. "Phineas?" he yelled out. He continued to turn frantically. His night vision allowed him to see the faces of the passersby. No Phineas. No Dax. He turned back to Hugo. Hugo saw his look and squeezed tighter on the railing.

"No!" Thaddeus heard the voice of his former valet. He turned and saw across the bridge the flash and the loud bang of pistol fire. He saw Phineas' shocked and frightened expression as Dax fell to his knees. Dax was attempting to pull himself up by the railing and dropped the pistol into the Seine River. Phineas saw the light reflect off the metal as it fell. He ran to the rail to see it fall onto a small boat.

Thaddeus quickly made his way over as the crowd on the bridge screamed and ran. The sound of police whistles wailed through the night air.

"Phineas?"

"Thaddeus. I- I didn't do this. He shot himself."

"I know. I saw everything from over there. Where's the gun?"

"He threw it over the rail, and it landed in a boat." Phineas looked at the Seine River. "There! That one!"

"Stay here. Say nothing. You are innocent. I am your witness."

Thaddeus ran to the far side of the bridge and then along the Left Bank. He ran with a speed faster than any mortal ever could and caught up to the boat. He took a leap that landed him square in the center of it. The crew was immediately shocked and frightened.

"Where is it?" he demanded.

They stood, too panicked to move.

Over their shoulders, he saw the flash of a second gunshot and then the piercing sound that rang through the panicked night air.

No. He feared the worst.

Thaddeus screamed out in pain. The crewmembers jumped into the river and swam towards the banks. Thaddeus took control of the vessel and turned it around to make his way back. Once close enough, he jumped from the boat and ran to where he left Phineas and Dax. The police held off the crowd, but Thaddeus burst through with a power that was unstoppable. He saw Phineas lying on the bridge with the bloodstain on his shirt growing larger. He grabbed him in his arms and looked him in the eyes.

"Thaddeus," Phineas choked his name. "Thaddeus. I- I-" He was unable to speak as tears rolled from his eyes and blood began to fall from his mouth.

"I know Phineas. I know."

Thaddeus pulled him closer and held him tight.

"I love you," Phineas said.

Thaddeus felt him go. He did not even get the chance to say it back. He stayed there, squatting over his love as rage began to grow inside of him. He held Phineas as tight as he could. He sniffed the air. The scent was fading. Phineas was gone.

Rage was now all that he had left. It was strong and focused. He made the smallest attempt to control it in honor of Phineas. However, then he saw Dax.

Dax shot himself in a way that would not kill him. He would be martyred, but alive. Dax would come out of this as a victim and be given a story to gossip and elevate himself in Paris society. Phineas was dead because of Dax's envy.

"No," Thaddeus demanded as he lowered Phineas back to the bridge planks. "I'm sorry, Phineas. But we will be together again."

He gave him a kiss on the cheek and inhaled one more time for the slightest aroma that always brought a smile to his face. Nothing. He saw through his pain that Phineas was holding a piece of paper. Thaddeus took it and read it.

"Pont Louis Philippe.

Midnight.

All my love, Thaddeus"

The handwriting was perfect. Dax had perfected Thaddeus' penmanship.

Thaddeus looked up with all the rage that he could muster. Dax fought through his public performance and gave the slightest smirk of accomplishment. Thaddeus drew his fangs and leapt onto Dax. He pulled him up as the crowd screamed in disbelief. Thaddeus held Dax high in the air by the throat.

"You killed him," Thaddeus screamed. "All of this to get back at me."

He was shaking Dax.

Dax kicked him in the face and Thaddeus dropped him to the ground.

The police piled on Thaddeus in an attempt to take control of the situation. They were not successful as Thaddeus pushed and threw them from side to side, over the rail into the flowing river below.

"Help me!" Dax screamed. "First Phineas tried to kill me and now Thaddeus! Someone, please!"

Thaddeus grabbed Dax and again held him aloft. He screamed out like an enraged animal. Dax was truly frightened as he struggled to free himself. Blood from Dax's wound fell directly into Thaddeus' mouth, which caused Thaddeus to immediately lose all control of his humanity. He dropped Dax to the ground, holding tight at his collar.

"Now it's my turn," Thaddeus spit out with Dax's blood coming back onto his face. "You will regret what you did… Forever!"

Thaddeus sank his fangs deep into Dax's neck. Blood spurted forcibly. The curious crowd that lingered on the bridge screamed and ran. Some just moved further back to avoid getting blood on themselves, mesmerized by what was happening. The police officers looked at one other, waiting for someone to take the first step forward.

"Forever!" Thaddeus demanded again as he looked deep into Dax's fading eyes and saw his wretched envious soul leave his body. "Peace will never come to you," Vampire said as he looked away.

Dax looked panicked as the last bit of life left his body. Thaddeus watched as the final essence left Dax's physical body; his spirit hovered above and watched the scene in disbelief.

Aside from one man with a multitude of crystals and several ruby rings, the crowd was unable to understand that Thaddeus was talking to the spirit that floated in the wake of the double homicide.

Thaddeus dropped the body and began to walk away. The crowd quickly parted, giving him distance in fear of becoming the next victim. The police continued to look at one another, unsure if they were courageous enough to attempt arresting Thaddeus.

Thaddeus walked back to Phineas. He lifted his lifeless body and sniffed the air again. The slightest scent of citrus hit his nose. It was there again. Phineas was fighting to stay alive, but then it faded and was gone. Thaddeus dropped his head to Phineas and sank his fangs into his neck. He slowly walked off with the body as the crowd watched, but maintained a distance.

Dax's spirit floated. He stared at his limp body and knew instinctively that he would never inhabit a physical form again. The crowds' attention was all drawn to Thaddeus' exit. There was no one paying any attention to Dax's lifeless body. Then, he saw the man with the crystals and the ruby rings walk towards his body. He was followed by Victor Hugo.

Victor shook his head and held his hand over Dax's eyes to close them. He shed a tear at the loss of his friend. The man with the rings looked up at the sky, seeing Dax's spiritual form. The man nodded. The spirit nodded back.

CHAPTER 40
The Entrapment

"Whether you care or not, now you know," Ghost told Vampire as the magical lights swirled around them.

"And now I know what?" Vampire spit out with venom in his words. "That I was right to destroy you?"

"No," Ghost continued with an air of superiority, ignoring his tone. "You now know what happened to me. And that this torture is of your own making."

"All of my tortures are of my own making, you fool!"

"Oh, my friend," Ghost laughed as he floated around in an irregular pattern. "You created me. But the Jeweled Dragon is not waiting for *me* to take revenge. And we do not have the time to quarrel about who was right and who was wrong. I finally understand that our argument is petty when compared to her agenda."

Vampire stared at the shimmers of the magical lights off the reflective grains of sand. The thoughts in his mind were spiraling. He knew that Ghost spoke the truth. However, he refused to hear it from the one who had killed Phineas back in 1891 and circled back in the form of this angry spirit.

"I have been trailing you for six years. I was sent back to this dimension with the purpose to find you and bring you to Mavi." Ghost floated around him. "She wanted to warn you about the Jeweled Dragon. But then I was introduced to the Peasant King in The Wastelands who wanted me to bring you to him… For The Dark Sisters." Ghost now held Vampire's attention. "Why? I do not know. But I can only assume that it was for the worst."

Vampire forced his arms across his chest and pulled tight upon his trunk.

"But now… After going back through this experience… I know that I too was at fault. I created the situation that caused my own downfall." Ghost stared off in reflection. "And I am responsible for correcting *my* mistakes."

Vampire relaxed his tension.

Ghost let out a sigh. "I know that this is difficult to hear, but Monk and Tinker are not part of the prophecy. You are."

Vampire looked to the top of the entrapment.

"An Immortal to destroy an Immortal. The Three of Legend. The Sword of Sansit. The Shield of Gnim and the eight Cez stones." Ghost was speaking with passion. "This is what is needed to stop the Jeweled Dragon." He waited. He watched as Vampire looked away longingly. "I am sorry, but Monk and Tinker are not included in that. Their loss is heavy, but you can still see him again."

Vampire turned to him.

"If we defeat the Jeweled Dragon and allow time and space to continue." He was now screaming. "That is the only way to allow Phineas another life… To return to you."

Vampire held his glare upwards and watched the particles of the entrapment move in their random pattern.

"The Jeweled Dragon will return," Ghost reminded him. Vampire gave a slight nod. "Only an Immortal can destroy an Immortal." He floated closer to Vampire. "The only way for you to find *him* again is to win this. That is the only way that Phineas can come back to you. Don't let this be the last goodbye."

Vampire realized he had spent his entire existence being ruled by his pride. And even now, his pride stood in the way of fully accepting the truth about himself, because it was *Dax* who was saying it.

He understood that his choice to save humankind altered his path from his beginnings when he was created to destroy it. However, upon that first encounter with Phineas, he realized that he found something equal but opposite himself. He found a force that was only human, only mortal; a force so mortal and delicate, yet so strong with humanity and kindness that it gave him a truer purpose. And from that point on, for thousands of years, he had worked to save what he was sent to destroy.

Vampire stood upright. He made a harsh body contraction that forced the dust from his clothes. He nodded his head and inhaled deeply. He held his hands to his mouth and looked up through the magical entrapment to the sky above.

"Monk is not mentioned in the prophecy." Vampire accepted the truth in that. "His presence was for me, not mankind. Yet, he served mankind with each life he lived."

Vampire opened his clenched fists and held his fingers to his puckered lips.

"And he is gone." He kissed his hands and lifted them up towards the top of the enclosure. "This is for his return."

"No!" Ghost rushed over to ensnare him in his own ethereal form. He was too late.

Vampire's hands had made contact with the light, causing a loud explosion. Ileana, Sorcerer, Axel and Princess were thrown off their feet as fire came off the electrical field of the entrapment.

Aldrick held his place. His eyes reflected fire. The flames and electrical energy rushed into his copper staff. It did not burn. Instead, Aldrick smashed his staff into the sand and the fire was gone.

Ileana and Sorcerer looked at one another with shock. Princess was quick to her feet. Axel ran to his brother.

"Aldrick!" he felt for any flames beneath his clothes.

Aldrick's eyes returned to their natural state. He looked at his brother with as much surprise as Axel expressed. "Fire." Axel whispered and looked him up and down. "You are the Champion of Fire."

They began laughing hysterically and hugged tight.

"Oh my-" Cadet began.

"The Three of Legend," Vampire said. He nodded to Sorcerer and then to Ileana.

Princess ran up to her brothers. "Are you okay, Aldrick?"

"Better than okay! I feel amazing!"

"Vampire," Sorcerer yelled out. "I am trusting that we do not have to keep you contained any longer."

"You do not," Vampire yelled back. "We have the Three of Legend and an Immortal. We still need to find the yellow Cez stone, the sword and the rest of the shield." He looked back at Ghost, who hovered nearby. "We need to stay committed."

He turned his attention to the others. "I have some things to finish here," he said. "Ghost! I need you to continue to protect me while I transition back into these previous lives." Vampire had retaken control of his fate, of his choices.

Sorcerer and Ileana looked at one another, then back at their children and Vampire. They all agreed.

"Phineas," Vampire pushed out a whisper. It took all his strength to do even that. "Phineas," he repeated in a slightly more audible voice.

Ghost glided closer, engulfing Vampire in his form to take him back to another point in his past.

"Seer?" AZ yelled as Seer began to convulse.

"AZ!" Princess yelled. "What is it?"

"I don't know," he yelled back.

CHAPTER 41
The Shadow Realm

Seer was surrounded by darkness. He heard the audible scratching growing louder and more aggressive. Rushes of hot air came past him. He was sweating and panicked. The heat became more intense and was coming from multiple directions. He turned again and again to try to see what it was, until he found himself spinning uncontrollably.

The heat was now surrounding him and the sound of the scratching became painful. Seer pulled his hands to his ears to attempt to stop the sound. It made no difference.

He was now rotating in all directions. He had no control over his body as the heat came at him from all sides. The pain from the burning overtook the pain from the scratching noise.

Kill me, was all he thought. The pain had become unbearable.

And then it stopped.

Seer was weightless. He was looking out of his red, fiery eyes at a vastness of black. The emptiness in front of him began to alter and reduce itself to three forms. Behind it was something familiar: the landscape of the Desert of Xedu.

Seer's only thought was to scream out. Yet, he was unable to.

As the three forms surrounded him, he felt the hateful presence of The Dark Sisters.

"Yes," they said in unison. "We are one again. You will aid in our escape from this place."

Tears fell from his red eyes.

"Where are you, my queens?" he asked. They said nothing.

CHAPTER 42
Hell, Fifth Circle

Tinker mired at the circus tent that seemed to have popped up in front of them through the misty haze. They were still a distance from the lights that illuminated the structure, but were now being joined by an assortment of characters that ran, wheeled and flew past them through the field.

Tinker, of course, was more curious in the unfamiliar beings and was making very detailed mental notes to understand their form and physical make up. He made attempts to interact, but they were all rushing towards the tent. He only made quick, side-eye glances at the ones that looked dangerous to get as much information about their appearance and movements as his fear would allow.

As they came closer, the dirt road that Monk, Sansit and he now found themselves upon was bordered by coaches that were linked together like a train. Each housed a different beast, who was to be exhibited in the main tent.

"This is incredible," Tinker said a bit too loud.

Monk and Sansit looked at one another with a different expression. They understood that something would show itself to be even more *incredible* but expected that it would most likely not be to their advantage.

Regardless, Monk could not help but appreciate Tinker's innocence. He did not want to interfere with his friend's appreciation, but he had to keep him focused.

"Tink?"

"I know. I know," Tinker said with a childish eye roll. "We are in Hell. This is all going to turn bad. That story is becoming exhausting," he told Monk and Sansit as they walked past beasts of all forms, sizes, and colors, some spitting fire and others turning objects into jewels with their touch. "But just give me a minute to take all of it in before it goes wrong." Tinker took the sketchbook from his backpack and started to feverishly draw and write notes.

Monk and Sansit looked at one another again. "Fair enough," Monk said with a shrug of the shoulders to Sansit.

Sansit slapped Monk across the face. "Focus, you idiot."

"Ouch!" Monk held his hand to his face. "Why did you hit me? Tinker said it."

"I got my point across," Sansit replied. "Keep him focused."

Back behind the row of coaches, Tinker's attention was caught by two beasts that were chained to a post in the ground.

"Dragons," he said with amazement. "One red and one green." He cocked his head with added curiosity at the playful way the dragons chased each other.

"Yeah, Tink," Monk interrupted, still rubbing his face. "Remember what happened with the last dragon."

"These are not like that one," Tinker told him with a gleam in his eyes.

"Which one?" Sansit asked.

"The Jeweled Dragon," Monk told him.

Sansit's eyes shot open.

"Get away from them, boy," Sansit demanded as he pulled Tinker back onto the road before he caught the dragons' attention.

"What?" Tinker begged. "Just look at them," he watched them fly around one another. "They're like puppies."

"Yes. Yes," Sansit agreed. "Like 'the Hounds of Hell' kind of puppies," he whispered with a harsh tone. "Those are very dangerous, even more so to you."

"Why even more so to us?" Monk asked.

"I did not mean *you*." Sansit looked around to make sure that they were not being overheard. "I meant *him*." He pointed at Tinker. "He's not meant to be here."

"You mean because I'm not dead?" Tinker asked.

"Shhh!" Sansit demanded. "I'm sure that you're not fooling everyone here, but you're at least getting by. Don't advertise it."

"How did you know?" Monk questioned.

"The Fourth Circle, you nitwit," Sansit reminded him. "I read about it as soon as you arrived in Hell." He continued to whisper so that only Monk and Tinker could hear.

Monk and Tinker quickly looked at one another.

"That's not good."

Monk knew by Tinker's facial contorts and biting of his lower lip that his mind was running in all directions.

"Tink?" Monk questioned with a sense of calm to keep Tinker from exploding emotionally.

"The books in the library?" Tinker asked with a jealous tone for he had not been able to take advantage of that knowledge.

"Wipe that look off of your face, son," Sansit barked. "Gluttony to envy? You are falling into a trap here."

Sansit slapped him across the face to break his decline.

"Ouch!"

"You're welcome," Sansit said and turned to walk towards the main tent.

"Hold on," Monk demanded. "There's something that you're not telling us."

Sansit stopped and took a deep sigh. He turned his head to watch the playful dragons.

"Puppies," he laughed out loud.

Sansit turned to Monk and Tinker standing with disapproving looks on their faces.

"Out with it," Monk demanded.

"Remember," Sansit told Monk. "I still don't like you."

"And I still don't care," Monk argued back.

"Sansit," Tinker softly called his attention. "Please."

Sansit let out a deep sigh and shrugged his shoulders as he explained.

"I kind of created the Jeweled Dragon."

"You what?" Monk yelled.

"Shhh." Sansit knew that Monk's outburst would gain unwanted attention.

"Please explain," Monk said in a lower but equally bothered tone.

"I knew that the Jeweled Dragon would be used for destruction," Sansit confessed. "It was not the first time that I had attempted to destroy humankind. But I did not know that she would be sent to end all of time and space… Not until I read about it after being stuck in that library," he said and looked between them.

"So, this is all your fault?" Monk questioned.

"No. It's Vampire's fault… And yours. I had no choice," Sansit spoke through gritted teeth, arguing his case. "The Enlightenment-"

"You had a choice," Monk countered. "Nothing that The Enlightenment offered should have let you agree to destroying all of time and space."

"I did not know that was the plan. But I also did not trust them. So, I hid a few things from them just in case I needed to stop them." Sansit attempted to justify his argument.

"And look where that has gotten us," Monk argued back.

"I know how to control destruction!" he argued through gritted teeth to bring them back to his side. "And that's why *I* wrote the prophecy… How to stop her… Just in case I needed to do it."

"Don't you mean, just in case *we* needed to do it?" Monk asked, still annoyed with Sansit.

Sansit shrugged it off. "When I brought the Black Plague, I watched the two of you figure out how to stop it!" Sansit continued to argue as Monk and Tinker held back any confidence in his statement.

"Wait a minute," Tinker ordered. "The two of us?"

"Yes," Sansit replied. "The two of you were doctors in Firenze and were able to control and stop the Black Plague." He looked at Monk. "It cost you your life." Sansit looked up at the night sky. "And Vampire was there when you died."

"Did he kill me?" Monk asked.

Sansit was quick to look at him. "No," he said, "he saved your memories. He did that with each of your deaths. Only once did he kill you." He pointed to Monk's side. "But then marked you so that he would be able to find you again."

Tinker was again distracted by the dragons while Monk and Sansit now stood in silence.

The dragons began flying in circles in opposite directions. The chains that bound them to the glowing diamond spike in the ground were becoming tangled.

Monk watched Tinker walk towards the beasts. Sansit too looked to see Tinker now running towards them. Monk and Sansit ran after him.

The dragons were flying in a much tighter circle as the chains became wound up.

"No!" Tinker screamed as the dragons smashed into one another and burst into flame and water.

The combination became a mist that was now slowly dropping over Tinker. He felt the moist air and breathed deeply. The warm vapor entered his lungs. He welcomed the humid air and extended his arms as if to take as much of it as he could.

Tinker felt a wetness on his hands. He opened his eyes and watched as the vapor began to take the form of a human woman. The misty droplets began to come together and, although still transparent, created the Element, Water. She glided to the ground with a smile. Tinker felt his heart race.

"Hello… Tinker," Water said to him.

"Hello," he replied with a smile. Tinker was lost in the sight of her. He felt immediately safe as Water pulled him in for an embrace.

Water's form was soft and warm. Yet, when Tinker released her from his embrace, he remained dry. He realized it but did not feel the need to question it.

"The dragons?" he asked.

"I needed a way for you to see me," she told him.

"I see you," he laughed. "I see you everywhere."

"Yes," she giggled. "I guess you do."

"I thought that I imagined you. It's nice to see you like this," he told her and spun her while holding her hand.

Tinker laughed and expressed his joy in his tearful eyes.

"What is it?" she asked with a shy smile.

"I'm trying to understand," Tinker said. "Can all the Elements show themselves like you?"

"Yes," Water replied. "But only to their champion. It requires the connection of elemental magic to see us."

Tinker nodded. "So, I am your champion."

"Yes," she replied with the same shy grin.

"I have been through so much," he told her, exposing his worries. "All of us. I should think that this is a dream, but as crazy as it is, I know this is real."

Water continued to smile. "This is real."

"Why do I feel like all of the problems have gone away?"

"It's the mist," she explained.

He returned the shy flirtation. "I'll accept that."

"Without question?" She laughed.

"Surprised?" he asked as she nodded. "Me too, actually. But all my life, water has always given me a sense of safety and peace."

He looked at the moisture that he rubbed on his fingertips as he nodded.

"And Sansit," she rushed. "His time in Hell has brought him to a new perspective. He has learned from his own mistakes and is about to be challenged by his past."

Tinker looked back to see the outlines of Sansit and Monk through the mist.

"We don't always see things from a greater point of view," Water told him.

"Even you?"

"Even me."

Tinker nodded with his head down.

"And Tinker," she continued. "Remember that not everything *in* the water feels the way that I do. I cannot always intervene, but I will when I can… For you."

Tinker felt himself blushing.

"I must go now," Water told him with regret.

"Please don't."

"I am always with you Tinker." She acknowledged the mist and the drops of water on his skin.

"I still can't believe that I am talking to you or that we are in Hell."

Water laughed. "*You* opened the portal with Lucifer's key," she told him.

"Lucifer's key?"

"The orb in your pocket," she said.

Ileana, he thought, remembering when she had gifted him the orb back in the City of Witches, before any of this started.

"I had to save Monk." He looked up at her face. "Thank you." Tinker looked back at the wet grass. "For helping us before. I know that you led us to the fireplace."

Water said nothing but dissolved into droplets and spread out onto the grass as the mist dissipated.

Monk and Sansit were both near where Tinker was standing.

Monk looked at him curiously. He had a wide smile on his face.

Monk pulled him up and into a hug. "Who were you talking to?" Monk asked him as he put his hand on his shoulder.

"You wouldn't believe me."

"Try me," he laughed.

Tinker opened his eyes and looked at Monk with the joy in his face.

"Water," he told him. "She helped us in the library. And she's helped me before."

Monk was silent.

"Told you," Tinker said and walked past him.

"I didn't say that I don't believe you," he said as Tinker continued to walk away.

"You didn't have to," he yelled back.

Sansit was standing near Monk. Monk looked down.

"Water," Monk told him.

Sansit nodded.

"That boy is amazing," Sansit told Monk.

"You have no idea," he told him.

Tinker walked past the empty chains that had held the dragons.

Monk and Sansit caught up with him on the road.

The carriages were crowded with onlookers. The attractions housed within them came directly from dreams and nightmares. They ranged from sea creatures that were able to conjure fire underwater to rogue mermaids that were paying off their karmic debt. There were food stands that were full of exotic aromas, colors, and tastes with some of the served delicacies still moving.

"Everything is free," Tinker told them.

"Nothing here is truly free," Sansit reminded him.

"And all of these beings are from-"

"Different dimensions," Sansit told him. "So many worlds and dimensions, each of them funneled into Gokyuzu and then the souls were put on trains to Hell before entering Heaven and either returning back for another run of it or entering The Enlightenment with the soul's purpose complete."

"Interesting concept," Tinker told him. "But Gokyuzu is no more. How is it going to go now?"

He looked back at Monk who stayed quiet. Sansit too said nothing.

"I'm not mad at you, Monk," Tinker told him. "But it was her. It was Water."

"I know, Tink. I believe you," Monk told him. "My reaction was wrong. I'm sorry. But with so much happening right now, I'm afraid that even you will be overwhelmed."

Tinker looked at his hand as he felt his palm becoming sweaty for no reason. He turned it upwards. Monk and Sansit looked to see the water droplets. They watched as the droplets began to come together and levitate above Tinker's hand.

Tinker started to think of moving the water that hovered in the air. It moved to his request. He thought of figures and forms. The water contorted to become what he had envisioned. "Don't worry about me, Monk. I am the Champion of Water." Tinker laughed with joy. "This is amazing," he told them. "I found who I am."

"You are a very special young man," Sansit told him.

"How long have you known?" Tinker asked Monk.

"I wasn't sure," Monk told him. "I had read about the Champions of the Elements many years ago. I suspected that it could be true when you were a child. You always found security in water, holding your breath and staying under it, playing and running out into the rain, staying in the snow until you were frozen, but never frostbitten. But it wasn't for me to tell you. It was for you… to see and understand."

"It feels very…" Tinker searched for the word, "normal?"

"Why not?" Monk threw back at him.

"I mean, she's *Water*… Like everything is made of water and that makes her everything."

"And you are her Champion," Sansit added. "You and she can work together to create peace and balance."

"I mean, who am I to question it," Monk said to him. "I've spent nine lifetimes in an endless life and death love affair with an Immortal vampire."

They all looked at one another and laughed. Tinker looked at the carriages, the creatures of attraction, and the vendors. His expression became guarded.

"Tink?"

"She told me that not everything in the water feels the way she does."

Sansit stepped forward. "You will need to keep your position quiet while here in Hell. As soon as it is known that you are her Champion, you will become a target."

"More than now?" Tinker asked.

"That will be strike two. Every sinner down here and the ones not here yet will look to take from you," Sansit warned him.

"But she chose me," Tinker told him.

"To be fair, she did not choose you. You just are her Champion, and she knows it," Sansit whispered and looked around for eavesdroppers. "But even the creatures in these tanks would look to manipulate or destroy you to attempt to take your position."

"But don't worry, Tink. We won't let that happen," Monk assured him.

They watched all the creatures start to make their way into the giant circus tent.

"Okay," Monk said. "It seems as though we have a show to watch." He emphasized the word *watch*. "To get out of here and to the next circle."

Tinker looked back at the dragons' collars and chains.

"Red and green." Tinker whispered his thoughts. "Mist." He scribbled notes in his sketchbook.

Monk and Sansit exchanged a look. Sansit was pushed as the crowd forced them towards the tent.

"Seems like it's time to go in," Sansit said. "Take these," he ordered Monk and handed him clothes that he grabbed from a drying line.

Monk quickly dressed in an attempt to draw less attention.

"Let's go," Monk ordered.

"Not in the front," Tinker barked with concern. "I don't want to sit in the front."

Monk was looking around the inside of the tent. He was not sure what he was looking for but felt the need to be prepared for anything.

Tinker was staring at the couple in front of them. He was making failed attempts to speak, his mouth gaping in shock.

"Kid," Sansit began. "I've been down here long enough to not be surprised by the looks, the sounds, the smells, and sins of anyone I encounter."

"What about the tastes and feel?" Tinker asked jokingly as Sansit had eluded those senses.

"No way," he rushed back. "I won't eat anything I don't recognize." His mind wandered as his mouth quivered.

"Sansit?" Tinker begged out of concern.

"Sorry kid," he said. "I haven't had the touch of anyone since…"

"Can I say it?"

"Yeah."

"Gnim?"

Sansit looked at him with sad eyes. "And I never will," he said as he teared up. "She was the only one for me."

Sansit looked at him.

"Ask," Sansit allowed. "You know that you want to. It's in your nature to want to know things."

Tinker smiled kindly. "Are you sure?"

"I am," Sansit said with his own slight grin. "It will be nice to remember."

Tinker motioned to speak as the lights went down.

A narrow spot illuminated the center ring. It came from three spotlights around the tent, coming from behind the top row of the seated crowd. The ring was empty. Tinker squinted, trying to figure out what was about to happen.

The crowd applauded as if this was the anticipated opening. Tinker looked back and forth to Monk who shrugged his shoulders and to Sansit, who was in awe. Tinker was still confused and growing increasingly curious because he was unable to figure out why the crowd was applauding

"The empty ring," began a feminine voice.

Sansit grabbed a hold of Tinker's thigh and squeezed. Tinker shot him a painful look and attempted to remove his hand, to not avail.

"An empty promise," she continued. "That is what I have and from it, what I have to offer you."

The three spotlights began to widen and separate. Grinding music began to play. The outer two lights began spinning. The spinning circles changed color, one red and one green. The images of the dragons outside were displayed in the circling lights, as the spinning lights created dust from the dirt floor.

The crowd applauded and whistled.

Tinker did not know if he was aggravated by not understanding what was happening or by Sansit's grasp that was digging into his leg. He elbowed Monk to get his attention.

Monk realized immediately what the problem was and gently placed his hand atop Sansit's.

Sansit loosened his grip and came back to his consciousness. He shook his head.

"Are you okay?" Monk asked.

"No," he replied and looked at Tinker's leg. "Sorry, kid."

"No problem," Tinker rubbed the spot. "What's the matter?"

The female voice continued with her opening monologue.

"The ring was full of hope once." She continued and told the tale of love and loss.

It sounded joyful but then sounded foul with sorrow. The voice broke through the darkness with both hope and regret. The three rings of light gave visuals to her tale of a lost love and her forever being envious of those who found love and kept it.

"The promise of eternal love was in that ring. But that ring, like that promise, was broken. Both destroyed and pulled apart. My forever sin is having found love, having lost it, and refusing to go and find it again. My forever sin is being envious as I am watching it happen for others but being too fearful to find my own."

The three spinning lights came back together and expanded to show the borders of the three performance rings. The outer two had a rugged edged jewel appearance, one ruby red and the other emerald green. However, the middle ring was borderless, aside from the light.

The crowd stood and screamed in applause, whistles, yells for more, and tears.

"What the…?" Tinker asked. "I still don't get it."

Monk nudged him and nodded towards Sansit. "Remember what you were about to ask him?"

"About Gnim?"

"I think you just got her side of the story," he said and leaned past Tinker to Sansit to whisper. "We should get out of the tent. We can talk outside."

Sansit nodded in agreement.

"Why can't I understand what's happening?" Tinker asked.

"Because you have never experienced this type of love and loss," Monk told him. "And if you ever do, you will have this to rely on to know that you are not alone and that it will get better."

"Would Vampire say the same?"

"He's always had the knowledge that I would be back. He just needed to be patient."

"Yeah. Vampire. Patient," Tinker joked. "Gnim does not seem to feel the same."

Monk and Tinker followed a step behind Sansit as he looked lost in thought again. The crowd was rushing to get out of the tent. They were being drawn to something.

"Now what?" Tinker asked.

As they came out to the night sky, Monk tapped Tinker and pointed to the red and green dragons flying unbound. They were making patterns in the sky in the form of hearts. Then they flew through them and broke them.

With each broken heart, screams were heard from the crowd and bodies vanished into smoke. Some left a shadow on the ground. The shadows vibrated and let out a scratching sound, before flying off.

"Yup," Tinker said. "Hell. Definitely Hell."

Monk and Tinker ran up to Sansit and squatted to grab hold of him by the shoulders.

"Sansit?" Monk looked into his teary eyes.

"It was her," he said with the most sorrowful voice.

Monk instinctually pulled him in for a hug.

"Get off of me, you fool," Sansit barked.

"Glad to see you're back."

"I haven't been able to touch anyone like that since her. And I'm surely not going to start with you."

Monk could not help but laugh at Sansit's immediate turn of emotion.

"But Sansit," Tinker spoke with hope in his voice. "She's here. You're here. Maybe…" he searched for his words cautiously. "Maybe, you can work this out."

Sansit looked at him with sorrow.

"Sansit?" The question came from a feminine voice in the darkness.

Sansit froze in place.

"H- Hello," Tinker offered a greeting to the giant woman who was wearing the circus tent as a dress. "I am Tinker… And this is Monk."

"I am-"

"Gnim," Sansit said with a quiver in his voice. "You wanted the story, kid. Well, here it is." He pointed behind him and up to the sky knowing that Gnim was a giant.

"Sansit? Is it really you?"

"It is," he told her without turning around.

"Sansit?"

"Can you please say something else," he yelled and turned to see her. His eyes immediately teared up.

"I just thought that I would never be able to say your name again, especially with you being present," she said as she fell to her knees.

The surface shook and knocked both Monk and Tinker off balance. Sansit rode the ripples in the ground as if he had expected it.

"The legend is real," Tinker said as if he had just become a believer.

"They all are," Monk whispered back. "Water. Vampire. Dragons…"

"Sansit and Gnim," Tinker added.

Sansit was frozen in place. Tinker gave him a questioning look as he tried to deduce if it was by choice.

Tinker walked towards him. Monk reached out to stop him but instead stopped himself. Tinker was making his own choices and his own mistakes. Monk had to let him. He was there to protect him, but he had to let him grow.

"Hell might not be the place to do that," came the rugged voice over Monk's shoulder. "Hello, Monk. Been awhile." Leviathan walked past him and made a reference to Monk's eyes. The Demon Ruler of the Fifth Circle of Hell extended his hand to Gnim. "Come to daddy. This piece of Hell filth has nothing for you," he said and snarled at Sansit. He launched his top hat high into the air and it landed on Gnim's head. She transformed into her smaller human form.

Sansit was still frozen. He did not react. Tinker was looking back at Leviathan with disgust.

"No," Sansit said and then looked up at Monk. "It's time that I confessed *my* tale. The truth will free me," he said and looked to the carriage that Leviathan and Gnim had disappeared behind. "And her."

Monk and Tinker shared a stare. Monk gave a nod and they both sat in the soft grass. Sansit turned to them and began to tell his tale.

"We were both warriors," he began. "More like mercenaries for hire and not always on the same side, but fierce warriors. We were not birthed like other Immortals. We were mortals who were forced into Immortality by The Enlightenment because of our skills. We were called upon at different times in history… Times of war. I always welcomed the challenge of Gnim being in battle either with or against me. I fought with my emerald blade and she with her ruby shield. I never protected her; I never had too. And she never protected me. She was my only rival but I never attacked her with the goal of destroying her, nor she of me. It was always like a dance. The battle would be over, but we would still spar. It was beautiful."

He saw that Tinker had a confused expression on his face.

"Battles are meant to be won, kid. If you were a hired mercenary, when it was won, it was over. None of this 'kill or enslave everyone' nonsense. You were hired to do a job and then to go home," he said with a sense of loneliness.

"And Gnim became home?" Tinker asked.

"Who's telling this story?" Sansit barked.

Tinker threw his hands up.

"But yes," Sansit admitted. "Gnim became home." He let out a giggle. "I have to admit, it was not a traditional introduction, and it was hidden from all, or at least I thought it was. Gnim and I were a team, but we were also individuals and hired separately. If anyone knew that we had come together, they would have all turned on us. They would have looked to destroy us." He shook his head as he thought back and spit when he spoke these words.

"But someone did find out," Monk added, to Sansit's displeasure.

"Yes," he said. "And not just someone. The Dark Sisters."

Tinker looked at Monk.

"They have been destroyed," Tinker told Sansit. "Ileana…"

"The Witch Queen?" Sansit asked.

"Not sure if she's going by that title, but yes," Tinker said in defense of her honor. "She recently destroyed The Dark Sisters. How did they find out about you and Gnim?" Tinker queried.

"The same way that Vampire destroyed him each time," he replied and nodded towards Monk.

"Pride got in the way," Monk added. "Your pride."

"Yes," Sansit told him. "They were in cohorts with Leviathan, and he granted them access to Hell. He made a deal with Beelzebub, and they discovered the Fourth Circle. The library. After finding a book that told the story of our transition to Immortality, they traveled back in time and found us in our mortal lives, before we knew one another. They altered our paths," he added with anger.

He continued to tell his tale. "Gnim's services and the armies that she commanded were being sought after for a higher price than mine. I became envious of her, and we started to fight. I mean, really fight in battle. It was no longer sparring with her but an angry fight to destroy one another."

"But now, you were both Immortals," Monk added.

"The Dark Sisters had been watching the change in us and now turned their game upon us. They looked to destroy us and all the Immortals. They wanted to challenge The Enlightenment and needed the essence of an Immortal to do it."

"But they are no more," Tinker told him.

"Not in your world, but they are still present in this one," Sansit said to Tinker's surprise. "Souls move on kid," Sansit reminded him. "The Demon Rulers have them under control-"

"For now," Monk added.

"For now," Sansit agreed. "But they took joy in looking to destroy us," Sansit looked back to the carriages, to the spot where Gnim had disappeared from view with Leviathan. "And it worked." He turned back to Tinker and Monk. "They enchanted my emerald sword and Gnim's ruby shield. Both objects were known to be indestructible, even to each other. But their curse was fed by my anger and my anger was fed by their curse. And the same happened with Gnim until…"

Sansit stared upward at the sky and let out a heart-wrenching scream. Monk looked at Tinker to make sure that he was not too shaken by the sound. Tinker's mind was elsewhere. Monk wondered if he had even heard the cry and what he was formulating in his ever-spinning thoughts.

"It was inevitable," Sansit said with a change in his tone to give a false sense of acceptance. "We never could have been. We were in perfect opposition to one another. That's why we were made Immortal."

"You were created as equals," Monk told him from a different point of view.

"Like you and that bloodsucker?" Sansit asked him with a condescending tone. "But my heart is still too broken," he added, returning to his sad tone. "Like my blade and her shield."

"Sansit?" Tinker asked as if waking from a dream. "Where is the center of Gnim's shield?"

"I do not know," he told him. "That was my main purpose in staying in that library. I read feverishly to discover its whereabouts, but nothing. I just kept reading more and more about other things and lives and then was so distracted that I lost sight of why I went in there to begin with."

"We have the frame of Gnim's shield. Her ring. We just need to find the center," he said and looked at Monk.

"Well, good luck. Gnim took it apart after our love ended," Sansit told them. "And besides, you need powerful magic to forge it back together."

"But your love did not end," Monk reminded him. "It never ended."

Tinker smiled. Monk did the same. They turned and looked at the dragons that were again chained to a post and flying playfully. The beasts wrapped their binding chains tighter until they crashed into one other and exploded. Just like before, their fiery ashes and mist fell to the ground. However, this time they formed back into their physical forms with the collars adhered around their necks.

"Well, I'll be damned," Sansit said.

"I think you already have been," Monk joked.

Sansit ignored his humor as he realized that the collars were ruby red. "Could this be true?" he asked.

"We're going to need those collars," Tinker told him.

Monk turned to Sansit and kneeled down to his height. "We need to find the missing part of your blade. Do you even have a lead on where it could be?"

"No. Nothing."

"The emerald blade and the ruby shield…" Monk began.

"Water and Fire…" Tinker added.

"The shield could protect from Fire," Monk continued.

"Fight fire with fire," Sansit understood.

"And the emerald blade could counter Fire with…"

"Water," Tinker concluded with a sense of hope.

Sansit looked off towards the carriages. He stepped away from Monk and Tinker without thought to his steps. Monk and Tinker were actively problem solving out loud, but Monk tapped Tinker to stop talking and to watch as Sansit began to nod his head.

"I may not have a lead on the blade," he said aloud and then turned to them as he pointed towards the carriages, "but I'm sure that I know someone who does."

Tinker looked at Monk who gave him a cautious smile. "Here we go again," Tinker said.

Sansit was already on the move. However, unlike before, he was now stepping hard with purpose. Each stomp of his small footsteps sent dust and dirt in all directions. The force of his foot contact and the resulting release from the ground caused Monk and Tinker to have to catch their balance. They looked at one another with surprise.

"I didn't expect that change of heart," Tinker said.

"We should follow him," Monk said with an impressed tone.

"Definitely," Tinker agreed as they ran to catch up. The ripples of energy in the dirt and rock continued to challenge their balance with each of Sansit's footsteps. "But maybe at a little bit of a distance."

They reached the carriages. The road was illuminated with carnival lights that were strung along and across the path. The patrons from the big tent were still in awe of the maritime attractions that were in the tanks in the moving carriages. Some creatures were leaping out of the water from tank to tank, leaving a golden light residue as the water droplets lingered in the air to illuminate the skin of the fair goers.

"Gnim!" demanded Sansit in a loud and echoing voice that was followed by a strong wind that blew the golden flecks from the patrons faces and shoulders. "Gnim!' he repeated, as his steps shook the ground and upset the water in the tanks.

The concerned expressions of the marine life within the tanks and the uncertainty of the patrons did not hinder his approach.

"Is this part of a show?" one patron asked as he wiped the water from his overcoat that had been drenched when the tank had shaken.

Monk and Tinker were not sure as to what to do. Sansit was committed to his course. They did not know what course that was, but trusted that it would lead them forward and hopefully, out of the Fifth Circle of Hell.

Monk sped ahead and saw that Gnim was lying with Leviathan on an elevated chaise. They were in a reclined position but her expression was concerned. Leviathan was at ease. He smiled as he chewed the exotic fruits that Gnim was feeding him.

Leviathan allowed his lower body to transform into its natural state. Squid-like legs slithered off the chaise as he stood. The coordinated movements of the eight extremities slid him forward to the edge of the platform. The sea beast was applauding Sansit as Sansit stopped his approach. Leviathan stood four body lengths above Sansit.

Sansit looked up and tried to maintain his committed expression. However, he battled his feelings for Gnim, his lost spirit, and the intimidation that he was feeling from Leviathan.

Monk and Tinker were quick to run up to his side. He turned and saw the support. He nodded at them in gratitude, which seemed to add to his confidence.

"Thank you. Thank you," Leviathan yelled out with a condescending laugh. He continued to applaud Sansit. He looked around at the crowd, which realized that was their cue to do the same.

Tinker looked at the crowd and understood that they were the lost souls of the Fifth Circle of Hell. Some were fading into shadows, and their applause made a painful scratching noise. Monk was staring at Gnim and the sadness on her face. He fell to one knee and was in Sansit's ear. *Shadows,* Monk thought. *Something is not right.*

"You are one of the greatest warriors of all time," Monk whispered to Sansit. "As is she. But look at the two of you now. Both broken by love. Both still sharing that love. What have you become, Sansit? And what has she become?"

Sansit's blood was boiling at Monk's words. He looked at Gnim. He saw the lack of character that had taken over her as she lay, still broken hearted on the chaise.

Sansit looked up to the sky and raised his hands as high as he could.

"What have you done?" Monk asked him.

Sansit dropped his arms and smashed them into the ground, causing an intense shaking and visible ripples. He let out a yell that began to blow hard at everything in its path.

The ground began to crack. The carriages began to topple as the wheels fell into the openings. The onlookers too were toppling over and falling. The screams were everywhere.

Leviathan slithered forward. The platform began to come undone and to fall. Gnim jumped and landed on her feet as she seemed untouched by Sansit's demonstration. Gnim's expression changed to anger.

"Thank you for that." Leviathan held a martini glass out to Sansit and then finished the contents before throwing it to the side. "I do appreciate an occasional night off." Leviathan's tentacles sucked their way across the road. "Let someone else torture these wretched souls so that I can watch and be entertained," he continued. "And even learn a new technique." He laughed. "Like that could happen."

Leviathan was directly in front of Sansit. Sansit was looking up at him, as were Monk and Tinker. Tinker's attention kept going back to Gnim. He could feel her sadness.

Gnim's face was hiding it well, but it was there. She felt Tinker's understanding and avoided his stare. Tinker was confused.

"Why don't you just say it?" Tinker yelled out.

"Alright," Leviathan said.

"I… I wasn't talking to you," Tinker mustered up the courage to engage with the Demon Ruler.

Leviathan was taken back by Tinker's spirit.

Monk saw Gnim's expression change. "You may rule this Circle of Hell," he told Leviathan, "but you too serve a master."

"I serve no master," Leviathan retorted.

"Oh, but you do," sounded the sweet voice of Water. "And I am she."

Leviathan stood strong but dared not turn.

Water droplets from the ground began to vibrate and rise as the air became humid. The droplets moved closer together as a misty vapor took form and became solid.

Tinker's expression widened with joy. Water saw herself reflected in the twinkle that appeared in his eyes. She smiled but went back to matters at hand.

"Who will do your bidding, if not I?" Leviathan questioned Water.

"Your position is solid, Leviathan," she told him. "Worry not about that. You serve me well… but remember that you serve *me*."

Leviathan was hesitant. "And if I choose not to?"

"Then you choose to lose everything, and you become one of your tortured souls, as someone else rises to your current position."

Water looked over to a carriage untouched by Sansit's outrage. It housed a floating darkness that was in flux, attempting to separate into three forms and then being pulled back into one.

"Remember," Water told Leviathan. "It was you who allowed them into Hell in an attempt to create chaos." She looked back at the floating blackness. "And it is your punishment to have to keep them contained here."

Tinker's expression took an immediate turn as his eyes widened in shock. He quickly looked at Monk, who had anticipated this and was already looking back. Monk mouthed the word *Trust.*

Leviathan held his head proud. He was not going to appear to back down. He needed to save face, but he also needed to maintain his position.

The black form began to float towards them. The humid air took on a tinged aroma. Tinker smelled the foul acidic scent and covered his nose with his yellow scarf. Sansit gripped tight to the handle of his broken blade. Monk stood unaffected. Water maintained her regal posture as Leviathan fought to keep his. Gnim had stepped back from Leviathan, but she too held a defensive position.

"There they are," Sansit quietly said to Monk. "The Dark Sisters."

The scratching noise from the shadowy souls became louder. The misty blackness began to come apart and form three equal parts at the front end, but stayed connected at the back. The blackness expanded slowly as it passed each of them. It quickly moved away from Tinker and paused by Monk, as the three heads curved around him without touching him. It came to Leviathan, who continued to fight to hold his position.

The blackness engulfed him, but he did not scream. It receded and took a position behind Water, where it changed into white mist and then evaporated. The scratching noise ceased. Water held an eerie coolness as she continued to stare at Leviathan.

Leviathan was catching his breath. His attempt at staying strong was admirable. He looked up to Water with an angered glare. He dropped to his knees and lowered his head.

Water nodded in acceptance of his agreement and began to evaporate. She looked at Tinker as she finally disappeared into mist and droplets.

"Sansit?" Gnim asked coyly.

He did not look at her.

Monk walked over to her. "I think that we can help."

Sansit turned to Monk as his expression softened. "It is time," Sansit said and then looked at Gnim.

Tinker watched Leviathan slither off into a guarded tent. He turned and saw Monk speaking with Sansit and Gnim. He ran over to them to hear what they were discussing.

Gnim was quick to turn to him and grab Tinker by the wrist.

"Do not judge her, boy," she said with a fierceness. "Water," Gnim continued but looked at Sansit, "has had to make difficult choices that may have been misunderstood. The Dark Sisters are here to keep Leviathan from making that mistake again."

"She could always just give up her fight," Sansit offered, overhearing her words.

"Would you?" Gnim asked him. "Did you?"

Sansit said nothing and looked off into the dewy night.

"I thought that we were talking about Water," Tinker queried.

"Umm, maybe we should just step back," Monk guided him a few steps away.

"Everyone here is like an emotional storm," Tinker said.

"Tink?" Monk smiled. "We are in Hell. What do you expect?"

"Point taken."

"Hey!" Monk yelled to Sansit and Gnim.

They ignored him as they continued arguing.

Monk yelled again but they did not stop. Tinker shielded his eyes as the blinding light came from Monk's back.

"Hey!" yelled Archangel with an added strength.

Sansit and Gnim immediately stopped their screaming and saw the Immortal in front of them.

Gnim walked over to inspect Archangel.

"How did you do that?"

"Sort of a long story," Tinker offered. "But the short version is that he fell into a hole in the ground. I accidentally opened a portal to Hell with Lucifer's key that was given to me by Ileana. Vampire's tear landed in Monk's eye as he died and voilà! He can transform back and forth from mortal, Monk, to Immortal, Archangel. That's what I've been calling him. And here we are in the Fifth Circle of Hell, listening to you two bicker on."

"I'm going to need the long version," Gnim told Tinker as she completed her inspection of Archangel.

"I'm still trying to figure out the details," Tinker told her.

Archangel transformed back to Monk.

"Like I said before," Monk told her. "I think that we can help."

He looked to the dragons that continued flying and wrestling.

"The collars," he said to Gnim's surprise.

"I do not believe that Leviathan knows," Monk told her.

"I'm sure that he does not," Gnim said. "He would have done something if he did."

She looked at the dragons as they played with such joy and force. They smashed into each other and then burst. The collars were left at the ends of the chains as the mist settled on the grass.

"It does not matter anyway," Gnim said with disappointment. "The rim of my shield is missing."

"Not anymore," Monk told her.

Gnim quickly turned with a shocked expression.

"We have the outer part," Monk told her.

"Where is it?" she demanded. "Give it to me!"

"It's not here."

"Where?" she continued to become outraged. "It's mine! Give it to me!"

"Gnim?" Sansit said, making an attempt to calm her.

"Where is it?" she screamed and began to transform back to the giant.

"Two can play that game," Monk transformed into Archangel with his back to her to momentarily blind and distract her.

Gnim was knocked off balance by the light and fell back with a great crash that shook the ground.

"It is not here," Archangel repeated in a thundering voice as his wings flapped in a calm manner.

"It's at the Caves of Waku," Tinker explained. "With friends. They are keeping it safe."

Gnim was fighting herself to accept that the "friends" were not stealing the missing part of her shield. She looked at Sansit. "You knew this?"

"I just found out," he told her.

"Where have you been?" She was still lying back and propped up on her elbows.

"Trapped in the Fourth Circle," he said with sadness. "Trying to find you."

She softened and transformed back to the smaller version of herself.

Tinker was quick to cover her. "I thought you needed that top hat to transform," he said.

"So does Leviathan. I let him think it," Gnim confessed. She turned to Sansit and knelt in front of him. They hugged. Tinker could not help but smile. Archangel transformed back to Monk and put his arm around Tinker.

"They will need a minute," Monk told him. He and Tinker walked away with his arm draped comfortingly around Tinker's neck.

"Are you okay?" Monk asked him.

Tinker paused in thought.

"The Dark Sisters," he said.

Monk waited as they continued strolling across the dewy grass.

"I mean, Water being associated with Leviathan is bad enough. I have to accept that. He's a sea beast. But The Dark Sisters?"

"Well, at least we know what happened to them," Monk offered.

"Ileana destroyed them," Tinker reminded him. "We already knew that."

"But now we know where they were banished to."

Monk stopped walking and turned to Tinker. "Tink," he began. "She is Water. She is an Eternal Element. She has to keep balance and that involves playing on both sides of the coin."

"I know… Or at least, I guess I know. I didn't really think about her like that…"

"You thought of her as just a girl."

"Well, yeah!" Tinker admitted. "This is new to me, Monk."

"I know," he said with comfort. Monk joked as Tinker led them back to Sansit and Gnim.

"Hey Sansit!" Tinker yelled as they continued towards them. "Grab your girlfriend and let's move on. And Gnim, would you please collect the center of your shield. We have four more stops and a few things we have to figure out."

"My shield," Gnim said as if lost in a memory and then ran over and did exactly that.

"Correct me if I am wrong, but the collars are rubies, fire stones," he said looking off.

She nodded.

"The outer part, the ring, was to be my wedding ring," Gnim said. "It was made from my shield."

Sansit held her hand to comfort her.

"A fire shield," Tinker thought aloud.

Gnim released the dragons from their collars and pushed the collars together until they formed a single circular form. She adhered it to her back.

Tinker shrugged his shoulders with a deep inhale and then released it all. "How do we get out of here?"

Gnim pointed towards a different circus tent that looked like a giant peacock.

"That's… ummm…"

"A lot," Sansit finished Tinker's thought.

They began walking towards it with a triumphant stride.

"Hey, Sansit?" Tinker asked. "Any idea where the rest of your blade is?"

Sansit looked at Gnim.

"Not yet," he squeezed her hand. "I guess I forgot to ask Leviathan. But we'll be able to figure it out… together."

CHAPTER 43
Caves of Waku

The sun was continuing to lower in the late afternoon sky. Ghost was right. The magical entrapment no longer held as the sun was setting. Ileana and Sorcerer had already delayed the inevitable, but only temporarily. The worry had lessened as Vampire had assured them that he no longer needed to be contained.

However, AZ was screaming as Seer had gone unconscious again. Ileana and Cadet were the first to reach them. Sorcerer had run to Tinker's cart to grab a case full of ointments and a variety of herbs and liquids to make potions. AZ was still holding Seer and calling to help wake him.

Seer was grinding his teeth and making a painful scratching sound.

"I know that sound. That is definitely a Jiggler," Cadet said with concern.

"Slap him," Aldrick yelled.

"Seer!" AZ called to him as his seizure-like appearance became more intense.

"Well?" Sorcerer asked Ileana as he came to Seer's side.

"Not sure," she answered. "AZ? Did he say anything before this happened?"

"No," AZ said in a panicked voice. "We were just trying to figure out how to get the Jigglers into the Entrapment."

"Jigglers?" Vampire asked with concern.

"No need for that now," Cadet replied with relief in her voice. "The Entrapment is down." She looked at Vampire with a cautious stare. "And you're good, right?"

"Yes," he replied, just to keep everyone to not ask again.

AZ looked at Princess who put her hand on his shoulder. "He is still trying to find Monk and Tinker."

Sorcerer was examining Seer. The red of his eyes was changing in its intensity. Sorcerer looked at Ileana.

"That's not supposed to happen," he said.

"What is it?" Princess asked.

"Well, he is somewhere," Sorcerer replied.

Seer continued to grind his teeth.

"All that I can think of is that some type of dark magic is involved," Ileana said.

"Yes. Jigglers," Vampire shot back with anger.

"This is more than that," she replied and squinted her eyes as she watched Seer's body tense.

Sorcerer was busy mixing the contents of different vials. He was rushing and turning. He did not realize that Axel had been handing him the vials. Ileana's eyes lit up and she gasped. Sorcerer too realized what Axel was doing.

"I'm just doing what feels right," he said. "And you're not telling me that I'm wrong. So?" Axel said. "I was able to protect Aldrick and Princess from the dragon," he said, retelling when he created a rock wall to save them from her attack. "And raised the ground under Princess when it collapsed. I just did what felt right."

"The Three of Legend," Aldrick said with a wink.

"Ghost," Vampire said. "We should leave them to it. Our journey is not yet complete." He laid himself in the warm sands as Ghost came over him and surrounded his body.

CHAPTER 44
Buenos Aires, 1750

The night sky was full of stars. Moonlight reflected off the water of the Rio Tigre. The deep brush hid the small vessel in the shadows and the rustling of the trees silenced the soft sounds of the oars paddling through the water.

"Shhh… Keep your eyes sharp." The order was whispered in the dark.

The air was thick. The dewy aroma of the river plants was enticing and overwhelming.

These scents would make for great perfumes, Phineas thought.

"This is where they usually find mangled bodies," the pompous smuggler told him, making it sound like he was not concerned.

"You mean like that one," Phineas whispered a casual response.

The smuggler was taken back by the sight of the man's body torn open and his guts ripped from him. His sudden gasp brought with it the smell of the foul flesh. He turned and vomited over the side of the boat.

"Shhh…" Phineas reminded him with the hint of a smile. "It's going to be hard to get anything in or out of here if you keep up the noise." He handed the smuggler a handkerchief to wipe his mouth. "Shouldn't you be immune to this kind of stuff?"

"I'm a smuggler, not a heartless Englishman." He vomited over the side of the boat again. Phineas held him to make sure that he did not fall in.

"Got it," Phineas said without any offense. "Are we almost there?"

"Yes," he whispered through a muffled cough.

"Where are we, anyway? I thought that we were going to Buenos Aires."

"We are near Buenos Aires. We are in Concha."

"So, what tore that guy up back there?" Phineas asked, hoping that it would not cause another vomiting episode.

"Tigre," the man whispered back and looked through the darkness.

"Tigre? There are no tigers here," Phineas told him.

"Really? Tell that to that guy."

"Fair enough."

"It's around the bend."

"I can smell wood burning," Phineas said with a slight smile on his face.

"I don't smell anything."

Phineas was lost in his imagination.

"Hey!" The smuggler elbowed him. "Stay alert."

They rowed around the bend and found a single light emanating from the high grass of what was expectedly an island. Phineas attempted to find a land bridge, but in the darkness, he would not be able to confirm it. This was his first interaction with smugglers. He was doing a good job of hiding both his concern and his excitement.

Phineas had come to the area with a Portuguese mission. He was a doctor interested in learning more about the properties of the natural medicines that he had heard about in a lecture back in England. Phineas had found his way to the Portuguese hold on the other side of the Rio de la Plata, in Colonia del Sacramento. Getting here came with a price. He was harboring goods that were considered illegal by the Spanish rulers of the land.

Spain had been forced to pay heavier attention to the Buenos Aires region. Illegal trade had continued to grow. Word had gotten out that across the Rio de la Plata, the Portuguese allowed free trade. The Spanish were still trying to control it, to continue to collect taxes on goods and services. Spain feared that England and Portugal would gain strength and take the lands.

"Light that," the smuggler ordered and pointed to a candle as he rowed on.

Phineas did as he was instructed. Another candle was lit at a distance and began to move through the darkness. Other flames began to show themselves. Phineas and the smuggler came around another bend and found the dock that the candles were leading them to.

Phineas knew that he would not be trusted by the people he was about to meet, but he also knew that what he brought to them was of great value.

They approached a dimly lit dock made of wood. It was narrow and well hidden in the low hanging tree branches.

Phineas tossed a rope to the armed man on the dock and jumped off the boat to adhere it as the smuggler pulled in the oars. "Secured."

The armed guard said nothing but motioned his head for Phineas to walk to the house at the end of the dock.

"No," Phineas argued. "First, we inspect what I brought… together."

The man smiled, exposing a gold tooth and walked away.

"So, maybe you're not new at this," the smuggler joked.

Phineas said nothing.

Another man walked the length of the dock. He was tall and did not hold the stench of the guard who had not bathed for quite a while.

"You reject our terms?" he asked Phineas.

"No," Phineas replied. "I just don't trust you."

The man laughed. "Nor I, you. You are an Englishman who has come here illegally." He moved closer to Phineas. "There is no record of you even being here. If you disappeared, no one would ever think to look for you here."

Phineas smirked. "Someone would," he lied. "I'm not stupid enough to put all my loyalties into a band of smugglers."

The man pursed his lips and nodded. "Good for you, Phineas."

Phineas was surprised to hear the man speak his name.

"You do not know this, but we have met before." The man turned to walk back to the end of the deck. "Come with me. Your things are safe."

Phineas did not move.

"Trust me."

He looked back at the smuggler and the crates, and followed the man.

"My name is Thaddeus, and I have been running this operation. I am securing rare scented plants to take over the European perfume industry."

"And I am looking for these plants for medicinal purposes," Phineas told him.

"Yes. I know," Thaddeus said with a grin. "You're a saint," he joked.

"I'm smuggling illegal arms to a guerilla war in the dark of night. I don't think that would be considered saintly," Phineas stated.

Thaddeus laughed harder and motioned for Phineas to board another boat. Phineas questioned what was happening.

"We are going to a party," Thaddeus told him. "In my honor. You will be my guest."

The crew rowed the boat back to the main tributary of the river. They were exposed to the other boats traveling in the night and were headed to the grand structure on the other side.

"My home," Thaddeus whispered, proud of his own words. "Temporarily."

Phineas nodded but gave no sign of being impressed.

"I have been looking for you," Thaddeus told him.

"I brought the weapons and I just want what I came for," he said.

"The plants. You will have them," Thaddeus stood as the boat came to dock. "Please." Thaddeus motioned towards the elaborate home.

Phineas followed but remained cautious.

As they entered, they were met by a room full of Thaddeus' business associates, who all pretended to be less impressed than they really were. Thaddeus reached for Phineas' face and traced the scar that ran across it.

"It's all about who you present yourself to be," Thaddeus whispered.

"It's all about who you really are," Phineas argued back. He walked towards the far side of the room.

Eyes followed and heads turned.

"What happened to his face?" a woman asked Thaddeus.

"El tigre," Thaddeus replied and walked away.

"You're already the center of attention," he told Phineas as he came to stand next to him at the bar. His drink was already waiting.

"You seem to be upset with that," Phineas said.

Thaddeus scoffed at his remark.

"Don't worry," Phineas told him. "As soon as I leave, this crowd will be yours again." He stepped through the crowd of what had become admirers.

Thaddeus was rapidly growing tired of Phineas' cat and mouse game. He wanted to be the one in control. He was the one to be chased, but he was increasingly intrigued. Phineas had never behaved like this before.

What has happened to him? Thaddeus thought. He meandered through the crowd but kept an eye on Phineas. *He's polite but completely disinterested in anyone here.* Thaddeus looked around the crowd. *Attractive. Rich. Decent conversationalists,* Thaddeus thought. Yet, no one held Phineas' attention. *Why is this time so different?*

Thaddeus followed Phineas outside. He found him seated on the dock. His drink was in his hand. His shoes were off, and his feet dangled in the cool water. Thaddeus followed suit and removed his shoes and socks. He came to sit next to Phineas. He took a sip from his drink and continued to look off into the night sky.

"There used to be a constellation there," Thaddeus told him as he pointed to the part of the starry sky that was void of light. "I stole the constellation eons ago."

Phineas shook his head. "You just can't stop yourself. Can you?"

"Stop myself from what?" Thaddeus questioned.

"From being so self-absorbed," he told him. "You are so full of pride that you don't even see what is happening around you."

Thaddeus cocked his neck.

"The people around you are being suppressed. They have to resort to smuggling. Yet, you sit here in this very opulent lifestyle with the other side and make no effort to make things right." Phineas raised his glass. "Cheers to your ignorance."

Vampire reacted. Thaddeus had not reacted when this argument originally took place.

"Your pride. Your ego." Phineas shook his head. "I came here under the naïve notion that I was going to meet the one who would change the world." He looked at Thaddeus who expressed shock on his face. "I would like to collect my plants and leave, please. I will make my way back to Colonia and then to England."

Vampire held Thaddeus' tongue as the two consciousnesses were present. Originally, Thaddeus had argued on his own behalf. He knew that Phineas was right, but he could not allow himself to look like a fool. However, in this reliving of the events, Vampire held back and took the judgement.

What would happen next was inevitable, but Vampire wanted Phineas to know that he was right about pride being a problem.

Phineas got up to leave. He began to walk back to the house.

No. Stop, Vampire thought. But Thaddeus was in control. He let him walk the length of the dock and then closed his eyes as the explosion shattered every window, sending shards of glass that sliced through Phineas. He fell back as blood drained from every cut and opening.

Thaddeus ran over to him. He grabbed him in his arms as Phineas fought for air. His lungs had been punctured and his death was inevitable.

"Damn you," Thaddeus said as Phineas fought for his life. "This is my fault, Phineas. I am sorry. You and I should have had a life together, not just a few hours."

Phineas continued to struggle.

"I can preserve the truth for you… For the future," he told him. But really, he said it for himself.

Thaddeus knew that it was his arrogance and pride that created the situation. He had ignored the advice to be more cautious with his business dealings. The Spanish controllers of the area were looking to stop the illegal trading and had been raiding homes and businesses. He thought himself above their law. "I should not have been…"

Phineas was dying. Thaddeus took in a deep inhale and caught the fading aroma of citrus. His fangs grew and he lowered his head down to Phineas' neck. He tasted the delicate balance of his blood and held him until his essence was no longer.

Vampire took control and lifted Thaddeus' gaze to the place where the Dracu constellation had once illuminated the sky. He brushed the scar that ran diagonally across Phineas' face and then placed his hand on the left side of his torso, where the mark of the constellation had been laid at the time of Phineas' first death.

He could see that the stars blinked back in their positions in the sky and then were gone.

CHAPTER 45
Hell, Sixth Circle

"Pride, right?" Tinker asked.

"The peacock entrance said it all," Sansit replied. He looked at Gnim as they walked holding hands. "And I am sorry for mine."

"You should be," she told him to his surprise.

"And you?"

"And me, what?" Gnim looked down at him. "Is this how it's going to be? I have to apologize for things that were not my fault?"

"No. You have to apologize for things that were your fault."

"Monk?" Tinker begged.

"Hey!" Monk yelled to stop them from arguing.

"Oh, I see what's happening," Tinker jumped in. "Pride. Your pride is what is keeping you from letting go of your mistakes, any mistakes, regardless of who made them."

"This is not going to be easy," Monk thought aloud.

The sound of slow and disinterested applause came from the darkness.

"That was faster than I expected," said the strong male voice. "Although I should have expected this much from the Champion of Hell," he added and stepped forward, looking between Monk and Tinker.

"Lucifer," Monk said with venom in his voice and a twitch at the side of his nose.

"Envy was the last circle, Phineas," Lucifer teased and stood flirtatiously close.

"No," Monk replied and walked past him.

Lucifer shook his head in disappointment. "Does he really have such a hold on you?" he asked him.

"Yup."

Sansit and Gnim were so engulfed in the exchange between Monk and Lucifer that they let go of their own bickering.

"That's too bad," Lucifer said.

"Why? What are you offering? Eternity here with you?"

"It's a good offer, Phineas," Lucifer took him by the hand. Monk was immediately aware of the golden bracelet on Lucifer's wrist that looked as though a part of it had been rubbed through.

Lucifer kissed Monk's hand and gave another flirtatious smile as he moved himself to stand body to body with Monk. Their mouths were just short of touching. A simple word would pucker lips enough to make contact.

Monk matched Lucifer's stare.

Monk leaned back. "Not happening."

"Wow," Lucifer replied and leaned in. He touched Monk's lips with his own as he formed the word. "Good for you," he added and again touched lips. Lucifer cracked a cocky smile.

Monk held his cool. Then, he met Lucifer's cockiness with his own flirtatious smirk.

Lucifer bit his lower lip as he felt Monk's smile grow bigger. Monk dropped his robes to the ground. Lucifer cocked an eyebrow. He dropped his robes as he saw the light from behind Monk. He looked disappointed but did not look away.

"You're welcome for that." Lucifer watched Monk transform into Archangel.

"You did this?" Tinker asked.

"The light bearer," Lucifer reminded them. "The fallen angel. Who else would have? Who else could have?" He walked around Archangel. "I must admit, I outdid myself... again. Reminds me of myself. But to be fair, it was a collaboration."

He felt along and through the feathers which held an air-like quality. As he waved his hand through them, they turned silver and gold in color. They returned to crisp white after he removed his touch. The feathers began to lose all color and resembled ripples in the air.

Lucifer stepped towards Tinker. "You're the one she sent to see the sculptor."

Tinker looked down in embarrassment, but it was because he was only now fully understanding why Ileana sent him through time to meet with the sculptor, Ricardo Bellver.

"Makes sense," Lucifer added without explanation.

"So, was this alteration intended for me to take over for you down here?" Archangel looked back and forth from Tinker to Lucifer. "As the Champion of Hell?"

"Options, Phineas." Lucifer touched an area of the wings in Archangel's vision to show him the change to gold.

"Again, no," Archangel replied. "Respectfully," he walked over to stand next to Tinker. He transformed back to Monk and took up his robes. "You're just in it for the competition with Vampire."

"The pestering beast," Lucifer said with a flick of the hand. "He's soulless."

"For now, maybe," Monk argued.

"You have a plan?"

"We have several," Tinker interrupted as his thoughts came back to the present and his courage returned with Monk at his side.

"Do tell, boy." Lucifer came to stand directly in front of Tinker. Lucifer felt a sharp coolness stabbing at his groin.

"Get away from the kid," Sansit demanded with his broken blade at Lucifer's crotch.

"You?" he kidded. "I had forgotten about you."

"Yeah well, this blade can easily remember what it is supposed to do, and it has the power to… transform you," he told him with a tap upon the bulge in his groin.

"You'd have to be fast enough."

"Oh, we are," Gnim told him with a growl.

"The party has officially started," Lucifer said with a hearty laugh. "How did you get away from that slimy offense, Leviathan?"

"I just walked away." Gnim looked to Sansit, "Once I remembered why."

"Awww, that's sweet," Lucifer said condescendingly.

Sansit stuck the blade in a bit.

"Leviathan is the one who forged that blade, you know."

"Any idea where the missing piece is?" Tinker asked.

The look in Lucifer's eyes changed to complete control as his irises turned deep purple.

"Idea?" he asked. "No. I've been a bit of a homebody as of late." He quickly looked at Tinker's jacket pocket. "Not really part of the idle gossip outside of Hell."

Tinker caught his interest, knowing that he held Lucifer's portal key in his jacket pocket.

CHAPTER 46
Caves of Waku

Seer took in a deep and painful inhalation. He awoke from the trance as if he had come back from the dead.

"Ileana!" Cadet screamed.

Everyone came running.

Sorcerer was the first to reach them. "Has he said anything? Even something that you did not understand. A different language?"

"No. Nothing," AZ reported.

"He just inhaled as he opened his eyes," Princess added.

Sorcerer was examining Seer. He was holding crystals up to his forehead.

"Anything?" Ileana reached them with Axel and Aldrick.

"Nothing yet." Sorcerer began to choose the crystals more carefully. "But I think that we are getting there."

He snuck a side glance towards Ileana as he reached for an opaque black crystal that was cut into a pyramid form. She gave a subtle nod.

Sorcerer took the crystal into his hand and closed his fingers around it. Ileana placed her hand on his shoulder as he thought the words of the incantation. In her mind, Ileana heard him speaking and thought in unison.

The others were focused on Seer and his breathing. They were holding him down as he began to flail about in an attempt to get up and run from whatever was haunting him.

Sorcerer placed the crystal on his heart, and Seer immediately went unconscious. The painful scratching sound came as he began grinding his teeth.

"What the fuck just happened?" Aldrick asked.

"We are getting to the source of Seer's torment," Sorcerer told him.

"By knocking him out?" AZ asked. "How's he gonna tell us if he's passed out again?"

"It is not for him to tell us," Ileana told them. "It is for the tormenter to be exposed. The right crystal will draw…"

"You bitch!" Seer screamed and tried to get up and choke Ileana.

AZ, Axel, Aldrick, and Princess held him down. Cadet pulled Ileana back and out of his reach.

"Well," Ileana said with ease. "No one's arguing that."

Seer spit at her, but Princess blew the air to have the black mucus miss hitting Ileana.

"Thank you."

Seer's eyes were completely black. His lips and tongue were also black. The blackness was spreading through his veins and across his skin. A thick, black mucus-like substance mixed with his blood was draining out of his mouth.

Sorcerer held a container to Seer's mouth to collect the foul-smelling fluid.

"You thought that you had destroyed us," the gurgled voice spoke and spit from Seer's mouth.

"Where are you?" Ileana demanded.

The voice was silent.

Ileana pushed on the black crystal over Seer's heart.

The voice screamed in pain. It echoed and was now coming out as multiple voices.

Ileana's eyes glowed emerald green. "Dark water," she said. "The Fifth Circle of Hell."

"It won't be long now," the voices all spoke in unison. "The Champion of Hell will fail."

Ileana attempted to disguise her confusion. Princess caught the look.

Sorcerer focused on Seer, who was now returning to his regular appearance. The last of the black mucus had drained into the container. Sorcerer put the top on and sealed it with a magical enchantment.

Seer was breathing comfortably. He was unconscious again.

"Tell us!" Princess directed her demand at Ileana and Sorcerer. "Were those voices The Dark Sisters?"

"Seer was possessed by The Dark Sisters?" AZ asked. "I thought that you had destroyed them," he said to Ileana.

"From this realm," she said and stood with her hands on her hips in thought. "They are in the Fifth Circle of Hell."

"Is that a good thing or a bad thing?" Axel asked.

"Not a thing at all," Ileana answered.

"Umm, I think that Seer would beg to differ," Aldrick said.

"We will have a few questions for Seer when he wakes," Sorcerer told them.

"The Fifth Circle?" AZ asked.

"How many circles are there?" Aldrick questioned.

"Nine," Axel answered to everyone's surprise. "What? No one but me and Tinker reads the classics?"

They all looked at one another and then to Aldrick, who shrugged his shoulders. Axel rolled his eyes.

"Being this good looking doesn't make me stupid," Axel told them.

Ileana pulled her lips tight but said nothing.

CHAPTER 47
Hell, Sixth Circle

Lucifer stared at Sansit's fractured sword as he sauntered around Monk. "Leviathan may know where the rest of your trinket is. But you will have to go back and deal with him and those three bitches," Lucifer said to Tinker as he then looked off.

"And they're just gonna tell us," Sansit stated.

"I doubt that very much," Lucifer replied with his cocky smirk.

Sansit did not advance.

Tinker looked among the others and then back to the broken blade in Sansit's hand. He thought of the Shield of Gnim. Part of the frame was wrapped around Monk's forearm, and the other pieces were all accounted for. Gnim was wearing the center piece on her back. Tinker was sure that there would be a way to reassemble the shield. However, the other part of the blade were still missing, as well as the yellow Cez stone.

Tinker's mind ran, but he did not speak his thoughts.

"Good for you, boy," Lucifer said to him. "I support your spirit."

Tinker's head shook. He did not realize that he had been so obvious with his reaction.

"How do we get out of here?" Tinker rushed.

Lucifer sauntered towards Tinker as he and the others were taken back by Tinker's change of subject.

"Traditionally, one would have to get through all nine circles," he told him. "And then get through…" He faked a shiver. "Heaven."

"Heaven?" Tinker questioned with surprise.

"Yes. Heaven," Lucifer told him. "It is the same path that every soul takes after death."

"What?" Tinker begged. "Every soul comes to Hell and then to Heaven and then…?"

"And then," Lucifer replied, surprised at his question, "returns back to its original dimension until it becomes pure and ascends into The Enlightenment."

Everyone was quiet.

He approached Tinker. "But you seem to have brought with you quite the conundrum." He was directly in front of Tinker and took a deep breath. "Your soul still inhabits your body. You did not die before coming here."

Tinker's eyes widened. His secret was exposed.

"Oh don't worry," Lucifer put his arm around his shoulder. "I won't tell. Afterall, it was my portal key that let you in."

Tinker's fearful stare was intense on Monk.

"Why not?" Monk asked. "Is there a reason that you wouldn't want to tell?"

Lucifer cracked a smile.

"Because it is not out of the goodness of your heart," Monk continued. "Something isn't adding up."

Lucifer let go of Tinker and walked to Monk. "You got me," he said in a friendly confession. "That key is a secret. It was gifted to me by my brother, Archangel Michael, so that we could meet up from time to time on neutral ground."

Tinker was feeling around the orb in his pocket.

"How about an exchange? My key for getting him out of here," Lucifer rushed back. "In the same form that he came in." He slowed his response and looked off as he walked with his back to them. "After all, that is why Vampire sent you. He promised to get me my portal key back in exchange for me telling him where I hid the Book of Spells."

"Vampire betrayed us!" Tinker could not control himself.

Monk paused. "Ileana has the book."

"Oh she's alive," Lucifer faked a shocked expression. "So glad to hear that."

Tinker grew increasingly angry. "I'm guessing that you can't just take the portal key from me… Otherwise, you would have already."

Lucifer laughed. "Very good. And yes. You are right. But I need it back. Otherwise, I won't be of any help to you. Think about it. If everything is destroyed, I lose too."

Monk met Tinker's stare. He nodded. "Your call," Monk said.

Tinker walked over to Lucifer. "I don't trust you, but I do believe you. However, before I agree, you need to tell us how we are going to get out of here."

"Gokyuzu," Lucifer told them. "It is in ruin. Not a single soul has come down here for some time now… Until you two showed up. And none have moved forward. Souls are just being lost. They are becoming those shadows and making that scratching sound. Gokyuzu is basically empty aside from the shadows that linger there. If you find your way there, there is a chance that you will be able to transition back into your own dimension and time… with my help."

"Are you going to help us?" Tinker asked.

Lucifer smiled. "I already have," he told him and turned into light. The light broke up into endless sparks and each drifted off into the skies to make what looked like stars.

"It doesn't matter what you think of him," Sansit said, shaking his head. "He is impressive."

No one argued.

CHAPTER 48
Hell, Sixth Circle

"So, now what?" Sansit asked.

Lucifer had left them alone in the empty space. It was white and vast. There were no details to the physical space.

"Do you think what Lucifer said is true?" Tinker asked. "Do you believe Vampire betrayed us?"

"No Tink. I don't," Monk replied. "He would never-"

Monk squinted his eyes and saw very subtle shadows that formed lines in what he realized were the corners of a pyramid. The height of the angled walls was lost in the distance.

"We are inside a pyramid," Monk told them. He looked at Gnim. "Would you mind seeing if you can assess the top?"

She nodded with a cocky smile and immediately began to grow into her giant form. She reached up to feel for the top of the pyramid but was unable to ascertain its apex. She moved along the walls of the pyramid and felt a flow of energy.

"It feels magical," she told them. "But with a negative feeling, like it is trapping or containing us."

Monk thought. He pulled at his lower lip as his mind raced.

"Oh, Lucifer," he whispered. "Why not just tell us?"

"Because we have to grow from this experience too," Tinker reminded him.

Monk smiled.

"Yes," he agreed. "All of us."

"Pride," Tinker said. "Whether he betrayed us or not, we know who that is," he added with a sigh.

Monk made a face. He knew exactly who Tinker meant.

Vampire had become increasingly aware of his pride being a source of his and all of their setbacks. However, being too proud to stop it, he continued to maintain the same perspective.

"He's like the definition of insanity," Sansit told them. "And you just keep allowing it."

"I'm on a learning curve," Monk told him with jest.

"Nine lifetimes? You're a slow learner."

Monk shrugged his shoulders, knowing that he could not argue.

Gnim returned to her human size.

"But there is something else," she told them. "It feels like we are not the only ones here."

Monk, Tinker, and Sansit looked around but saw nothing.

"Something shadowy. Sinister."

Tinker looked at Monk.

"But something loving too," she added.

"Gnim," Sansit addressed with caution. "You're talking-"

"Crazy," she said, finishing his thought. "I know that it sounds like that. And it feels like that. Crazed. Confused. Fearful. But I'm just telling you what I am experiencing."

"Fair," Monk allowed.

A foul rotten aroma entered the space.

"Don't look at me," Sansit told them.

"Jigglers," Gnim yelled. "The shadows of lost souls."

Tinker felt around his belt and pockets but could not feel what he had hoped. "Damn it!" he exclaimed. "The one time that I am not prepared."

"But you are," sounded the familiar voice in the air.

Tinker's eyes shot open in surprise.

"Seer?" Monk asked, recognizing the voice.

"I found you," he said.

"Yes. Yes, you did!" Tinker rushed back with joy. "How?"

"Where are you?" Seer asked.

"Hell," Tinker told him.

Monk grabbed him by the arm to stop him from saying anything else. He held his finger to his lips to make sure that Sansit and Gnim did not speak.

"Where is Monk?"

Monk held Tinker's hand and signaled him in Morse Code to explain that Jigglers cannot be trusted.

But what if Seer sent them? Tinker signaled back.

Monk shook his head.

He can get information from them, but he can't control them, Monk signaled. They are shadowy creatures that seek to cause pain.

Tinker nodded, although disappointed.

The silence held.

Monk kept eye contact with the others to be patient and quiet. He wanted the Jigglers to give information and to not receive it.

The foul stench was gone.

"They are gone," Gnim told them.

"That was not Seer," Monk added with disappointment.

CHAPTER 49
Hell

Tinker was walking throughout the pyramid. It continued to expand away with every step. He could not calculate where it ended and did not see anything that was changing on the horizon. As he looked up, he could still not see the top.

"I don't understand what is happening," he said. "Or rather, why *nothing* is happening."

"We are still waiting for someone to get beyond their sin," Gnim told him.

"Vampire," Tinker, Sansit, and Monk said in unison.

Gnim looked at Sansit.

"Maybe I should sit," she said. "This will take a while."

Monk was lost in thought. He was playing with his lower lip. His consciousness had disappeared into a reverie of himself in another life. He started to smile as he saw himself and Vampire being playful in a snowy mountain chalet. He felt the heat from the fireplace; he smelled the burning pine; he tasted the peppery Malbec on his tongue;

he heard the crackles from the fire; he felt Vampire's accidental touch and remembered how whenever that would happen, neither would move away.

"Monk!"

Tinker had been calling but with no response. He gently touched Monk's shoulder.

"Yeah," Monk said as he came back to the present.

"Where did you go?"

Monk smiled. "Just remembering something pleasant."

Tinker smiled at Monk's joy.

"Sorry to cut it off, but is there any way that you get *him* to fly up and see if there is a way out? Or at least to get us some more information? Gnim is only able to grow so big."

Monk looked up to the endless white and then back at Tinker with a smile. The bright white light illuminated from his back.

Archangel held that same kind smile that Monk had. Tinker found that surprising.

Without a word, Archangel took to flight. Tinker watched as he flew directly upwards and climbed until out of sight.

As he was ascending, Archangel was feeling a sense of concern as he was unable to find the top. He flew in all directions to see if he could reach any border of their surroundings but was unsuccessful. He came back down to Tinker, who was standing with Sansit and Gnim.

Archangel shook his head and then transformed back to Monk.

"He better get over himself," Sansit said to Monk. "Your boyfriend is holding us up."

"I could not even find the borders that Gnim felt," he told them. "It's expanding."

"Is that a good thing or a bad thing?" Sansit asked.

Tinker was quiet in thought. He began his regular problem-solving approach in which he moved around and talked to himself with erratic arm and hand gestures.

"Is he a Witch?" Gnim asked.

"No," Monk told her, "but he is a genius."

"His arm and hand movement suggest otherwise," she said. "That boy is full of magic."

Monk looked at Tinker and after hearing Gnim's comment, saw him in a different light. She was right. He was moving his arms and hands in magical patterns. Monk knew that although Tinker had read about magic, he had never expressed a formal aptitude for it.

"Water magic," Monk whispered.

"Definitely Water magic," Gnim agreed.

Tinker gave a final grand swing with both arms as ice formed and was pushed from the air in front of him. The ice flew off, out of sight. An explosion was heard in the distance.

Tinker looked back at Monk with icy blue eyes.

"Do you smell the water?" Tinker asked as the blue of his eyes returned to their normal color.

Monk hesitated.

"Let's follow the ice," he told them.

CHAPTER 50
Caves of Waku

Vampire inhaled deeply and sat upright. Ghost had released him from within his form and hovered just above him.

"Hey," Cadet said with a kind smile. "You're going through it, huh?"

"Nothing I haven't experienced before," Vampire replied.

"Do you mean all those lives or the bullshit that you created?" she laughed.

He let out a slight laugh as well. "Yeah. I guess I am to blame for a few things." He looked at her and brushed her hair from her face. "And you stood beside me," he reminded her with a sense of gratitude.

"Through most of it. It was fun," she told him. "But we need to get this show back on the road." Cadet stood and offered a hand to help Vampire up from the sands. "We don't know when the Jeweled Dragon will return. But we know that she will."

Vampire looked off at the sun in the lower western sky.

Cadet put her hand on Vampire's shoulder. The corners of her mouth pulled tight and showed her dimples.

Vampire nodded. "Hit me, Ghost," he said with his eyes closed and his arms stretched out to the side.

Ghost immediately engulfed Vampire and took him on his next journey.

CHAPTER 51
Hell, Seventh Circle

Tinker was quick and ahead of the others. Monk, Sansit, and Gnim followed him as he ran towards the explosion and discovered the end of the pyramid. Monk led Sansit and Gnim through the opening that Tinker had smashed open with the ice.

"Water," Tinker said with continued excitement as he stood on the other side of the opening.

He slowed his pace and walked forward. His joy was maximized as he looked around with rapid head movements.

"Squirrel," Monk joked to Sansit and Gnim.

"What?" Sansit asked as he laughed at Tinker's twitching.

"I thought of naming him that because of this exact reason."

"I'm glad that you did not." Gnim grabbed his attention "How did he do that with the ice?"

"Not sure," Monk admitted. "I am learning so much about the boy that I saved all those years ago."

Tinker had stopped dead in his tracks as Monk came to stand next to him.

"Monk?"

"Your gifts are coming forward," Monk told him without Tinker asking the question. "Whatever is to come, I will always be with you."

"Yes. I know," he nodded with his gaze to the sky. "So what do you make of that?"

Monk and Tinker stared at the concrete columns that stabilized a doorway which towered high. They looked up but saw the solid structure lost in the gathered clouds that were now becoming electrified. Lightning had been igniting, changing the color of the storm clouds from purple to blue and then back to gray.

"Seems ominous enough," Tinker said with a shake of his head.

His initial instinct to pause and analyze was no longer. He was already feeling the stone columns. He sniffed the air. He closed his eyes and listened. Tinker was experiencing things differently but his mind still turned everything into a mathematical equation.

Monk watched as Tinker absorbed the information and deduced his conclusion. Monk saw the white light that was glowing through the crack between the doors.

"Immortal strength," Tinker told him. "No other way to open them."

"Your wish," Monk said and transformed into Archangel, "is my command."

Archangel approached the doors, but before he could make contact, they began to open.

"Seems more like magic words than Immortal strength," Archangel joked.

"Oh, you're funny now?" Tinker shot back. "Monk's all serious, reminiscent and heartbroken and you're the funny one?"

"Seems that way."

"Come on."

"Wait!" Archangel ordered.

"No. It's the next step. The Seventh Circle of Hell." Tinker walked through the doors, into the high narrow passageway that led towards the source of light.

Tinker turned and as Archangel stepped across the threshold, he transformed back into Monk. As they looked up, they saw that there was no visible ceiling, only what looked like the cloudless night sky. Monk's eyes were drawn to the place in the sky with the missing constellation. His left side began to feel warm.

"Why do I feel like you didn't choose to do that?" Tinker asked about his transformation.

"Because I didn't," Monk replied. They looked back and saw that Sansit and Gnim were not crossing into this circle of Hell. "Maybe this is not a place that Immortals can enter." He again placed his hand on his side.

They walked back to the opening but were unable to cross. They looked back at Sansit and Gnim who stood on the outside.

"It appears that our collective journey ends here," Sansit told them.

Tinker looked between Monk and Gnim. Gnim nodded and smiled.

"Take this." She removed the ruby from her back and pushed it through the opening. "Return it to me after you defeat the Jeweled Dragon."

Tinker took the crimson stone which was heavier than he anticipated and strapped it to his back. His backpack served as a cushion between him and the hard jewel.

"Thank you," Tinker told them. "We would not have gotten this far without you."

"Nor we," Gnim replied.

"You," Sansit began, "are the hope. You are the Champion of Water."

Tinker lowered his head, embarrassed.

He turned to Monk. "And you, the Champion of Hell. I mean, those wings of yours and the gifts that came with them were the only way for us to get this far."

Monk nodded respectfully but with only a suspicion of what that meant.

"Gnim and I are unable to travel any further with you." He looked down and pulled something from under his jacket. You're gonna need this." Sansit handed him his broken sword. "You will do my blade proud."

Tinker shed a tear.

"And Monk," Sansit continued. "I do like you. You have endured so much and have stayed true. You. You are the reason that this needs to succeed."

"I am sorry that we cannot help to get you out of Hell," Monk told Sansit and Gnim.

"But you did," Gnim told him. "Being apart was our Hell. We are out."

"We are Immortal," Sansit reminded them.

"Go," Gnim told them. "Stop the Jeweled Dragon."

Tinker and Monk nodded and continued forward. It was snowing. Tinker looked back to see Sansit and Gnim holding hands as they walked away from the opening.

As Tinker and Monk moved through the thin covering of snow, a pair of snowless footprints was left where Tinker trekked. Monk's steps left no trace.

"Hell doesn't make sense," Tinker said. "There is horror, sadness, pain, but also growth and understanding."

"I think that is the point of it," Monk told him. "For each of us to learn and to do better."

They continued along the narrow path in a self-reflective silence. It opened to a wide chamber, with a rounded ceiling and multiple openings.

Monk looked at the snowy ground. He became immediately aware that he had not left any footprints.

"Nine openings," Tinker walked into the center and turned in a circle.

"Nine lifetimes," Monk added as he inspected the ones on the other side. "This was the last," Monk said with assurance.

"No," Tinker replied.

"I died, Tink. You saw it. You told me."

A red light was floating through the air. As it moved closer to them, it revealed as a floating flame.

The flame stopped moving in front of them, lingering. It felt alive but tortured. It gave off an aura of instability and fear. It was in a constant state of flux.

Tinker and Monk looked at one another and saw the flame's reflection burning in their eyes as if it were a part of them.

"Yes. I feel it too," Monk turned to look at the flame. His side began to feel warm again.

"Sadness," Tinker too was drawn to stare at the flame. "Our sadness."

Monk felt the tear drop from his left eye.

"Not just ours," he said.

Monk turned to Tinker, who was crying fully. Monk felt a loss, along with an overwhelming sadness. He held Tinker as he lost his strength to stand. They both dropped to their knees and let out all their sadness in tears.

"The pain," Tinker said as the tears continued to flow "Seer's pain is so deep."

Monk said nothing. He let himself cry. Tinker was face down in the snow. Monk took in a deep inhalation through his nose. He regained his composure and aided Tinker back to his feet.

"We will speak nothing of this," Monk told him.

Tinker nodded in agreement as he wiped the tears from his eyes.

"And we will withhold our judgment," Monk continued with his orders.

Tinker nodded again.

"Good," Monk said and pulled him in for a comforting hug.

"Nine," he said.

Tinker held a bit longer.

"I can't go with you, Tink," Monk told him.

Monk looked back with sorrow. "Archangel is not allowed any further along this path." He looked away. "And I died," he showed him the single path of footprints in the snow.

Tinker saw an increased brightness in the distance. Monk turned to face him. "My soul has to leave you and figure a way to complete my journey." He held Tinker by the chin and looked into his eyes. "You can do this."

The light now resembled the sun during the Golden Hour. "And when you do, that will be my path."

Tinker knew that what he said was true.

Monk pulled him in for a tight embrace. "You are what I am most proud of in this life."

Tinker was crying but he understood. He nodded and forced a smile at Monk.

"Go," Monk told him as he held him at arm's length. "You are protected."

Tinker stood in place as Monk backed away.

"Tell him to defeat the Jeweled Dragon so that I can be reborn and see him again."

Tinker nodded through his tears.

"Go, Tink," Monk said just above a whisper. "Go."

Monk watched as Tinker turned and walked off with his head hanging low. Monk sighed and felt all the sadness of this loss.

"Come with me," Belphegor, the Ruler of the Seventh Circle of Hell, said to Monk with labored breath as he appeared through the falling snow.

CHAPTER 52
New York City, 2005

Vampire relaxed into the bond with the version of himself as he blinked and felt the wet snowflakes hitting his face. This had now become familiar. He stood ankle deep in the still falling snow. He peered around and saw the bundled individuals in their heavy coats and winter accessories. Saddened colors of black, navy and charcoal reflected the mood after a blizzard dumped three feet of snow on 'The City That Never Sleeps'. New York City had come to a dead stop.

Those few brave souls who were weathering the storm on foot were doing it out of necessity. The buses were shut down. The subway was operating with limited service as exposed tracks were impassible and local power outages temporarily imprisoned those commuters in the dark tunnels that crossed under the city.

Yet, there he stood, under the marquee of the Joyce Theater, with his hands in his pockets. He did not seem to be affected by the torturous winds blowing the frozen bits of ice and snow. He stood on the corner of Eighth Avenue and Nineteenth Street in a fitted suit, with his deep purple scarf blowing in the wind. The scarf was more for fashion than for warmth. He did, however, wear a pair of high boots. He was particularly fond of this season's sleek line of footwear. His long salt and pepper colored hair was blowing in the wind. His face seemed younger than his hair coloring. And although a bit pale in skin tone, most would excuse that to… Winter in New York.

He watched the few passersby huddled in pairs as one helped the other through the high snow. Yet, with everyone shielding their exposed faces from the elements, few noticed him. They stumbled past the striking man in black who seemed to be unaffected by the torturous weather that was attacking the city.

Slim pickings, Vampire thought to himself. He was, after all, out for dinner. But the limited heartbeats that he encountered did not offer a sense of fulfillment.

And then, there it was. The rush of adrenaline pumped through his Immortal body. It was intense and grabbed at Vampire's heightened senses. He started sniffing into the air like an animal stalking its prey. The scent was as intense as the rush of adrenaline. *He* was near. The blizzard was blowing hard now, and no one could be seen on the street.

The scent was carried on the winter winds. It was crisp and familiar, a touch of jasmine on the citrus scent, very grounded at its base. Vampire knew this scent. He had even tried to bottle it in the past, but no one, not even he, was ever able to get the combination exactly right.

The wind started blowing in all directions now. The ever-changing breeze reminded Vampire to be patient.

He closed his eyes and spoke the mantra, "You are always where you are supposed to be."

"Funny," he heard the light joyful voice over the whistle of the wind, "I say the same thing."

Vampire dared not turn until he took in a deep inhale.

Yes, he thought as the true fresh citrus scent was finally present. He opened his eyes and turned around to find a young man in yellow water-proof boots, medical scrubs, a down-filled, blue coat with hood up and his hands in his coat pockets.

As he turned to see the smiling face, the man's expression quickly changed to confusion.

"Do I know you?" the handsome stranger asked. "You seem… *very* familiar."

Vampire smiled as the wind blew his long locks and the icy snow forced him to squint his eyes. His smile lingered. He did not yet speak.

"No. I guess not." The man answered his own question. "I definitely would remember you." He continued to smile at Vampire.

Eight lifetimes later, it still impressed Vampire that the response was always the same. Full. Easy. No change in pulse. No fearful responses to have to charm. He came with the same love that reminded Vampire why he ripped the constellation from the night sky; the reason he did not destroy humankind. He could not exist without him.

This time, Vampire had been waiting for him to return for over one hundred years from his previous death in Paris in 1891. He knew that he would be back. He knew that his previous life had ended without him fulfilling his true purpose, whatever that would be. So, he waited. He was Immortal after all and could wait forever, if he needed to. But he did not want to wait forever. He was a proud and selfish being and even more selfish when it came to-

"Phineas," the man broke the silence with an extended and exposed hand. "My name is Phineas."

Vampire extended his own hand.

"Thaddeus," Vampire replied. As he made contact with Phineas' hand, a shock forced him back. Phineas laughed but he did not retract his hand.

"I guess, it's all the wool and down," he said looking at Thaddeus' suit and his own coat. "Static electricity."

"Yes," Thaddeus added. "Makes sense."

Vampire reached in again to shake the still extended hand. He was surprised.

"How is your hand so warm?" Thaddeus asked. "No gloves? In this weather?"

"The coat, I guess. Deep pockets. I tried to get this homeless guy near the hospital inside, but he refused."

"And now he's the proud owner of a pair of warm gloves…"

"And a hat," Phineas added, removing the hood of his dark blue parka.

"I'm surprised you kept the coat," Thaddeus joked. "I've known other men like you who would give the shirt off of their backs."

"Generous, but not stupid."

Phineas smiled as he said it. Thaddeus smiled back but said nothing.

"And you? Where is your coat?" he looked him up and down. "I ask from a professional point of view. I am a doctor and don't want you to get sick."

"I'm exceptionally warm blooded."

Phineas stayed silent as he tried to process what that meant.

"So," Phineas broke the silence again. "How is it that two warm handed men with strange names come to be standing under the same marquee on this God-awful night in New York City?"

"Luck?" Thaddeus retorted.

"Nah. No such thing," he answered, shaking his head. "Like you were saying when I invaded your *meditation*. 'You are always…"

"…where you are supposed to be.' It's uncanny how true that is when you look back. Isn't it?"

Again, the silence came between them, but it was not uncomfortable. The sound of the wind was almost musical at this point.

Phineas began to feel the cold.

"The coat is good and warm, but I've had to walk all the way from the Eastside. My sweat is starting to turn to ice, so…"

"Dinner?"

Phineas laughed with a surprised expression.

"Sure. Yes! If we can find something open."

"Ah. Good point."

Phineas looked in any direction for lights to signal an open restaurant. They saw no signs of open restaurants.

"Well…" Phineas began with a hint of a pause. "I do live… down the block."

Thaddeus began to smile.

"I'm a good judge of character, and I don't think that you're a serial killer."

Thaddeus laughed. "If only you knew."

Phineas laughed. "I hope you say 'yes'." He paused. "But maybe another time…?"

"No," Thaddeus casually replied. "I mean 'yes'!" he quickly corrected himself. "I mean," he continued more flirtatiously, "you are always where you are supposed to be."

"Exactly."

Phineas' smile lit the night.

"This way," he guided by physically turning Thaddeus to walk down the block with his shoulder against Thaddeus' upper arm as he kept his hands in the coat pockets.

The two men disappeared from the avenue lights heading west to the garden apartment that Phineas called home.

CHAPTER 53
Caves of Waku

Ghost had released Vampire from his cold embrace. Vampire walked away from the others and found himself sitting atop one of the cave openings. He was staring at the sun that was lowering in the sky.

"Something is different," Ileana told him as she came to sit beside him, in the orange-colored light of the setting sun.

"That one was the hardest," Vampire, still feeling the sting of having lost Phineas back in New York City. He turned to look at her. "Phineas died after fifty years together." He looked down. "He died of old age… Natural causes. Like we may have gotten it right."

Ileana smiled and put her head on his shoulder.

"Maybe you did," she told him.

CHAPTER 54

Hell

Tinker walked alone through the darkness of a tunnel. He had put his goggles on. His pace was strong and direct, but he feared not being able to make out the end of the shaft. He sighed to calm himself.

He had walked for what he felt was an hour, consumed by his thoughts. He smiled and laughed, but also pulled his mouth tight into a hard line while his nose twitched. He remembered Monk. He remembered the only family he ever had.

Tinker stepped faster. He had to succeed. That was the only way to assure that Monk would return for another life. He promised himself that he would make it.

As he reached the opening at the end of the tunnel, the smoky air was warm. The breeze was gentle.

"Is that a frozen lake?" Tinker thought.

CHAPTER 55
Caves of Waku

Ileana and Vampire returned to the others. Sorcerer and Axel were holding crystals to Seer's head.

"The green one," Sorcerer pointed to a stone that looked like a thick pin.

Axel held it to Seer's forehead and immediately felt the rush of pain and anguish that came from physical contact with him. Sadness. Everything was sadness. Every memory. Every moment was tinged with pain.

He felt them all differently, as if he was experiencing what a seer experienced when he touched another… A heightened emotional level to everything and it felt like pain.

"Axel?" Sorcerer asked with concern. "What is it?"

Axel put his hand to his mouth and walked away from Seer. "Sadness," he said with a tear falling from his eye and looking into the distant sky. "Pain," he continued as he lost his breath and buckled. Sorcerer caught him. "Complete darkness."

CHAPTER 56

Hell, Eighth Circle

Tinker's mind was reeling, but he had to wipe his tears and figure his way out. He had the center of Gnim's shield and the handle of Sansit's sword. He had to get them back to the others for a chance to destroy the Jeweled Dragon and allow Monk's soul to return.

And I'm supposed to trust Lucifer, he thought. "Well, where the Hell is he?"

"Interesting choice of words," the demon appeared from the air.

"Lucifer," Tinker said. "I am going to trust you."

"Like you have a choice."

"Like you have a choice." Tinker showed him the glowing orb. It immediately turned orange and pulsed like a speeding heartbeat.

"Follow me," the demon told him.

Lucifer led Tinker along the snow covered path and to a narrow bridge that expanded over the frozen lake. It was wide enough to walk single file. Tinker was eager to get to the other side and hopefully, out of Hell.

He followed Lucifer onto the unstable crossing. He noticed that even the lightest snowflake that made contact with the lake erupted in a fiery release. But Tinker's exhaustion made him less reactive and more focused on crossing.

Tinker felt his left foot sink as the plank under it fell through.

"Careful," Lucifer said, jokingly. "You've come too far to lose now."

Lucifer assisted Tinker back to a standing posture.

"Thank you," Tinker said. "Hell sucks."

Lucifer cracked a smile. "And that's why I want my portal key back."

"Looks like it narrows even more," Tinker said, remarking about the slimmer path ahead.

"We will have to walk sideways."

"Can't you just fly us across?" Tinker asked him.

"Hell is a journey. A constant test. This is your version of Hell. I am limited by your experience. Your personal Hell."

Tinker faced right. "I'm trying to trust you but-"

An explosion came from the lake.

"Step on your count," Lucifer faced left for balance.

"Okay," Tinker agreed with a nervous quiver.

"Don't look down, Tinker," Lucifer ordered. "Stare ahead."

Tinker's attention was drawn to something in the sky. The painful scratching sounds could be heard.

"Lucifer?" Tinker squinted. "Something is coming."

"On my side too," Lucifer informed him.

Lucifer looked down to see the columns of the bridge covered by bodies of underlings crawling atop one another.

"We have to move, Tinker."

"Yeah," Tinker agreed. "Hell really sucks."

Lucifer felt him tense.

"Are you sure that you can't just get us off this bridge?"

"This is your journey," Lucifer reminded him.

"That's unfortunate," Tinker said. "On my count." He held his stare to the other side of the crossing. "And step," Tinker commanded.

Lucifer shot intermittent looks down and kept a watchful eye on the sky.

"Step," Tinker continued as they braced each other and continued to sidestep across the narrow passage. "Step."

The underlings kept climbing and whatever was flying towards them was getting closer.

"Step," Tinker repeated. "Step." Lucifer looked to the sky and was surprised by what he thought he was seeing. "Step."

Tinker looked back and saw that the underlings had reached the top of the bridge; they were crawling over each other towards Tinker and Lucifer. Tinker turned his head towards the end of the bridge. "We are almost there," he said. "Step," Tinker repeated.

The underlings were moving faster. Tinker looked ahead to see that they had reached the edge of the frozen water.

"Step," Tinker yelled.

The underlings were trying to jump off each other. Some missed the bridge and fell into the lake. Fire erupted with each hit of the surface.

"Hurry!" Tinker yelled. "We are almost there."

One of the underlings launched itself and flew over their heads. It landed between them and the end of the bridge.

"Keep going Tinker," Lucifer demanded, "and don't touch it."

Tinker saw that there was no way they would be able to jump over the underling. "Backup plan," he yelled and jumped for the edge of the cliff. He pulled Lucifer with him.

They slid down the surface of the icy cliff until they caught hold of a ledge. They caught their breath and began climbing up the slippery rock surface. Tinker looked over his shoulder and saw the underlings as they continued to climb over one another. He and Lucifer reached the top of the cliff. They rolled over and let out an exhausted sigh.

"You seem so human," Tinker said through labored breaths.

"I am part of your Hell. This is your journey," Lucifer reminded him.

"And them?" Tinker pointed to the underlings.

"They are the souls that cannot move on," he said. "They are trapped in the Eighth Circle until they end up as shadows." Lucifer helped Tinker to stand. "And that is why you must succeed."

Tinker looked at the blackness that was flying around the sky.

Lucifer followed his stare. "Those are lost souls. They have been destroyed and will never return." The scratching sound continued.

"And Monk?"

"Since the Jeweled Dragon destroyed Gokyuzu, there is no way for any soul to continue their journey."

Tinker looked back with piety.

"You didn't answer my question."

Lucifer still offered no answer regarding Monk. "Gokyuzu is your way out of here. We are going through a backdoor," he told Tinker. "We're almost there."

CHAPTER 57
Hell, Ninth Circle

Tinker and Lucifer walked along the snowy path. No words were spoken. Tinker still held his unanswered question regarding Monk. They came to the bank of another icy lake. Tinker saw bodies in the ice from the waist down. Some were shivering and begging for help. The rest were completely frozen over. Only their stare and the loud clicking of their chattering teeth reflected their pain. Some had eye movements that expressed the torture they endured. Others tried to call out, but the only sound that came out was the loud clicking of teeth on teeth.

"No soul will move beyond this point until balance is restored," Lucifer told Tinker. "The attack on Gokyuzu was meant to keep Hell out of the battle, but also to destroy every soul. No one can move forward and therefore, each soul will be destroyed and become a shadow, a Jiggler."

Tinker looked at Lucifer. "And that will happen to Monk."

"That will happen to every soul in time, if you do not succeed," Lucifer repeated.

Tinker's eyes squinted.

"Your way out is over there." Lucifer pointed to a cave with a partially hidden entrance, across the lake. Tinker looked with concern. "The ice will hold. Your soul is still with your physical self."

"And you?" Tinker asked.

Lucifer laughed. "Oh, I'm coming with you." He walked onto the frozen surface. "I am getting my portal key back and getting out of Hell."

Tinker was hesitant but followed after seeing that the ice did hold under Lucifer. *Not scared; just smart,* he told himself.

Tinker was still hesitant with each step. He walked cautiously through the maze of frozen bodies. He saw eyes move and even fingers bend and straighten. The chattering teeth became painful to his ears. As he reached into his bag for something to put over his ears, a hand grabbed at his ankle.

The surprise forced a deep scream from Tinker as he pulled himself away.

"Hel-" was all he could barely hear from the mouth that was frozen in an open position.

Help, he thought to himself.

Tinker was quick to catch up to Lucifer.

Snow was falling and blowing hard. The bodies that were frozen in the lake began to break into pieces and flake off into the swirling wind and snow. Blackness formed from them and fell off.

Tinker pulled his goggles over his eyes.

"They are gone," Lucifer told him. "Their souls have been destroyed. Nothing more than the shadows that make that scratching sound."

Tinker felt the ache in his stomach.

"The longer this takes, the less souls there will be to save… Until there are none," Lucifer told him.

"If we don't make Gokyuzu operational again, the Jeweled Dragon has already won," Tinker thought aloud.

Lucifer's expression showed that he knew that to be true.

Tinker and Lucifer made their way across the ice and to the hidden entrance of the cave. As they entered, Tinker was surprised to find the other Demon Rulers present.

"What is this?" Tinker asked. "You lied to me!" he yelled at Lucifer.

"No," Satan told him. "He did not."

Asmodeus moved closer to Tinker. "We are present here to remind you that the rest of your journey affects all of us."

"Every dimension," Beezelbub added.

Mammon stood. "We will have no purpose and be destroyed if you do not succeed."

"And Monk will not have an opportunity to live again," Leviathan added.

Belphegor said nothing, only pointed ahead to a tarnished door.

"It used to be golden," Lucifer told Tinker. "But turned to this after Gokyuzu was destroyed."

"Will the key still work?" Tinker asked.

"We're about to find out."

CHAPTER 58
Hell

"Well," Tinker said, taking the glowing orb out of his pocket. "It is your key."

Lucifer's eyes widened with excitement.

The other Demon Rulers stood nearby. They, unlike Lucifer, did not have a portal key. They did not have the opportunity to exit Hell aside from being summoned.

"Let's make sure that it works first," Tinker reminded him. "And there is no telling what we will find on the other side."

Lucifer heard his words but was focused on having his portal key back.

Since giving the portal key to Ileana, he had not been able to leave Hell; an agreement that he regretted.

"Lucifer," Tinker whispered. "We have to hurry. The longer we hesitate, the more souls get lost forever," Tinker reminded him.

"Yes," Lucifer replied, snapping out of a reverie.

He stroked his hand over the glowing orb and watched as it changed color from bright white to a deep purple. He moved his hand along the borders of the door. There was a dim light.

"It's not working."

Tinker moved closer. He placed his hand upon the orb, and it began to pulse. "Let's try it together," he said. "Life and death."

Lucifer nodded and traced the same pattern. Increasingly bright light came through the edges of the door. The door itself became less tarnished as they watched with anticipation.

CLICK.

Lucifer looked at Tinker.

"We will have to work together to save all of time and space." Tinker looked around at the other Demon Rulers. He mentally retraced his journey through each of their circles. "Until we meet again."

One by one, they each nodded in respect to Tinker for his strength and bravery, but mostly, for his humanity and kindness.

"Let's go," Lucifer said. Tinker followed him through the golden door.

It immediately closed behind them and the light went out. Each Demon Ruler returned to their circle.

CHAPTER 59
Caves of Waku

Seer gasped and came into consciousness with panic. "Something is happening."

Vampire was upon him, holding him tight by the shoulders. "What? What is happening? Do you see them?" Vampire quickly asked. "Monk? Tinker?"

He looked at Vampire in the eyes. "Tinker."

"What?"

His eyes were glowing crimson red. "I can see Tinker."

"Where is he?" Princess rushed.

"Everything around him is damaged... in ruin. Broken. Fallen," he said. His eyes returned to their neutral state. "Gokyuzu."

Vampire looked at Ileana. The Twins and AZ were looking up at the sky.

"It is in ruin but not erased. It still sits between dimensions," Seer told them. "And is part of ours."

"Where?" Ghost asked as the others all looked for a slightly purple cloud in the sky. "Can you lead me to it?"

"What will you do when you get there?" Sorcerer asked. "You won't be able to bring him back."

"I can," Cadet said with one hand on her hip and swinging her pack of rainbow dust in the other.

CHAPTER 60
Gokyuzu

Lucifer stepped lightly. Gokyuzu was now a shadow of its former self. Lucifer's portal key had opened the door to an underground train platform. The overhead lights were flickering. Sparks emanated from exposed wires gracing the train tracks.

"If this is what it looks like down here-" Lucifer lost his words in thought.

"I'm afraid to see what we will find," Tinker followed.

"We need to be cautious."

"Oh, believe me," Tinker replied and gripped the blade of the Sword of Sansit. "I am thinking the same thing."

They reached the stairs that led up to the street.

"Ready?"

"Ready," Tinker assured him with his grip tighter on the blade's handle.

CHAPTER 61
Caves of Waku

"I can see him," Seer repeated. "He is moving." He looked at Cadet.

"I'm shocked there is even a piece of it to return to," Sorcerer told them.

"Well, as long as that piece is in our dimension, I can get there. Ghost!" Cadet yelled. "Where am I going? I need a destination to create the right intensity of colors for the rainbow."

Ghost faded to a ripple of lightly green air and then returned.

"It sits in the sky above Tamsu," Seer said. His eyes widened. "Tamsu was my home as a child."

Vampire held his reaction. *Of course,* he thought. *You're the boy that I led to the monastery all those years ago.*

"Get him and bring him back here," Sorcerer told Cadet.

"Why can't you just create a portal to Gokyuzu?" AZ asked.

"Because that portal would open for anything else that is there to possibly return here," Ileana replied.

"Then, the Rainbow Network it is," Cadet said with confidence and nodded. Vampire walked over and pulled her in for a hug. "Bring him back safe," he pleaded. "I need to protect him… For Monk."

Cadet's lips tightened across her mouth, neither a smile nor a frown. She nodded again.

"Cadet! Wait," Ileana yelled as the Leprechaun moved into position.

Ileana breathed deep. "There is something I must tell you before you go."

CHAPTER 62
Gokyuzu

Lucifer continued to lead the way up the stairs and out into the orange and purple daylight. The sight was total devastation. Buildings had crumbled. Fires continued to burn. The sweet smell of burnt flesh lingered in the air. The only movement came from papers and debris blowing in the hot breeze.

"You're looking for life," Lucifer said matter-of-factly. "You will not find any. These souls were destroyed, never to enter Hell. Never to travel to and through Heaven, or enter The Enlightenment. Lost for good. Shadows."

Tinker sighed with disappointment. His heart was devastated. He thought of Monk. *Is his soul lost forever too?*

He and Lucifer needed to figure a way back to the others. But he did not know what had happened with the others. *Are they safe? Alive? Did the dragon return?*

"Tinker?" Lucifer asked.

"Focus. I know," he said with a nod of the head. Tinker looked around. "Monk and Vampire were given wings made from angel and demon feathers to descend when they were here. Mavi had given them to them."

"Well, she too is no longer," Lucifer reminded him. "So, unless you have something in your bag of tricks that can help us, we are not getting anywhere." Lucifer looked around. "I used to get on one of the trains back. The souls did not have recollection of who I was. It was perfect. But now-"

"The trains are gone. The tracks are gone," Tinker said. "We need to find our way somehow."

"I think that I can help with that." A voice came from behind them. They turned ready to fight. Tinker held Sansit's blade out in front of him.

"Cadet?" Tinker questioned. "Is that really you?"

"Sure enough," she replied and met his tight embrace. "Seer found you here." Cadet looked Tinker over at arm's length. She saw the ruby shield on his back and looked down at the golden handle of the blade in his hand. "Looks like you've collected a few new things," she kidded him. She looked at Lucifer. "I would ask where you've been, but the answer is obvious. Hello, Lucifer."

"Hello, Cadet," he said and leaned in.

"Na na!" she replied. "You're as alluring as ever, but I've smartened up."

He nodded and laughed.

She looked kindly at Tinker. "I'm afraid to ask, but-"

"Gone," Tinker told her with his head held down. "Monk died. He was unable to complete the journey out of Hell. All the souls in Hell are not moving forward into Heaven. Gokyuzu needs to be restored for that to happen. And until then, they are lost forever."

"Oh, Tink." She wiped a tear. "Well, let's get you home. Everyone will be relieved to see you."

Tinker's smile turned to confusion. He sniffed again and again. His eyes widened with fear.

"Bergamot-"

EPILOGUE

B olts of lightning whipped through the air. The angel was bound to the hard stone floor by chains of fire that vibrated and pulled tighter with every muscle contraction.

He screamed out as the energy split his tattered wings, the white feathers now singed and burnt to charcoal. His long locks of hair were dripping with sweat and covered his face. Blood dripped from his wounds.

He could not fight back. The whips of fire crashed upon him and knocked him flat to the hard stone beneath him. He did not have the energy to scream any more.

The angel gasped and panted awaiting the next bout of torturous strikes. Instead, the sound of footsteps made their way closer. His labored breathing continued. He controlled his panting and looked up to see who approached. His left eye was swollen shut and blood fell from his lip.

He stared at the golden sandals that made their way forward.

"Citrus?" he heard and then a deep inhale followed by another. "No."

The angel looked up. A scar ran diagonally across his face.

"Phineas," the Archangel Michael said, surprised. "We have to get you out of here."

ABOUT THE AUTHOR
James Voorhees

For James Voorhees, creating the world of **The Ambassador Chronicles** has been a long lived passion. This sprawling cinematic fantasy saga started modestly with *The Ambassador Chronicles*, a book of ten interconnected prequel stories that first introduced readers to the extraordinary "Ambassadors."

The full-scale epic launched with the trilogy's first installment, *The Dragon Constellation*, and now plunges into the depths of peril with *The Nine Circles*. James believes that the greatest adventures are found in the characters who struggle against overwhelming odds.

He is already hard at work on the thrilling final volume of the trilogy.